CW00506317

BETRAYAL

KERRY KAYA

Boldwood

First published in Great Britain in 2022 by Boldwood Books Ltd.

Copyright © Kerry Kaya, 2022

Cover Design by Colin Thomas

Cover Photography: shutterstock

The moral right of Kerry Kaya to be identified as the author of this work has been asserted in accordance with the Copyright, Designs and Patents Act 1988.

All rights reserved. No part of this book may be reproduced in any form or by any electronic or mechanical means, including information storage and retrieval systems, without written permission from the author, except for the use of brief quotations in a book review.

This book is a work of fiction and, except in the case of historical fact, any resemblance to actual persons, living or dead, is purely coincidental.

Every effort has been made to obtain the necessary permissions with reference to copyright material, both illustrative and quoted. We apologise for any omissions in this respect and will be pleased to make the appropriate acknowledgements in any future edition.

A CIP catalogue record for this book is available from the British Library.

Paperback ISBN 978-1-80162-942-3

Large Print ISBN 978-1-80162-941-6

Hardback ISBN 978-1-80162-940-9

Ebook ISBN 978-1-80162-943-0

Kindle ISBN 978-1-80162-944-7

Audio CD ISBN 978-1-80162-935-5

MP3 CD ISBN 978-1-80162-936-2

Digital audio download ISBN 978-1-80162-939-3

Boldwood Books Ltd
23 Bowerdean Street
London SW6 3TN
www.boldwoodbooks.com

For Callum

1

Tracey Tempest had never been the type of woman to keep her opinions to herself, especially when it came to her mother-in-law Patricia. But seeing as she had a garden full of guests, today of all days she was begrudgingly prepared to make an exception, if for no other reason than to keep the peace. After all, the very last thing she wanted to do was cause a scene on her husband Terry's birthday.

Brunette and petite, and with a penchant for wearing leopard print, Tracey was a beautiful woman. But as she moved around her immaculate fitted oak kitchen lifting tin foil away from plates of ham sandwiches, sausage rolls, and large bowls filled with salad, she gritted her teeth into a scowl.

'Why don't you get out from under my feet and go outside Pat?' she urged her mother-in-law with a flick of her head towards the garden where Terry's fiftieth surprise birthday party was already in full swing. 'Terry will be here at any moment and I'll be bringing the cake out soon,' she said with a glance at her watch, 'and you wouldn't want to miss out on that, would you?'

Patricia turned up her nose as she eyed the single-tiered iced sponge cake with a measure of distaste. In the middle of the thick white icing two red candles bearing the numbers five and zero had been pushed haphazardly into the sponge.

'Cake,' she remarked in a loud shrill voice. 'Is that what you bleeding well call it? I told you I would have baked the cake myself and believe me, it would have been a darn sight better than this monstrosity.' She flicked a remnant piece of icing away from the gold-coloured cake board and on to the worktop. 'But oh no, my baking wasn't good enough for you, was it?' She paused to catch her breath and squinted to look up at the clock on the wall, the alcohol she'd already sunk making it difficult for her to focus. 'Besides, it's a bit early, ain't it? You've not even brought out the buffet yet.'

Tracey closed her eyes, then silently counted to ten before answering. In her mind, the sooner Terry put in an appearance and the cake could be served, the sooner one of her sons could drop their grandmother off home and the real party could begin. 'Well go and spend some time with the guests then.' She gestured impatiently in the direction of the many family and friends who were gathered in the garden. 'What do you want to be cooped up inside with me for?'

For a few moments Patricia was thoughtful as she patted her peroxide blonde hair that she'd painstakingly back combed to within an inch of its life. 'What time did you tell Kenny to get Terry here for?' Her blue eyes twinkled as she asked the question. Kenny Kempton was not only her son's childhood friend but he was also Terry's business partner and it was no secret that Patricia had a soft spot for him.

Taking a second glance at her watch, Tracey took note of the time. She'd told Kenny to make sure he brought Terry home for two o'clock, and with just a few moments to spare, she still needed to finish setting up the buffet. 'They're due any minute, so why don't you go outside and wait for them,' Tracey said, ushering her mother-in-law out of the kitchen.

Patricia all but skipped out the back door, her slim body practically jigging from side to side with excitement as she tottered outside on impossibly high stilettos.

Heaving a sigh of relief, Tracey shook her head and resumed the task of tearing away sheets of tin foil from the finger buffet. Her mother-in-law's cloying scent still filled the kitchen and, wrinkling her nose, she waved her arm in the air to help clear the stench.

'Was Nan giving you grief again?' As he strode into the kitchen, a hint of amusement could be heard in Ricky Tempest's voice. The hostile relationship between his mother and grandmother was legendary on their estate and it was fair to say there was no love lost between the two women. To be more precise: they despised each other and had done so from the very first moment they had clapped eyes on one another.

Throwing the discarded sheets of tin foil into the bin, Tracey looked up at her eldest son and rolled her eyes. 'As much as I love your father,' she sighed, 'if I'd have known back then that I would have to put up with his mother day in and day out, I would never have agreed to marry the man.'

Ricky chuckled out loud; for all her talk, he knew for a fact his mother adored his father and would be lost without him. His parents were not only a match made in heaven but also had the kind of marriage that he and his younger brother Jamie could only hope to one day emulate.

'Do me a favour darling, as soon as the cake has been eaten take your nan home.' She tapped the side of her head. 'There is only so much I can take of her in one day without blowing a gasket and believe me, it's taking every ounce of my strength not to wrap my hands around her throat and throttle the life out of her.'

'Will do.' Ricky chuckled even harder. Shifting his weight slightly, he cleared his throat and became serious. 'I'm thinking of popping the question to Kayla.'

Tracey's mouth dropped open. 'What, here? Today?' she asked.

Ricky shrugged, and as his three-year-old son Mason ran into the kitchen he was saved from answering.

'Oh, go on, do it today.' Tracey beamed up at her son. 'We'll make sure it's one of the biggest celebrations this estate has ever seen! We'll put on the works, a proper East End knees up, and as for your dad,' she said with a laugh, 'he can pay for the bloody lot; it's about time the bugger came in useful for something,' she said.

'She hasn't even said yes yet Mum,' Ricky reminded his mother.

'Oh, she'll say yes, don't you worry about that.' Peering through the kitchen window, Tracey spotted her son's girlfriend Kayla attempting to make small talk with Patricia and loved the woman even more for her effort. She of all people knew just how difficult it was to get a decent conversation out of her mother-in-law. 'That girl loves the bleeding bones of you and it's about time you made it official, made her a Tempest. She's already one of the family and she's got a good head on her shoulders too.'

'We'll see,' Ricky answered as he scooped his son up into his arms before he could swipe one of the iced fairy cakes that his mother had set out on a cake stand just moments earlier.

'Oh let him have one, there's plenty to go around.' Peeling away the paper casing, Tracey passed across one of the cakes and as her grandson took a large bite she gave him a playful wink.

'Just remember to keep schtum about it for now Mum; I don't

want Kayla catching wind of it before I've even had the chance to get down on one knee and propose.'

Tracey chuckled and, leaning in towards her son, she pretended to pull a zip across her lips. 'I'm the queen of keeping schtum, and believe me, if I can keep quiet about the skulduggery your father has been involved in over the years then I think I can keep a lid on this,' she said.

With an impending wedding on the horizon, even Pat's presence wasn't enough to dampen Tracey's mood and with another glance at her watch she wondered for the umpteenth time that afternoon if it was too early to bring out the birthday cake? And more to the point, where was her husband? She bit down on her lip. It was so typical of Terry; he'd be late for his own funeral, not that she entirely blamed him considering he had no idea about the party, but Kenny on the other hand, now he did know, and more than once she had specifically instructed him to make sure that he brought Terry home on time.

* * *

In quick succession, Kenny Kempton snorted two lines of cocaine from a compact disc. 'This,' he said with an approving nod, 'is the fucking bollocks.'

Beside him in the passenger seat, Terry Tempest grinned. 'I told you it's the nuts and believe me, there's plenty more where that came from.' At six-foot-two in height, Terry was not only a handsome man with dark brown hair, hazel eyes and a chiselled jawline, but he also had a muscular physique and menacing presence about him, all of which his two sons had inherited.

Licking his index finger, Kenny greedily gathered up the remnant traces of cocaine and rubbed them across his gums. Then, looking up at the rear-view mirror, he set about wiping away the excess white powder from around his nostrils before smoothing down his greying hair. Unlike Terry, he was a portly man and a good three inches shorter than his business partner. The only thing he and Terry shared in common was the fact that they could both hold their own. Even as children they had inflicted fear and intimidation amongst their classmates. They had ruled the playground in pretty much the same way as they ruled Dagenham, with brute force.

Up ahead of them, a white transit van turned into the breakers yard that Kenny and Terry owned. Kenny waited until the van had pulled up beside them before leaning across Terry, pulling open the glove box and taking out a loaded semi-automatic pistol.

'What took you so long?' he demanded as he stepped outside the car, his gruff voice loud and harsh.

Kenny's son Shaun jumped out of the van, his plump cheeks flushed pink, and ran a hand through his blond hair, making it stand up on end. 'Bianca,' he spat. 'Her and the rest of the Murphys are threatening to up the price; reckon they're sick and tired of babysitting the merchandise.'

Kenny narrowed his eyes. Bianca, or 'the bitch' as he'd nick-named her, was beginning to get right on his tits. And as for the rest of the Murphys clan, not only were they the equivalent of snarling dogs, but they were severely lacking when it came to brain cells. They had no sense for business, a fact which should have sent alarm bells ringing in Kenny's ears long before he and Terry had finalised any form of deal with them. He cocked his head towards the van. 'What about the goods?'

'All present and correct.' Shaun grinned. Moving around the van, he glanced over his shoulder, checking that the coast was clear, then set about unlocking the rear doors. 'She said they want double the price next time, otherwise the deal's off.'

Passing the gun across to his son, Kenny gave a nasty chuckle. As far as he was concerned, Bianca and the rest of her family could go fuck themselves. Not only had they laid out the terms of their business transaction but they'd also shaken on it and like fuck were the Murphys going to double back on their word six months down the line. Not unless they wanted to cause serious ructions. 'You need to sort her out,' he growled, giving Terry a sidelong glance. 'The bitch is getting above her station.'

Despite the flash of anger that tore through him, Terry could see Kenny's point and so begrudgingly gave a nod of his head. As of late, Bianca had begun making more and more demands, not only on their business deals but also on him. She didn't like to share and on more than one occasion had let it be known that she wanted Terry all to herself. Terry didn't have the heart to tell her that that wasn't how he was made. He already had a wife, Tracey or his Trace as he affectionately called her. Tracey was a good woman and a blinding mother to their two sons, but as much as he loved her, he also liked a bit of variety, always had done; in fact, before the ink had even dried on their wedding certificate he'd shagged one of Tracey's bridesmaids in the gents toilets where they had held their wedding reception.

As for Bianca, he'd been seeing her on the side for the past six months. It wasn't the first time that he'd played away from home and certainly wouldn't be the last, but for the time being he was more than happy to string Bianca along. She had all the attributes that he liked in a woman. Not only was she beautiful, but more importantly she was good in the sack. Still, as good as Bianca was between the sheets, it wasn't enough to tempt him to leave Tracey. And even if he did, give it a month or two and he would be up to his old tricks again shagging other women. It was who he was, he couldn't change even if he wanted to. After all, a leopard never changed its spots, did it? Only, Bianca was too dense to realise this.

With the van doors now unlocked, the three men peered eagerly inside. Huddled towards the rear, four women looked fearfully out at them, their bodies trembling, their faces pale, and their eyes wide and terror stricken.

Kenny looked the women over. Despite himself, he was somewhat impressed; not only were they all young, slim and fair haired, but from what he could see of them they were also clean, unlike the last shipment of whores the Murphys had sent their way. Not only had the women looked ropey but they had stunk to high heaven. In fact, they had looked so dog rough that Kenny had been hell bent on taking a trip to Bianca's flat with a sawn-off shotgun in tow to have it out with the bitch. He would have done too if it hadn't been for Terry smoothing the situation over. Months it had taken for them to recoup the money they'd paid out for the tarts, a fact that Kenny wasn't going to take lying down. The Murphys had taken the piss out of them and that was the understatement of the century.

'Out,' Kenny ordered, waving his arm in the air in an attempt to make himself understood.

Cowering away from him, the petrified women clung to one another, their cries of fear becoming louder and more desperate by the passing second.

'Come on, get out.' Never one to have much patience, Terry jumped up into the van, yanked a woman to her feet then shoved her none too gently towards the open doors.

As the women were frog marched through the front door of a rundown house that was positioned towards the rear of the remote breakers yard, their frantic cries for help fell upon deaf ears.

'What are they saying?' Tilting his head to one side, Shaun studied the women through narrowed eyes.

'How the fuck would I know?' Terry pointed out as he pushed a terrified woman towards the wooden staircase which led up to where the bedrooms were situated. 'Do I look like I speak Slovakian or Romanian or wherever the fuck it is they've come from?'

Shaun shrugged. For all they knew, the women could be telling them they were riddled with every venereal disease known to man. The mere thought was enough to make him shudder. Twirling the van key around his index finger, Shaun backed out of the house. 'I'll go and fill the van up with petrol and meet you at the party.'

Locking eyes with his son, Kenny raised his eyebrows. 'Don't be late,' he warned, his voice holding a hint of menace. 'You wouldn't want to miss out on the festivities now, would you?'

His gaze drifting back to Terry, Shaun solemnly shook his head before bolting out of the door.

* * *

An hour later, as he turned the car off the A13 and drove towards Dagenham, Kenny gave a disgruntled shake of his head. Despite the wealth he and Terry had accumulated over the years, Terry had refused point blank to leave the estate where they had grown up, fully believing that staying in the area would keep his two sons grounded. He hadn't wanted them to grow up to become pompous, spoilt, arrogant bastards; no, he'd wanted them to graft for their dough, had wanted them to know the value of money and more importantly had wanted them to know where they had come from. In Kenny's eyes, the notion was ludicrous and at the first opportunity, he'd upped and left the council estate and bought himself a detached house in Elm Park. And as far as Kenny was concerned, his own son had turned out all right considering he'd not only grown up in a more affluent area but that he'd also attended a private school. The school fees alone had been crippling and he'd almost needed to take out a mortgage just to pay for the uniform, but it had been worth it; his boy had had the best education that money could pay for. Fair enough Shaun didn't have the same menacing presence about him that Terry's two boys had, but he could still hold his own, and would still be able to have a tear up as and when he needed to.

Still shaking his head, Kenny tutted loudly as he looked around him. 'This place never changes,' he stated. 'It was a shithole back in the day and it's still a shithole today.'

Beside him, Terry lit a cigarette and gave a nonchalant shrug, already bored with the conversation. Anyone would think that Kenny had been born with a silver spoon in his mouth the way he carried on. 'It ain't that bad. Let's face it, the place never did us any harm did it?'

'Not that bad?' Kenny sneered. 'Look around you; they should have bulldozed this place to the ground years ago.'

Moments later, Kenny brought the car to a halt outside the house Terry owned. As much as he hated to admit it, his friend had done wonders with the place. In fact, the house wouldn't have looked out of place in his neck of the woods and considering he'd paid just under half a million pounds for his gaff that was saying something. Unclipping his seat belt, he turned his head. 'Remember to act surprised,' he said, nodding towards the house. 'Tracey will have my guts if she finds out I let slip about the party.'

Groaning out loud, Terry unclipped his seatbelt and stepped out of the car. Tracey knew that he loathed surprises, and as his birthday had approached he'd warned her time and time again not to spring a surprise party on him. In his mind he could think of nothing worse and would have much preferred an evening out at the dogs followed by a meal in a curry house.

On seeing Terry's expression, Kenny chuckled. 'Just smile in all the right places,' he suggested as he sprung open the car boot, 'and with a bit of luck she won't be any the wiser.' Retrieving a velvet-lined wooden box containing a twenty-six-year-old bottle of Glenfiddich that he'd tossed into the boot earlier that afternoon, Kenny grinned. He'd paid a hefty price for the whisky and when he handed the gift over to Terry he hoped that his generosity would be noted by more than one person. In fact, he was counting on it.

* * *

Before Terry could even pull his keys out of his pocket, the front door was flung open and standing there on the doorstep was Tracey, her hands on her hips and a scowl across her beautiful face. As always, she looked immaculate, not a single hair out of place, her slim figure encased in a fitted cream dress with leopard print piping around the neckline. 'Where the bleeding hell have you been?' She directed her question at Kenny, who had the grace to look sheepish. 'Two o'clock I said.'

Taking a quick glance at his watch, Kenny shrugged. It was almost four. 'We had car trouble,' he said by way of an explanation. The truth was, they would have arrived much earlier if Terry hadn't insisted on sampling the merchandise before leaving the breakers yard. Not that he could tell his friend's wife this; as it was, she had no idea of what her husband got up to behind her back. Fidelity wasn't a word in Terry's vocabulary. The fact he was married made no odds to him; he was a randy bastard whose main goal in life was to screw as many women as he possibly could. The only stipulation he had was that the woman in question still had her own teeth and a pulse.

'More like you were in the boozer.' Tracey rolled her eyes. 'Some surprise party this has turned out to be,' she said, leading the men into the kitchen. 'And your mother's been chomping at the bloody bit waiting for you to arrive. Here Tel' – she smoothed down her dress and gestured towards the iced sponge cake – 'now that you're here, shall I bring the cake out, get it over and done with?'

'Bit early, ain't it?' Shaking his head, Terry afforded his wife a knowing grin. 'I've only just got here. Give it another hour or two sweetheart,' he said, slinging his arm around his wife's petite frame and squeezing her towards him. 'My old mum will fuck off soon enough and then you can let your hair down and relax.'

Tracey's cheeks flushed pink. Terry had always been able to see right through her, and so he should considering they had been together since they were teenagers. In fact, it would be fair to say that he knew her inside and out, especially when it came to the strained relationship between her and his mother. It was just one of the many reasons why she loved him so much; he understood how difficult Patricia could be and had never once tried to excuse his mother's poor behaviour. Not only had they grown up together, but they had also built a life together and had raised two wonderful sons. How could she not love him? Terry was her everything, she worshipped the ground he walked on and had done so from the very first moment she had clapped her eyes on him.

Picking up her wine glass, she took a long sip. 'I'm going to hold you to that,' she laughed between mouthfuls. 'Two hours tops and then I'm bringing this cake out if it's the last thing I ever do.'

* * *

Amid a raucous cheer, Terry stepped out into the garden and gave his best impression of feigning surprise. A glass of his favourite tipple – whisky – was thrust into his hand and a Cuban cigar into the other.

As he lit up and took several short sharp puffs, Terry grinned happily. He may not like surprises but he could see just how much effort his wife had put into organising the party, and loved her even more for it, even if that was in his own haphazard way.

Minutes later, Terry began opening an array of gifts. Taking the wooden box from Kenny, he opened it to reveal a bottle of vintage whisky inside.

'Fuck me, this must have set you back a few quid?' Terry exclaimed as he whistled through his teeth.

Taking pride of place beside her son, Patricia gasped out loud. She may not have been much of a drinker, but even she could see the gift hadn't been something that Kenny had picked up last minute from the local supermarket. No, she'd bet her life on it that a great deal of care and thought had gone into the present. 'You're a good man you are Kenny.' Patricia beamed up at him. 'Your old mum would've been proud of you.'

As Kenny waved the comments away, he couldn't help but smirk as he looked around him to see if anyone else had witnessed the elaborate gesture. He loved nothing more than to flaunt his wealth, and actually got a kick out of others knowing that he was loaded, that splashing out over five hundred pounds on a bottle of whisky meant nothing to him.

* * *

Two hours later, Tracey ever so carefully tottered out of the house in a pair of leopard print stilettos. In her hands she held the birthday cake complete with the lit candles that flickered precariously in the light breeze.

'Happy birthday my darling.' Placing the cake on the patio table in front of her husband, Tracey stood on her tip toes to plant a kiss on Terry's lips, savouring the familiar pull of him. Even after thirty years of marriage she couldn't get enough of him and still to this day could hand on heart state that he was the only man for her. Oh they'd had their ups and downs, of course they had, what couples didn't, but still she was unable to envisage a future for herself without him by her side. And if truth were told, she didn't want to.

'Make a wish Grandad.' Barely able to contain his excitement, Mason jumped up and down.

Laughing heartily, Terry hauled his grandson up on to his shoulders, whispered into the little boy's ear then leant forward so that together they could blow out the candles.

Amidst cheers and shouts for a speech, Terry grinned. He plonked his grandson on the floor, picked up his glass then swallowed down a large gulp of the whisky.

'Come on Dad,' his youngest son Jamie called out to him, 'give us a speech.'

'All right,' Terry called back to his son good naturedly, 'give me a fucking chance.' He cleared his throat and as he opened his mouth to deliver the much-requested speech, a deafening gunshot resonated through the air.

Pandemonium broke out and as the terrified guests ran for cover, shock was etched across Terry's handsome face. Staggering forward, he reached around to clasp at his back. The sharp, piercing pain just below his shoulder blades was enough to alert him to the fact that he'd taken a hit, and as warm, sticky blood seeped through his fingers, staining the white linen shirt he wore crimson, the high pitched, piercing scream that came from Tracey rang loud in his ears. As he locked eyes with his wife, Terry's lips ever so slightly parted before his eyes rolled to the back of his head and he crashed face first to the floor, bringing the glass table, birthday cake and the gift box containing the expensive bottle of whisky down on top of him.

2

The funeral of Terry Tempest was a large, sombre affair and as four magnificent black horses pulled a glass carriage through the streets towards Saint Margaret's church in Barking, onlookers lined the pavements and craned their necks to not only get a better view of the solid redwood coffin but also to catch a glimpse of the grieving widow.

For the entire journey, Tracey had kept her head facing forward, her gaze remaining focused on the carriage that contained her husband's body. She was still unable to comprehend that Terry was gone from her life. Her heart had shattered into a million tiny pieces that day, the pain she felt ripping through her mind and body at a pace that almost took her breath away.

'It's going to be okay Mum.' Beside her, Jamie clutched her cold tiny hand in his. 'We're going to get through this.'

Without answering, Tracey bit down on her lip in an attempt to fight down the urge to scream at her son, to tell him that she would never be okay again, that a piece of her heart had died with her husband and that each and every time she closed her eyes the horrifying scene as Terry took his last breath still haunted her. Instead, she gave Jamie's hand a gentle squeeze back. Her boys meant well; after all, they too were grieving the loss of their father, the man they had looked up to their entire lives, and as much as they would understand her outburst it would be unfair of her to take her grief out on them.

As expected, the church was filled to the rafters. Tracey took a seat in the front pew, flanked on either side by her two sons. From directly behind her she could hear the pitiful sobs that came from Patricia. There and then her heart went out to her mother-in-law. She may not have been Pat's biggest fan but even she knew the loss of her only child would hit the woman hard – it was bound to. For the past fifty years Terry had been the mainstay of Patricia's life, her sole purpose for waking up in the morning. Many times over the years Tracey had heard her mother-in-law recount with a measure of pride, how as a single mother she had worked two jobs just so that she could keep a roof over her and her son's heads and put food in his belly. Very little had been known about Terry's father other than that he'd originated from Liverpool and had been a travelling salesman. Tracey had often wondered if Pat herself had even known who Terry's father was. She'd heard enough stories over the years to know that in her youth her mother-in-law had been considered a good-time girl who'd always been up for some fun, not that she had ever broached the subject with Pat to find out if the rumours were true, least of all with Terry himself.

The church service had been a long-winded affair and as much as Tracey had wanted to bolt out of her seat, flee from the church and gulp fresh air into her lungs, another part of her had not wanted the service to come to an end, knowing full well that when it did Terry's body would be interred into the ground, forever out of her reach.

Forty minutes later, as the mourners made their way out of the cemetery gates and headed across the road in the direction of the Captain Cook public house where the wake was being held, they offered Tracey their condolences. Dutifully she gave them a tight smile in return and thanked them for paying their respects.

'I'm sorry for your loss; Terry was a good man.'

Tracey glanced up to look at a young woman and was momentarily taken aback. The makeup she wore had been plastered on so thickly that Tracey wouldn't have been surprised if she'd used a trowel to apply her foundation. Her full pink lips were glossy, her dark eyebrows a startling contrast compared to the thick blonde hair which framed her face. The words should have been said with sincerity but to Tracey's ears there had been a lack of warmth in the woman's voice.

As the woman walked away, Tracey's gaze followed her with interest. 'Who's that woman?' she asked.

Ricky turned his head in time to witness Bianca Murphy and Kenny share a few words.

'That's Bianca Murphy,' he answered. Narrowing his eyes, Ricky gave a shrug. He hadn't even known that his dad was on friendly terms with the Murphys; he'd certainly never heard Terry have a good word to say about them. It was well known that the family were thugs, that they were given a wide berth by those who were unfortunate enough to know them, and Terry had more than made his opinion of the family known. He'd regarded them as scum, a drain on society, a sentiment which was widely agreed on by the locals.

For a few moments Tracey continued watching her husband's best friend and Bianca and as they turned to look in her direction, Tracey looked away, reminding herself to ask Kenny about the interaction at some point during the wake.

* * *

'He's really gone, isn't he?' Patricia cried. 'My boy is dead.'

Pulling Patricia into his arms, Kenny whispered words of comfort. He could understand Patricia's disbelief of her son's death. Terry had been a larger than life character and his absence would be a large void to fill, even for Kenny. Ever since they had been kids, he and Terry had been the best of mates, they had done everything together from fighting in the playground to fighting on the football terraces to finally making a name for themselves on the streets. They not only had reputations as hard men, but they were also both feared and well respected within the community. It would even be fair to say that they ruled Dagenham with an iron fist; nothing went down without their prior approval, and every drug sold on the streets went through them first.

'I mean, who would even do such a thing?' Patricia continued to cry.

'I wish I knew darling,' Kenny lied. Despite his and Terry's close friendship, in recent months, Terry had become the equivalent of an albatross hanging from around Kenny's neck. They were meant to have been partners, best mates even, but oh no, it was Terry who wanted to run the show and he threw his weight around left, right and centre, fully expecting everyone around him to jump to his attention and toe the line, Kenny included. Take the deal with the Murphys for example; it had been Kenny's suggestion to do business with Bianca and her brothers – they were so dense that it wouldn't take much work on his part to pull the wool over their eyes – yet within days of negotiating the deal, Terry had taken over, shouting the odds as per fucking usual. And, to make matters worse, Kenny's gut instinct had told him that between them, Terry and the bitch were keeping him out of the loop. In other words, there was a lot more money being made than either one of them were letting on.

Patricia's sobs broke Kenny's reverie and as her shoulders heaved, he pulled her even closer. 'I still can't get my head around it.' He blew out his cheeks and made a show of wiping away a solitary false tear. 'He was cut down in the prime of his life and believe me darling, when I get my hands on the culprits responsible, I'm gonna string 'em up by their fucking bollocks. They'll pay for what they did, you just wait and see.'

'You always were a good friend to him.' Patricia's sobs turned to hiccups and as she downed the remainder of her drink, she swayed on her feet feeling somewhat tipsy. 'Even as children the two of you were as thick as thieves.'

Motioning towards the barmaid for another round of drinks, Kenny leant against the bar. 'Terry was a good man,' he stated. 'I would have done anything for him, fucking anything.' He pocketed his change, then passed across a glass of white wine all the while studying Patricia, knowing for a fact that he was only telling her everything she wanted to hear.

'And you did an' all.' Patricia took a long sip of her wine. 'Look at that bottle of whisky you bought him for his birthday; he was made up with it.' Fresh tears stung her eyes and she began to sob even harder. 'He never even got the chance to open the bottle.'

Kenny forced away the smug grin that threatened to spread across his face. As much as the whisky had been an elaborate gesture, he was also banking on the fact that the gift would help cement his innocence. After all, what man in his right mind would shell out over five hundred nicker for a present all the while knowing that he was planning to bump the recipient off? They'd have to be crazy, wouldn't they? At least this was the conclusion that he hoped the old bill would come to.

As it was, the filth had been sniffing around a little too much for his liking and Tracey, the stupid cow, was actually encouraging them. She'd even told him that she rang the police station several times each day just for an update, hoping that by some miracle they would tell her they had caught the culprit responsible for Terry's death. It was ludicrous really. The old bill didn't care about the likes of them. He'd even heard more than one whisper through the grapevine that the filth had thrown a party when they'd heard that Terry had been gunned down; it was a case of one less face on the streets as far as they were concerned.

'Looks like your Shaun's had a skinful.'

Kenny snapped his head up.

'Your Shaun,' Patricia reiterated as she dabbed a sodden tissue to her eyes. 'He's three sheets to the wind.'

Kenny turned his attention to his son. Across the far side of the pub, Shaun was swaying unsteadily on his feet, the contents of his pint glass sloshing over both the floor and any unsuspecting mourners within close proximity.

Irritation swept through Kenny's veins and as he shot a surreptitious glance towards Terry's sons, anger filled him. Unlike Shaun, Ricky and Jamie Tempest sat dutifully beside their mother, their hard eyes watching everything that went on around them. They were alert, just as their father had always been, and no matter how much booze they sank Kenny knew that they would remain on their guard. From an early age it had been ingrained in them that they were Tempests and that meant there was always some bastard out there ready and waiting to have a pop at them. Slamming his glass down on the bar, Kenny made his way across the pub and, grasping his son by the elbow, he pulled Shaun round to face him.

'You're pissed,' Kenny hissed in his ear.

As he looked up at his father, Shaun staggered on his feet. His eyes were glassy, his skin pale and his lips pinched. 'It's a wake ain't it?' he slurred. 'I'm entitled to have a drink.' He belched loudly and refocused his gaze on his father. 'And if anyone's allowed to have a drink it should be me,' he said, stabbing a stiff finger into his chest, his lips suddenly curling down at the corners. 'I deserve it after what I did, after what you made me do.'

His expression becoming murderous, Kenny shoved his son towards the exit. The pint glass slipped from Shaun's fingers and smashed to smithereens on the hard wooden floor, causing several mourners to turn their heads at the commotion.

Once outside the pub, Kenny's breath streamed out ahead of him as he slammed his only son roughly up against the brick-work. 'Listen here you little fucker,' he snarled, 'watch your mouth; do you understand me?'

Shaun flinched, and as he brought his arms protectively up towards his head, he cowered away from his father. The action only served to fuel Kenny's anger.

'Do you understand me?' Kenny growled, his voice low and menacing.

Shaun swallowed deeply and, blinking rapidly up at his father, he choked out a reply. 'I'm sorry Dad.' Tears filled his eyes and he hastily wiped them away, not wanting to give his dad even more ammunition or another reason to lash out at him.

Kenny taking his anger out on his son was nothing new, only he didn't usually do it out in public. After all, he had an image to maintain and being an abuser of women and children didn't go down too well in his world. Outwardly, father and son appeared close; after all, Shaun was Kenny's only child, his rightful heir and namesake. The reality however was very different. Kenny had a vicious streak inside of him and the fact Shaun was his son meant nothing. In fact, Shaun had lost count of the number of times Kenny had taken his fists or his belt to him. The belt being Kenny's favourite form of punishment, he even kept a worn leather belt hanging up on a hook in the hallway to serve as a constant reminder of what would happen should his son disobey him. Kenny had even had the front to call the beatings tough love, claiming that it would harden Shaun up, that it would turn him into a man.

'I can't help it,' Shaun cried, pointing to his temple. 'What I did is up here, and it won't go away. It's eating away at me, I can't think of anything else, it's suffocating me. I killed him... I murdered Terry.'

Gripping his son by the jaw, Kenny forced Shaun to look at him. 'Forget about him,' he implored. 'Terry was having me over. Him and that bitch were raking it in and were trying to treat me like a fucking muppet. You know it, and I know it, and that,' he said with a shake of his head, 'is not something I was prepared to let slip. Terry deserved everything he had coming to him.'

Shaun swallowed deeply and his concerned gaze shot towards the pub. 'But what if they find out it was me?'

As he followed his son's gaze, Kenny screwed up his face. 'Who?' he demanded, genuinely perplexed.

'Ricky and Jamie,' Shaun answered, fear clearly evident in his voice.

Stepping away from his son, Kenny shook his head and let out a low chuckle. 'They won't,' he reassured him.

Shaun's voice took on a desperate measure. 'You know what they're like, they've got too much of Terry inside of them to be any different, they're like dogs with a bone once they've set their minds to something and they're not stupid, they keep looking at me,' he complained. 'They know what I did, that it was me, and what about...' Beads of cold sweat broke out across Shaun's forehead. 'What if they want in on the business – you know, the women,' he whispered. 'Or what if they go to the old bill? The filth would throw the book at us; they'll start snooping around, they'd question us, they'd question me. What if the old bill suss out the truth, that it was me who killed Terry, I'd go to prison, and I can't,' he cried. 'I can't do time Dad, you know that, I wouldn't cope, I'd fall apart.'

Dismissing his son's fears, Kenny rolled his eyes before glancing around him to check that no one else was within earshot of their conversation. 'Trust me,' he said, his voice low, 'Ricky and Jamie are clueless. They know fuck all about the shooting and as for the tarts, do you really think that Terry would have involved them in something like that?'

Unconvinced, Shaun took a deep breath. 'You don't know that for certain Dad...' he began.

'Yes I do.' Slinging his arm around his son's shoulders, Kenny nodded towards the pub. 'Terry didn't want the boys involved; he wouldn't have wanted them to know that his and Tracey's marriage was nothing other than a sham – at least on his part anyway, I'm not sure the same can be said about Tracey. You know as well as I do that he'd fuck anything with a pulse.' He afforded Shaun a wide grin. 'Now sober the fuck up before you end up causing us a shit load of aggro.'

'Is everything okay out here?'

Both Kenny and Shaun swung their heads round in time to see Ricky step outside the pub, his head tilted to one side as he studied them.

'Yeah.' Kenny grinned. He jerked his thumb towards his son and gave a wink. 'He's had a bit too much sherbet, if you get my drift.'

Ricky Tempest narrowed his eyes. 'It's my old man's funeral,' he said, taking a step closer. 'My mum is already in bits so rein it in a bit, yeah? I don't want her any more upset than she already is.'

The abrupt way in which Ricky spoke rankled Kenny, making

his back instantly stiffen. It was like listening to Terry bark out his orders all over again. Resisting the urge to tell his friend's son to fuck off, Kenny held up his hands, his expression becoming one of mock contrition. 'He'll behave himself, don't you worry about that; I've already given him a talking to.'

Giving a satisfied nod of his head, Ricky retreated back inside the pub.

As he watched Ricky go, Kenny's eyes became hard slits and his lips curled into a snarl. 'Who does the little fucker think he is, eh, telling me' – he poked himself in the chest – 'to rein it in, like I'm no one, like I'm some kind of mug. The prick needs to remember who he's talking to. I was having tear ups before he was even a twinkle in his old man's eyes.'

Shrugging, Shaun made the wise decision to keep his mouth firmly closed. The last thing he wanted to do was rile his father up even further than was necessary. As it was, he had a feeling that his dad was already teetering on the edge of sanity, he had to be if he truly believed that they could get away with murdering Terry Tempest without bringing any repercussions on themselves.

As they walked back into the pub, Shaun kept his head down low. Despite what Kenny thought of the two brothers, Ricky and Jamie were Tempests through and through. They could be hard bastards when they needed to be; it was one of the many reasons why Terry had put them to work as enforcers, whereas he had been given the task of guarding the women they trafficked. It just about said it all really, didn't it? Even his own father didn't believe he was capable of anything other than collecting the tarts from Bianca Murphy, and to make matters even worse, Shaun knew it too. The problem was he hadn't had the same upbringing as his father or the Tempests. While he'd been learning Latin at private school, Ricky and Jamie had been learning their trade by getting into scraps in the playground. Their worlds were poles apart, and it was only now with the fear of Ricky and Jamie's wrath hanging over Shaun's head that this fact bothered him.

* * *

Once he'd returned to his seat, Ricky nodded towards his brother, indicating that he'd had a word in Kenny's ear. He was determined that nothing and no one would ruin his dad's send off and that included Kenny Kempton and his son.

'Are you all right Mum?' Grasping his mother's hand, Ricky gave a gentle squeeze.

Tracey sighed. Picking up her wine glass, she took a long sip. How was she supposed to answer? Of course she wasn't all right. How could she be when across the road in the churchyard, her husband's corpse had been lowered into the ground, in what would become his final resting place. She still couldn't believe that Terry was gone, that she would never see him again.

'I just want to know why,' she finally answered. 'Why would someone have wanted to see your dad dead?'

Turning back to look at the crowded pub, Ricky was quiet for a few moments. He didn't have the answers that his mum so desperately craved; all he knew was that his dad had been a good bloke and that he'd been well liked and respected. The wait for his dad's body to be released for burial had felt like torture and all these weeks after the murder, Ricky was still unable to get his head around the fact that someone had wanted to top Terry; it just made no sense to him. How had the gunman known that his dad would be at the party, that there even was a party, and more to the point how had he carried out the execution? The shooter hadn't been in near proximity, that was one thing Ricky knew for a fact. In the aftermath of the shooting, he and Jamie had searched the alleyway directly behind their parent's house and subsequently come up empty handed. The only conclusion left open to them was that the bastard responsible for gunning their dad down must have somehow been watching the party unfold through the cracks in the garden fence, then once their father had been successfully executed, the shooter had promptly had it away on his toes. What other possible explanation could there be? It hadn't been someone at the actual party; his father had been shot from behind, his upper back taking the impact of the bullet, and seeing as his dad had been about to give a speech, he'd been facing the guests. As for Terry, of course he'd made enemies along the way. It was inevitable, a part of life, especially when you considered the world he'd lived in, but his dad had never mentioned any active feuds, at least not to him or his brother anyway.

'We'll get to the bottom of it Mum,' he sighed. 'Someone will know who did this.'

Tracey let out a bitter laugh and as she followed her son's gaze, her eyes became hard. 'Oh, you can bet your life on it that I'll find out who was responsible,' she answered, grasping both of her boys' hands. 'I'll turn this town apart if I have to because believe me, if it's the last thing I ever do I will find the bastard who killed my Terry.'

Ricky and Jamie shared a knowing glance. As tiny as their mum was, she had a vicious temper on her, one that even their dad had been loath to get on the wrong side of. It was no secret that Tracey was a strong, feisty woman; she had to be to have survived being married to Terry Tempest for as long as she had.

As she continued to stare out at the mourners, anger coursed through Tracey's veins. It had been no lie; she would find out who'd murdered Terry, and when she did the bastard was going to wish that he had never been born.

3

The moment Kenny stepped foot inside Terry's kitchen he knew instinctively that something was off. It was a few days after the funeral and at Tracey's persistence, he'd finally decided to get it over and done with and pay her a visit. Tracey for her part looked a state and that was saying something. Not only did she look as though she'd been dragged through a hedge backwards, but she also looked as though her hair hadn't been washed or brushed in days. She didn't have a scrap of makeup on and if that wasn't bad enough, the light grey lounge suit she wore was so badly creased he wouldn't be surprised if she'd slept in it the night before.

'What's all this?' he asked, nodding down at the solid oak table which was covered in a mound of paperwork.

Flicking the switch for the kettle to boil, Tracey took four mugs out of the overhead cupboard then set them on the kitchen counter.

'I'm looking for answers,' she sighed with a glance over her shoulder at the documents. 'I need to know why my Terry was murdered; I mean, could he have stumbled across something illegal?' She looked inquisitively towards her two sons who leant casually against the worktops with their arms folded across their chests. 'Maybe he'd been a witness to something, and someone killed him to make sure that he kept quiet.'

'Yeah, maybe Mum,' Ricky was quick to answer. Unable to fully meet his mother's eyes, he shifted his weight slightly then shot a glance in Kenny's direction, hoping that his dad's business partner wouldn't laugh in his mum's face and tell her that it was more plausible for Terry to have been the one to carry out an execution. As much as his mum thought she knew everything there was to know about her husband, Ricky knew for a fact that his dad had kept his wife in the dark when it came to his criminal activities. To Tracey's knowledge, her husband had earned a living ducking and diving, that he'd sold knocked off goods and counterfeits from the back of a lorry, and in recent years had started up a successful debt collecting service.

Before his death, Terry had run a criminal empire, and had been a very dangerous individual with a short temper and more fool anyone who'd thought that they could take him on and win. His reputation had been warranted, and he wouldn't have thought twice about plunging a knife into a man's gut if he'd had the audacity to try and muscle in on what Terry considered to be his turf. And, considering his dad's patch spread across the entire length of Dagenham, there wasn't much room for anyone else to try and wade in. Not that Terry would have given anyone the chance to; he would have had the geezer wiped out at the first hint of a takeover.

From Kenny's position, he could see that Tracey had pulled out what looked like every one of her husband's bank statements alongside a shoe box crammed full of receipts.

'Have you found anything?' he asked, making sure to keep his voice steady.

Distributing out the steaming cups of coffee, Tracey wearily took a seat at the table, and wrapped her hands around her own mug, glad of the warmth spreading through her fingers. 'No, nothing yet,' she sighed.

It took all of Kenny's strength not to allow his shoulders to sag with relief, not that he'd actually thought Tracey would find anything. Terry may have been a lot of things, but he hadn't been stupid. The last thing he would have done was leave a paper trail linking him to organised crime. After all, it was the number one rule, wasn't it? You wouldn't rob a bank and then keep the plans to the heist in your possession; even the densest of criminals weren't that daft.

Joining Tracey at the table, Kenny took a sip of his coffee. 'So' – he glanced warily across to Ricky and Jamie – 'what was it you wanted to see me about?'

'This.' Passing across a glossy brochure, Tracey attempted to smile. 'You weren't only Terry's best mate, you were like a brother to him, and I thought that maybe you'd like some input into his headstone.'

Kenny's eyebrows rose a fraction. 'I don't know what to say,' he said, taken aback. He offered a tight smile, then went back to browsing the catalogue. From what he could see, headstones didn't come cheap. Not that money was an issue; he was more than good for it, and he knew for a fact that Terry would have left Tracey a fair few bob, maybe even millions.

'He deserves the best,' Tracey added as she studied Kenny over the rim of her mug. 'I was thinking this one.' Leaning across the table she pointed to an elaborate granite memorial, bearing a huge, winged angel complete with a golden halo, that stood perched on top of a heart-shaped headstone. The whole ensemble had to stand at least six feet tall by Kenny's estimation, maybe even taller.

Almost choking on his coffee, Kenny looked at Tracey, his jaw dropping slightly open. It had to be a joke, surely? But the seriousness of Tracey's expression told him otherwise. Raising his eyebrows, he glanced down at the price and almost keeled over in shock. Fifteen thousand quid! For that price, surely it had to be made of gold or some other precious metal?

'What do you reckon?' Tracey asked, breaking his thoughts. 'Do you think it's too much?'

Looking back down at the catalogue, Kenny was at a loss for words. Too much was an understatement. The memorial would have been better suited to royalty instead of the local villain. 'It's smashing darling,' he lied. 'A fitting tribute.'

For the first time since Kenny had arrived, Tracey smiled, not what he would call a genuine smile, but it was still a smile, nonetheless. 'I like it,' she said, 'and I want him to have the best.' Tears filled her eyes and as her sons pushed themselves away from the kitchen counter to offer comfort, she waved them away. 'I'm okay,' she said, wiping her eyes with the cuff of her sleeve. 'I don't have any other choice.'

* * *

Forty minutes later, as Ricky and Jamie made their way out of their family home, Jamie tugged on his brother's arm.

'I'm worried about Mum,' he said with a jerk of his head towards the house. 'I mean, what exactly is she hoping to achieve by going through Dad's paperwork? It's not like she's going to stumble across a written note from the shooter, is she?'

Looking back towards the house, Ricky was thoughtful for a few moments. Like Jamie, he too was worried, only unlike his brother, he'd tried to brush his concerns under the carpet. If he didn't have to think about them then they weren't real and, besides, it had to be a lot better than the alternative and admit that their mum wasn't exactly coping. 'She's grieving bruv.'

'Grieving or not,' Jamie hissed, 'she's not acting right... up here.' He tapped his temple. 'And as for that fucking monstrosity she's picked out, Dad wouldn't have wanted that, and you know it.'

Ricky raised his eyebrows; he had no other choice but to agree with his brother. Their dad would turn in his grave if could see the memorial his wife had picked out for him. 'If it makes her feel better...' he began.

'You've got to stop her,' Jamie interrupted. 'Put your foot down and tell her we don't want it. She's going to end up making a laughing stock of dad. It's an embarrassment bruv.'

Ricky grimaced. 'Why me?' he exclaimed.

'You know why.' Shoving his hands into his pockets, Jamie gave a knowing grin, a smile that was so like their dad's. 'Because you're the eldest. She'll listen to you, you know she will.'

Ricky wasn't so sure. Their mum had never listened to anyone her entire life and that included their dad. 'Are you really that worried about her?'

'To put it in a nutshell bruv, I think she's lost the plot. We should have seen this coming; she's been with dad since she was sixteen, it's all she's ever known, she was hardly going to take his death lying down, was she?'

His brother was right and as Ricky lit a cigarette, he pulled the smoke deep into his lungs and ran a hand through his dark hair. Maybe he should ask Kayla to have a word. She and his mum got on like a house on fire, and surely it would be better coming from a woman; perhaps she could even guide his mum towards a more appropriate headstone, something less gaudy. 'I'll speak to Kayla, ask her to chat with Mum. She's good at that sort of thing.' Fishing out his car keys, he made to open the car door when Jamie tugged on his arm a second time.

'What about Dad's stuff?' he asked, motioning towards the house. 'She's going to end up driving herself out of her mind if she stays up all night again. It's not like she's even going to find anything; Dad wasn't stupid was he?'

Ricky shook his head. Jamie was right, their dad wouldn't have kept anything incriminating in the house. If it was the breaker's yard on the other hand, then maybe his mum might just find something of interest. Terry certainly seemed to like spending a lot of time there and some days you could barely prise him away, not that Ricky had ever been able to see the attraction. Every time he visited the yard he came away covered in dust, grime and slobber from the two German Shepherds who guarded the premises. 'Maybe it would be better if I have a chat with her instead.' He opened the car door and climbed inside. 'Not that she's likely to listen to me.'

Satisfied, Jamie nodded and with one last look back at the house, he made his way towards his own car. With a heavy heart, he pulled away from the kerb. He hated the fact that they were leaving their mum all by herself, not that she wanted him or Ricky to stay the night with her, she'd made that more than clear when they'd offered to keep her company. But that was Tracey all over; she could be as stubborn as a mule when the mood took her and he had a nasty feeling she was going to be just as stubborn when it came to the garish granite memorial she'd chosen.

* * *

Pouring herself a much-needed glass of wine, Tracey took a long sip then replaced the bottle back in the fridge and nudged the door gently closed. Setting the glass on the kitchen counter, she leant back against the cabinets and surveyed the kitchen. This part of the house had always been her domain, her pride and joy. She'd kept the kitchen spotless and Terry had often joked that you could eat your dinner off the floor, it was that clean. Tears sprang to her eyes and blinking them away, she lit a cigarette, her hand ever so slightly trembling.

The house was so quiet, it didn't feel like a home any more. Oh, she was used to being alone, especially in the evenings. More often than not, Terry wouldn't return home until the early hours of the morning, and she would usually be in bed fast asleep by the time he finally crawled into bed beside her. Only she'd never felt *lonely* back then. Despite the fact she rarely saw her husband, there had always been some background noise, the washing machine, the television, or maybe one of her favourite CDs would be playing. She was a particular fan of David Bowie and would often sing along to his songs while she did the housework. She'd even joked that Bowie was the only man who could tempt her away from Terry.

The memory made her smile. The truth was, as much as she loved Bowie, not even he would have been able to come between her and her husband. She'd loved Terry so much that in all the years they had been together she'd never so much as looked at another man. How could she when Terry was buried so deep under her skin that even the notion of being without him felt alien to her. She'd been sixteen, and Terry eighteen when they had got together, nothing more than kids, yet from the very first moment she'd clapped her eyes upon him she'd known that he was the only man for her. After their first date she'd even told her mum that she'd met the man she was going to marry. The memory made her smile even wider. Not only had she married him just as she'd predicted she would, but she had also given birth to his two sons. They had been a family, and they had been happy.

'What am I going to do without you Tel?' she said out loud. There was no response – not that she'd really expected one – just an earie silence that engulfed her entire body, making her inwardly shudder.

With one last drag on the cigarette, she stubbed the butt out in a glass ashtray, knocked back the wine then took a seat at the table. Spread out before her were Terry's bank statements. She'd already gone back six months and as of yet nothing had screamed out at her as being out of the ordinary, just the usual outgoings: petrol, meals in various restaurants, the jewellers where he'd bought her birthday present – a stunning gold tennis bracelet that he'd paid a small fortune for – and then the bill that he'd paid for the kitchen extension. As for incoming assets, five months earlier it looked as if he'd sold a car and thirty thousand pounds had been deposited into his account. Her forehead furrowed. Terry's silver Audi still sat on the drive, and hadn't moved since his death and she had no recollection of him ever owning another car. Perhaps it had been one of the boy's cars that had been sold, not that she could remember either one of them saying that they had sold a car either. Giving a slight shrug, Tracey went back to work and, with a highlighting pen in her hand, she highlighted anything that she was unsure of.

It was on the second page that she found another car Terry had sold, this time for twenty-five thousand pounds. Her heart pounding, Tracey sat up a little straighter and frowned. Flicking through the statements, she found a further six cars. Each car had been sold to a company called Hardcastle Limited. A quick google search told her that Hardcastle Limited was a car dealership based in Southend-on-Sea, the director a Maxwell Hardcastle. The name meant nothing to her and pressing her fingertips together, she leant her elbows on the table and stared down at her phone screen, unsure of what any of it meant, if it even did mean anything.

But the questions still remained: where had the cars come from and why had Terry never mentioned them to her? It wasn't as though they were talking about a few thousand pounds. Tallied up, the sales came to a staggering two hundred and twenty thousand pounds! So where was the money, and what had Terry done with it? Other than the extension on the kitchen they hadn't been splashing the cash, they hadn't holidayed abroad in recent years, and hadn't even gone on any shopping sprees, nor had they dined out every evening.

A sickening thought spread through Tracey's veins. Perhaps he'd come by the cars illegally, perhaps they had been stolen, but even that made no sense. Surely if this had been the case, Terry wouldn't have deposited the money into his bank account, would he?

There were so many questions that she needed the answers to. Taking note of the time on her phone, Tracey bit down on her lip. It was nearing midnight, far too late to call the boys and ask them to come back over. As it was, she had a feeling that they were worried about her. They hadn't said as much but they didn't need to, she'd seen the glances they shared, the look in their eyes whenever she mentioned their father. It was almost as though they wanted her to forget about him, to put him to the back of her mind and get on with her life as though he'd never existed. Easier said than done as far as Tracey was concerned. She would not stop fighting for Terry; he deserved justice, and she was deter-mined to fight for him until she took her very last breath.

As much as she didn't want it to, her mind wandered back to the moment Terry had been murdered. There had been no clues as to what was about to come, there had been no masked marksman bursting into the house, no angry shouts, no noticeable change in Terry's stance. No, her husband had been just as unaware of the tragedy which was about to unfold as both she and their guests had been. And yet there must have been something she was missing. Had there been a movement, or a sound that had been out of place? Had Terry perhaps seemed on edge in the days running up to his murder? No, was her answer, there had been nothing to alert her to the fact that something so heinous was about to occur, that her entire world would be turned upside down.

* * *

Early the next morning, a bleary-eyed Ricky reached out to grab his mobile phone from the bedside table. The shrill ringing had awakened him from a fitful sleep and he felt more tired now than he'd felt before going to bed the previous night.

'Mum.' His voice was thick, and he slid his tongue over his teeth before taking the phone away from his ear and noting the time. It had only just turned seven o'clock. 'You haven't been up all night again, have you?' he asked, rubbing the sleep from the corners of his eyes.

As Tracey answered, he groaned out loud and turned over on to his side. Beside him, Kayla lay on her back with one arm folded above her head. In that instant she'd never looked more beautiful to him. Her soft snores alerted him to the fact that she was in a deep sleep, and throwing the duvet away from himself, he sat up, swung his legs over the edge of the bed, and planted his feet firmly on the floor. 'You have to get some sleep Mum,' he scolded, his voice low, careful not to wake his girlfriend. 'You're going to make yourself ill if you carry on like this.'

Padding out of the bedroom with the phone tucked between

his ear and shoulder, he headed for the bathroom. Once there he placed his hand on the cool tiles and bowed his head, the conversation he'd had with his brother just hours earlier at the forefront of his mind. Jamie had been right, and no matter how much he'd wanted to ignore the warning signs, it was pretty obvious that their mum was on a downward spiral. She was becoming obsessed with their father's murder. Ricky wanted answers too; he'd give anything to know why his dad had been killed, and more importantly he wanted to know who had been responsible. Fair enough, his old man hadn't been a saint, and when it came to business his dad had been more than a little bit shady; in fact, it would be fair to say that Terry had been a big player in the criminal underworld. Unlike Tracey though, Ricky wasn't obsessing over the killing. And as much as he missed his dad, he didn't want to think about the murder night and day. It had been horrific enough to witness the shooting let alone relive it over and over again in his mind. He and Jamie had already put their own feelers out, and had let it be known that they were gunning for the bastards responsible. They were Tempests and that had to mean something, didn't it? Their surname was enough to put the fear of Christ into people, and although Ricky had never been the type of man to inflict fear, if it meant getting answers he was more than prepared to do just that.

As she switched off the call, Tracey had to fight down the urge not to throw her mobile phone at the wall. She had never felt so incensed. Her own son, her own flesh and blood who she had not only given birth to but who she had fed, clothed and cared for his entire life had spoken to her as though she were nothing more than an errant child. Who the fuck he thought he was she didn't know. How dare he tell her to go to bed and forget about her husband? Fair enough, he hadn't used those exact words, he hadn't needed to, the sentiment had been there.

Willing herself to calm down, Tracey retreated back to the kitchen and flicked the switch for the kettle to boil. While she waited, she lit a cigarette and inhaling deeply, she noisily blew out a thin stream of smoke.

She was smoking far too much of late. Before Terry's death she'd hardly smoked at all, maybe the odd one every now and then when she was feeling stressed or whenever Patricia had come over for a visit, but even then she could take them or leave them. Now she couldn't seem to stop and had already smoked her way through half a pack since climbing out of the shower in the early hours of the morning.

Once the kettle had boiled, she made herself a strong cup of coffee then arranged the documents out on the table so that she could question the boys when they arrived. They had to know where the cars had come from; they had worked for their father since leaving school and were a part of the business. Briefly she wondered if she should have bypassed her boys and gone straight to Kenny. After all, he had been Terry's business partner and surely he would have been able to give her answers as to who Maxwell Hardcastle was.

A quick glance up at the clock on the wall told her it was too late: Ricky and Jamie were already on their way over. Still, she decided, if they weren't forthcoming with information she would pay Kenny a visit and demand he tell her what the hell was going on. Satisfied that she now had a plan in place, Tracey stubbed out the cigarette and reaching under the sink, she took out a can of air freshener. The last thing she wanted was for her sons to find something else to complain about.

With the kitchen now smelling reasonably fresher, Tracey

took a seat at the table in what had once been Terry's chair. It was a calculated gesture, one that she hoped her sons would recognise. Whether they liked it or not she was now the head of the family and tapping her fingernails on top of the documents, she hoped for their sakes the boys gave her the same respect that they had afforded their father, because she was done playing games. She wanted to get to the bottom of Terry's murder and was as determined as she had been on the evening of his funeral when she had vowed to bring the bastard responsible to his knees.

4

Two hours later, Ricky stepped his foot on the brake and switched off the ignition. Up ahead he watched as Jamie climbed out of his own car and took a wild guess that his brother had been waiting for him to arrive, more than likely dreading the idea of tackling their mother alone. Not that he could entirely blame him; he himself didn't want to deal with her, and certainly didn't want to admit to himself that his mum might need help.

'What the fuck is this all about?' Jamie demanded. He tapped his watch, his expression one of annoyance at being awoken so early. 'I told you that she's lost the plot, that she's gone fucking cuckoo.'

Wearily, Ricky glanced across to their parents' house. 'She's grieving...' he began.

Jamie screwed up his face, his eyes hard. 'If you say that one more time bruv, I'm going to end up swinging for you.' He stabbed a stiff finger towards the house. 'Grieving or not this isn't normal, and you know it isn't. Take your head out of your arse for five minutes and wake the fuck up; she needs professional help.'

Swallowing down a retort, Ricky sighed. As much as he hated

to admit it, Jamie was right: their mum's behaviour was erratic. 'Come on.' Shoving his car keys into his jacket pocket, he nodded towards the path. 'Let's get this over and done with.'

At the iron gate they both paused. 'Well go on,' Ricky said, pushing his brother forward.

'Nah, fuck that.' Digging his heels into the floor, Jamie shook his head. 'You're the eldest you go first.'

'She's not dangerous,' Ricky hissed. 'This is our mum we're talking about, not some maniac.'

Jamie raised his eyebrows; he didn't look so sure. 'Then you won't mind going first then will you.' He smirked, shoving his brother forward.

Moments later, they entered the house, the stench of stale cigarette smoke assaulting their nostrils. 'Mum,' Ricky called out, his gaze darting around the hallway on the lookout for anything out of the ordinary.

'I'm in the kitchen,' Tracey called back.

Giving his brother a hard stare, Ricky shook his head. Anyone would think their mum was unhinged the way Jamie was carrying on, and yeah, admittedly she was behaving out of the ordinary, but she was still their mum. Not only that but from the tone of her voice it was more than clear that she still had all of her facilities, that she hadn't entirely lost the plot as his brother had so eloquently put it.

As he entered the kitchen, Ricky instantly rocked back on his heels. As bold as brass, his mum was sitting at the head of the table. No one had ever sat in their dad's chair before. It was an unspoken rule; it was his, and where he'd always sat. In that instant, he felt his shoulders sag and rubbed wearily at his forehead. 'What's going on Mum?' he asked with a measure of trepidation.

'This.' Lighting a cigarette, Tracey squinted through the

curling smoke and nodded down at the bank statements. 'What do you know about your dad selling cars?' Her cold stare flashed between her two sons. 'And who the bloody hell is Maxwell Hardcastle?'

Taken aback, Ricky and Jamie shared a surreptitious glance.

'Well,' Tracey asked, 'cat got your bleeding tongues? What do you know about your father selling cars and who is Maxwell Hardcastle?'

Shooting Jamie a glance, Ricky swallowed deeply. 'It was just business Mum.'

'Don't,' Tracey warned, wagging a finger at her sons, 'try and treat me like a fool. Where did the cars come from because I know for a fact they weren't your dad's.'

A moment of silence followed, and, as she banged her fist down on the table, Tracey's eyes flashed dangerously. 'Well come on,' she shouted, 'answer me. Any other day the pair of you can talk the hind legs off a donkey so don't you bloody dare come over all coy now.'

'It's like Rick said, it was just business Mum,' Jamie volunteered.

'Just business?' Throwing up her arms, Tracey gave a sarcastic laugh. 'We've already established that it was just business and believe me when I say this, you had best start talking and fast before I end up losing my rag and batter the pair of you. What the fuck has been going on behind my back?'

Stuck between a rock and a hard place, Ricky sighed. 'It's simple Mum, Dad would...' He momentarily paused, his loyalty to his father once again rushing to the fore. Terry had never wanted his wife involved in his business dealings and had done everything in his power to ensure that Tracey was kept in the dark.

'Well go on,' Tracey urged. 'Your dad, what?'

'He acquired one or two cars, then sold them on to Hardcastle and they would split the profit. It was simple really and everyone was a winner.' Noting the confusion in his mother's eyes Ricky explained himself further. 'Dad would sell a car for say thirty grand and then Hardcastle would double the price and sell the car on for sixty grand, meaning they both had thirty grand in their back pocket.'

Tracey's eyes widened. 'What do you mean he *acquired* one or two cars?'

Wishing that he'd kept his mouth firmly shut, Ricky shrugged. 'The majority of them he took as debts owed to himself.'

'And the rest?' Tracey hissed.

'Fell off the back of a lorry.' Jamie laughed, amusement clearly audible in his voice.

'You mean they were stolen?' Tracey gasped.

Ricky and Jamie both nodded. 'Well, sort of,' Ricky volunteered.

Tracey's eyebrows shot up. 'What do you mean sort of? They either were or they weren't.'

Looking to his brother for confirmation, Ricky cleared his throat. 'Not all of the cars were kosher. Like I said, some Dad took as debts owed to himself, and some, well... they sort of found their way into his hands. Once the licence plates had been changed over they were usually then sold to a private buyer.'

'Oh my God.' As she grasped on to the edge of the table, a shard of fear shot down the length of Tracey's spine. Right from the very beginning she'd known that Terry was no angel, but a thief? She would never have believed him capable of it.

'It's not a big deal.' Jamie shrugged. 'And it was a good earner, more than a good earner. In fact, Dad was raking it in.'

'Not a big deal?' Tracey screeched at the top of her lungs.

Leaping out of her seat, she clipped her son around the ear. 'It's theft and highly bloody illegal, not forgetting immoral.' Breathing heavily, she reached out for her cigarettes. 'I can't get my head around this,' she cried. 'I know he wasn't exactly a choir boy but not for one single minute did I think your father could be so devious.' Opening the box, she went to take out a cigarette before stopping herself and instead tossed the packet back on to the table. She was sick to the bloody back teeth of smoking and if she ever saw another cigarette again it would be far too soon. 'And what about this Hardcastle fella?'

Ricky narrowed his eyes. 'What about him?'

'What was he getting out of this arrangement?'

Jamie shrugged. 'Like Rick said, the profit was split fifty-fifty, everyone was happy.'

For a few moments Tracey stood thinking, then sitting back down at the table, she began to hastily leaf through the bank statements. The last car had been sold five months previously, and her sons were right, a lot of money had passed hands, but then Terry had suddenly stopped doing business with Hardcastle?

'Oh my God,' she cried, 'don't you see what this means?'

Bewildered, both Ricky and Jamie shook their heads.

'It was this Hardcastle, he killed your father. It has to have been him. He didn't like the fact that your dad had ended their arrangement and, he had a grudge to bear, he wanted revenge.'

'Nah.' Jamie shook his head. 'I don't think so Mum. Hardcastle's all right; he's a nice geezer.'

Tracey gave a bitter laugh. 'He can't be that nice. He sells stolen cars for a living.' She tapped the paperwork. Everything had become crystal clear to her even if her sons refused to believe it. Maxwell Hardcastle was her husband's murderer.

* * *

An hour later Tracey was in her bedroom putting the finishing touches to her makeup. Dressed in a simple black shift dress, she'd pushed her stockinged feet into her trademark leopard print heels and standing back, she inspected the final ensemble in her full-length mirror. Other than the fine crow's lines around her eyes, she looked well for her age and could easily pass for a woman ten years younger.

Grabbing her Prada handbag, she made her way down the stairs. In the hallway she paused for a moment before reaching out for Terry's car keys that he kept on a hook beside the front door. She may as well go all out she decided. Maxwell Hardcastle would not intimidate her and despite the fact she fully believed him to be her husband's murderer she wasn't afraid of the man. In her eyes he was nothing other than a coward; he'd proved as much by shooting Terry in the back rather than face him head on like a man.

Moments later, she slammed out of the house and made her way towards the car. She'd never driven Terry's car further than around the block and as she slipped behind the wheel, the leather seat felt cool against her legs. She started the ignition and the car purred to life. As she pressed her foot down on the accelerator she was reminded once again of just how powerful the Audi was, certainly more powerful than her Mini Cooper.

Within ten minutes, Tracey was pulling up outside the breakers yard that Terry had owned. She had only visited the property once before and that had been on the day the sale had been finalised and Terry had collected the keys. Careful of where she trod, Tracey made her way across the forecourt. To her left was a single-story brick-built building that served as an office and screwed across the windows were a series of metal grills. In the distance she could hear the sound of dogs, their deep ferocious barks enough to halt her in her tracks. With a nervous glance over her shoulder, she noted that the gates were wide open and took a wild guess that the animals were chained up. Surely Kenny wouldn't allow them to roam free when they could easily escape, would he?

Satisfied that she wasn't about to be mauled to death, Tracey picked up her pace and reaching the office, she placed her hand on the door handle and gave it a hard tug. When the door didn't budge she looked around her; she'd seen Kenny's car outside and so knew he was around somewhere.

'Hello,' she called out.

When there was no response, she set off towards the house. Just like the office, the windows had been covered in metal grills, even the windows on the upper the floor. Frowning, Tracey stared up at the building. She couldn't remember seeing bars at the windows when she'd last visited and briefly wondered why Terry had needed so much security. Had he been concerned that he would be burgled? Not that she could see much being stored in the house, at least nothing of value anyway. Perhaps the bars were to keep squatters out?

'Hello,' she called out a second time. Again, there was nothing but silence. Tentatively she took a step closer to the house. She reached out to push the door when suddenly it opened.

Stifling a scream, Tracey placed her hand across her heart. 'Kenny,' she breathed, 'you scared me.'

For the briefest of moments, Kenny's eyes were hard before he hastily composed himself, his expression breaking out into a stilted smile. 'Tracey.' His gaze darted behind her as though he was looking for someone. 'What are you doing here?'

Tracey sighed and opening her handbag, she took out the bank statements. 'I want to have a word,' she said, brandishing the documents towards him. 'The boys have told me everything.'

* * *

Kenny's skin paled and as he hastily closed the front door behind him, beads of perspiration broke out across his forehead. Had Terry told his sons about the tarts? He'd been under the impression that Ricky and Jamie were oblivious to the fact their father bought and sold women, at least this was what his former business partner had told him whenever Kenny had suggested they bring the boys in on the deal. Terry hadn't wanted his sons involved, hadn't wanted them to know just how despicable he really was. Besides, he wouldn't have been able to keep seeing Bianca Murphy on the side in Ricky's or Jamie's presence would he? At least not without opening up a whole can of worms first. As it was, his sons believed that his and Tracey's marriage was rock solid, as did Tracey herself.

Narrowing his eyes, Kenny eyed the paperwork warily, his fists involuntarily clenching at his sides. He was more than prepared, if need be, to crack Tracey one on the jaw and lock her in the house until he'd thought through a plan of action. After all, just one wrong word from her and the whole deal would come crashing down around him, taking with it his freedom if the old bill were to get wind of the operation.

Careful to keep his voice steady, he nodded down at the documents. 'What have the boys said?'

Tracey rolled her eyes. Considering the mood she was in, now wasn't the time for Kenny to try and squirm his way out of his wrongdoings. 'As if you don't know.' She gave a hard stare and shook the paperwork in front of his face. 'The cars Terry acquired.'

Relief surged through Kenny's veins and he had to stop himself from laughing aloud. Was that it? She'd decided to confront him over a few poxy cars Terry had sold to Hardcastle? 'Let me make you a cup of tea.' Placing his hand on the small of her back, he guided her towards the office and away from the house where four women were currently padlocked inside a room at the far end of the property. 'And then me and you can have a proper chat.'

5

Tracey's eyes were narrowed into slits as she watched Kenny make the tea. She was so angry; no, more than angry, she felt hurt, devastated even, that her husband had kept so much of his life hidden away from her. Hadn't Terry trusted her? Did he think so little of her that he'd thought she would open her trap and go running to the police at the first hint of trouble? In all the years they had been together she'd only ever kept her mouth firmly closed and had never once said or done anything that could have jeopardised their marriage.

Right from the off she'd known that Terry dabbled on the wrong side of the law, but she'd wrongly assumed her husband had done nothing more than earn his fortune by running a successful debt collection service and on the odd occasion sell a few knocked off goods, such as televisions, microwaves, or designer garments. One year he'd even sold Christmas trees. The pine needles had been a bugger to clean up, and no matter how many times she'd vacuumed, months later she'd still found the needles clinging to the carpet. It had been enough to put her off a real Christmas tree for life. The fact the goods Terry had sold had also been stolen was wiped from her mind. Everyone loved a bargain, didn't they, and in her mind that was all Terry had ever done – supplied items to people who in normal circumstances wouldn't have been able to afford to buy them. He was simply doing them a favour and was the equivalent of a modern-day Robin Hood. It wasn't as though anyone got hurt, and like Terry had always told her, most people had insurance anyway, so it wasn't as though anyone was actually out of pocket.

'So.' Placing a mug of tea in front of Tracey, Kenny eased his body into a chair. 'What did you want to have a chat about?'

Shaking her head, Tracey glanced down at the paperwork. There were so many questions she wanted the answers to that she didn't know where to begin. Finally, she cleared her throat, deciding not to beat around the bush and to get straight down to business. 'Maxwell Hardcastle,' she said, barely able to keep the animosity from her voice. 'How well do you know him?'

Kenny shrugged. Hardcastle was a face in his own right and behind the façade of being a businessman he was a hard fucker, one that even Kenny was loathe to get on the wrong side of. 'I've known him for years. Both me and Terry went to school with him, we used to knock around together, well until he ended up being sent down for a lump that is. Eighteen years he got. He topped his mother's bloke.' Kenny shook his head and blew out his cheeks as if recalling the memory. 'They had to identify the poor sod from his dental records, the beating had been that severe. From what I can remember he served a year or two in a youth detention centre then was moved to Belmarsh just after he'd turned eighteen. We lost contact with him for a while, then when he was released from nick he fucked off to Southend and has been there ever since.'

'Terry had known him well then?' Tracey's mouth dropped open. Not for a single moment had she expected her husband's murderer to be someone he'd known from childhood. As for Hardcastle, Terry had never once mentioned him, not even in passing. Not for the first time did she wonder how many more secrets her husband had kept from her; it was almost as though he was a stranger to her.

'Yeah.' Kenny shrugged. 'Like I said, we used to knock around together.'

Tracey raised her eyebrows and Kenny shifted his bulk, wondering what her reasons were for the sudden interest in Hardcastle. Had she already met with him? Had Terry bragged to Hardcastle that he and the bitch were stealing the profits, that together they were mugging him off, or had Tracey put two and two together come up with five and guessed his part in her husband's death? Nothing would surprise him where Tracey was concerned; she'd always been astute, unless it involved her husband's womanising ways that was, then she'd been as green as grass. Terry could have told her the sky was pink and purple and she would have believed him hence how he'd got away with shagging his way across half of London for as long as he had.

'Hardcastle might have been a pal once but believe me darling, he's a slimy fucker; he'd kill you as soon as look at you that one. It's common knowledge that he can't be trusted.' Of course, it was all lies. Max Hardcastle was not only well liked and trusted but he was also highly respected amongst the criminal fraternity and considered a big player.

It was exactly as Tracey had suspected and nodding, she leant forward, her expression one of anger. 'It was him,' she hissed through gritted teeth. 'He murdered my Terry.'

Kenny's eyes ever so slightly widened, the only sign he gave away that Tracey's words had caught him off guard. To be more precise, if he hadn't have been so shocked he would have burst out laughing, a huge belly laugh that would have had him bent over double and wheezing for breath. Not only was she barking up the wrong tree, but she was also a million miles away from the truth. Terry and Hardcastle had got along like a house on fire, they'd respected one another and, as for the car scam, it had been more than a good earner while it lasted. So much so in fact that it had taken a lot of persuasion on Kenny's part to steer his business partner away from Hardcastle and towards the Murphy family and the plan to pimp out prostitutes. Not that Terry had complained once he'd come to realise the deal meant he would have the whores on tap whenever he so wished, but that had been Terry all over. He'd always been ruled by his cock, and other than being a greedy, back stabbing bastard, it had been one of his biggest downfalls.

As quick as a flash, Kenny composed himself, and following Tracey's stance, he leant forward and brought his head close to hers as though they were conspiring. 'Nothing,' he growled, 'would surprise me when it comes to Hardcastle. Like I said' – he leant back in the chair and spread open his arms – 'he's a law unto himself, always has been. I should have worked it out for myself really. I mean, him and Terry weren't exactly the best of mates; they'd had more than one run in over the years. The situation got pretty nasty at one point and a war was on the cards.'

Tracey frowned then looked back down at the bank statements, her mind working overtime. 'But if he and Terry didn't get along, then why would they go into business together?'

Silently cursing himself for his slip up, Kenny gulped at his tea, giving himself a few moments to think through a plausible answer. Finally, he shrugged. 'It's called keeping your friends close and your enemies closer, and trust me,' he snarled, 'Terry considered Hardcastle to be his enemy.'

Her eyes blazing with fury, Tracey's expression hardened. In her gut she'd known that Hardcastle was the reason her husband was dead, and nothing and no one would be able to convince her otherwise. She gave a half laugh that bordered on hysterical, and lifting her head, she looked Kenny in the eyes. 'I'm going to bring him down,' she snarled.

There and then Kenny didn't know whether to laugh or cry. Hardcastle taking the fall for a murder that he himself had orchestrated was the answer to all of his prayers and was certainly one way of taking any suspicion away from himself or his son. Raising his mug in the air, Kenny pretended to propose a toast. 'And I sincerely hope that you do darling,' he stated, his voice coming across as genuine.

'Oh I will.' Tracey knocked her own mug against his. 'You can bet your fucking life on it.'

* * *

Max Hardcastle was a good-looking man. Standing at six feet tall he had a hard body, light brown hair and steely grey eyes.

Amongst his other business interests, he'd owned Hardcastle Limited for the past five years and it was a good little earner. The car dealership only dealt with prestige cars that sold from forty grand upwards, and currently sitting on his forecourt he had three Mercedes-Benz, five Range Rovers, six Audis, and four brand spanking new Teslas, each one worth a staggering eighty grand.

Sat behind his desk, he flicked through the paperwork before him. He'd always considered himself to be a grafter and was proud of that fact. The truth was he didn't need to get his own hands dirty and could easily afford to get someone in to manage for him, but that wasn't who he was. He liked to keep an active role in his businesses, including the four book makers that he also owned.

After a quick glance at his watch, he pushed back his chair and strode out of the office. As he walked across the forecourt, one of the sales reps caught his eye. Trudie was an attractive girl, and it didn't escape his notice that whenever he was in the vicinity she would thrust her chest out towards him and seductively bite down on her bottom lip, in the hope that she would catch his attention. Once upon a time he wouldn't have thought twice about bending her over the desk and giving her one – he would have viewed the encounter as a welcome distraction from a hard day's graft – but as of late he couldn't be arsed with the all drama. It was inevitable that one thing would lead to another and before he knew it she would demand more and more of his time until eventually he would have no other choice but to let her down gently. There would be tears of course and he'd be called all the names under the sun, and all because he hadn't been able to keep his dick in his trousers. At the end of the day, it just wasn't worth the hassle he decided. Not only that but he'd never been the kind of man who'd wanted to settle down. Oh, he'd had flings of course, he'd even had a long-term relationship once, but he didn't want marriage and definitely didn't want children, and for most women that was a deal breaker.

'Trudie,' he called out as he made his way towards his car.

Flashing a wide smile, Trudie flicked a lock of blonde hair over her shoulder and pushed out her chest, her large breasts straining against the thin cotton shirt she wore.

'I'll be back in a couple of hours,' he said. 'If anyone calls, take a message.'

Trudie beamed even wider, glad of the attention. After all, Max Hardcastle was a catch; not only was he a good-looking man, but he also exuded power and wealth. 'Of course, Mr Hardcastle,' she trilled.

Max didn't bother to answer, and climbing into his car, he

sped away from the forecourt without even giving her so much as a customary glance.

* * *

An hour later, Tracey was driving down the A13 towards Southend-on-Sea. The fact that she was about to put herself into a precarious position was pushed to the back of her mind, and although actively seeking out Hardcastle wasn't one of her better ideas, she had to see the man who'd murdered Terry with her own two eyes. Kenny had made Hardcastle out to be the devil incarnate, a monster who not only needed to be brought down but who also needed to be destroyed, and she was just the woman to do that.

Beside her on the passenger seat her mobile phone began to ring. Tracey didn't need to look at the device to know who it was; it was bound to be one of her sons. This was the fifth phone call in as many minutes and just like the times before, she left the call to ring off. She didn't want the boys involved, didn't want to put them in any unnecessary danger, at least not until she'd sussed Hardcastle out for herself. It was bad enough that she was walking into the lion's den, she didn't want her sons to follow her.

The sign for the Southend turn off came into view, and pressing her foot down on the accelerator, Tracey forced herself to relax. She wasn't a fool; she wasn't going to do or say anything to give the game away or give Hardcastle a reason to lash out at her. All she planned to do was test the waters, get a measure of the man, so that when the time came she would know exactly how to destroy him.

* * *

Ricky leant back in the chair and toyed with the mobile phone in his hand. It was so unlike his mum to ignore his phone calls. Biting down on his thumbnail, he couldn't help but feel as though he had the weight of the world on his shoulders.

'Is she still not answering?'

Ricky looked up and as Kayla perched on the arm of the chair, he snaked his arm around her waist and hugged her to him.

'I'm worried,' he admitted. 'I don't know how to handle this. This isn't like my mum. Jamie thinks she's lost the plot. What are we supposed to do with her?' He looked up, his expression one of hopelessness. 'I mean, do we need to think about getting her professional help, or how about getting her sectioned?'

Kayla gave her son's father a sad smile. 'She's grieving,' she reminded him. 'She doesn't need medical help; all she needs is her family around her and time to adjust.'

'Exactly,' Ricky was quick to answer. 'You know what Jamie's like, he's putting all this shit into my head.' He stabbed his finger against his temple to emphasise his point. 'The way he's carrying on, anyone would think that Mum's gone fucking cuckoo. If it was left up to him he'd have her carted off to the nearest psychiatric unit.'

Kayla raised her eyebrows. 'You just have to give her time sweetheart. As for Jamie, he's as worried as you are. This is his way of dealing with the situation; he doesn't mean anything by it. He's scared, that's all. Your mum has always been strong, she's the backbone of the family, and it's hard to watch her fall apart knowing there is nothing you can do to stop her from hurting. But when she's ready, she has us to help her get through it. And you know how much she adores Mason; if anyone can put a smile on her face it will be him.' Standing up, she kissed the top of Ricky's head then left the room.

As he watched her go, Ricky was deep in thought. Kayla was

right, all his mum needed was a bit more time to adjust to life without his father. They couldn't just expect her to bounce back as though nothing had ever happened. Giving a moment's pause, he pressed redial and brought the phone up to his ear. As much as he'd needed to hear Kayla tell him that his mum would be okay, it wasn't enough to stop him from worrying about her.

Trudie took one look at the woman as she stepped out of the Audi and plastered a wide smile across her face. She knew money when she saw it and the woman who was walking towards her screamed loaded.

She watched as the woman bent down to look inside one of the Bentleys and Trudie's smile grew even wider. She was in desperate need of a sale and considering the majority of her earnings were based on commission, she decided to put on the charm.

'Can I help you?' she asked. As she approached, she made a show of giving the car a wistful glance. 'Beautiful, isn't it.'

Straightening up, the woman looked over the vehicle. 'Bloody expensive too I bet.'

Taken aback, Trudie frowned. Not for a single moment had she expected to hear an East London accent. Still, she decided, it didn't take away from the fact the woman had money, and from what she could make out, a lot of it. Audis didn't come cheap, and although the woman's outfit wasn't to Trudie's taste, the Prada bag on the other hand was to die for and unless she was very much mistaken, a limited edition. 'What else would you expect from a car of this quality?'

The woman held up her hand and cut Trudie off. 'I'm not here to buy a car darling so you can save the sales pitch.' She glanced towards the office. 'I'm here to see Maxwell Hardcastle.'

Trudie's frown deepened. It had been a long time since a woman had turned up to see Max, not that she would have said the woman before her was his usual type. He usually went for blondes, with large breasts, and long legs. They were considerably a lot younger too. Perhaps she was his sister, although she'd never heard him mention one, not that he'd ever discussed his private life with her before. 'I'm afraid he's not here at the moment. Can I take a message for him?'

'It's okay,' the woman called over her shoulder as she strolled towards the cabin. 'I'll wait for him.'

Trudie's mouth fell open. 'You can't just go in there without permission. That's Mr Hardcastle's office.'

The woman's eyes flashed dangerously as she spun round 'Do you wanna bet?' she called back before marching towards the office.

* * *

Switching off the ignition, Max climbed out of his car, pressed the fob to activate the central locking system then walked casually across the forecourt. Outside his office, Trudie was waiting for him.

'Oh Mr Hardcastle,' she cried, wringing her hands together. 'I tried to stop her but she wouldn't take no for an answer.' She looked nervously towards the cabin then back to him. 'I thought that maybe she could be your sister or something.'

Max frowned, his gaze following Trudie's. 'What are you talking about?' he snapped.

Taking several deep breaths to stop herself from hyperventilating, Trudie gestured behind her. 'A woman,' she answered, her voice barely louder than a whisper. 'She turned up and just stormed inside. Like I said, I tried to stop her; I told her it wasn't allowed, that you wouldn't be happy with her just turning up unannounced.'

'A woman?' he asked, his gaze flicking to where the office was situated.

Trudie nodded, her eyes wide.

Max sighed. It wasn't the first time a woman had turned up at his place of work demanding to know why he hadn't been in contact. Only it had been months since he'd last taken a woman out for the evening and even then he hadn't given any inclination that he'd wanted to see her again. As far as he'd been concerned, they'd had fun and that was as far as it was ever going to go. A sickening thought suddenly struck him. He'd always been careful, but accidents did happen. What if a woman had turned up to tell him she was pregnant? What if she demanded he play an active role in the child's life? The mere thought was enough to bring him out in a cold sweat. He was hardly a good role model; he was too set in his ways, he enjoyed living alone, enjoyed the solitude.

'It's okay,' he reassured Trudie, his voice coming across a lot more confident than he actually felt. 'I'll take care of this.'

Trudie gave the cabin one final surreptitious glance then nodded her thanks. Max made his way inside. He knew the young sales rep would have loved nothing more than to eavesdrop, and she probably would have done too if he hadn't given her a knowing look before firmly closing the door behind him.

Seated inside Hardcastle's office, Tracey Tempest glanced around her. She couldn't help but notice how tidy it was. Nothing appeared to be out of place; even the pens had been placed in a neat line beside an equally neat stack of paperwork.

As the door opened she looked up, the hint of a citrusy after-shave filling her nostrils. She saw Maxwell's eyes widen in surprise or maybe even relief and was momentarily taken aback. In her mind's eye she had formed a mental image of him, but the reality was very different. Instead of the monster she'd been expecting, Maxwell Hardcastle appeared handsome, his hard torso encased in a light grey shirt that not only matched his eyes but also showed off his muscular shoulders and biceps.

As he opened his mouth to speak, Tracey hastily interrupted him. 'Maxwell...'

'It's Max,' he corrected her. 'My old mum was the only one who ever called me Maxwell and even then it was more than likely because I was in the dog house and believe me, that was often.' He smiled. 'You could say I was a bit of a scallywag as a kid.'

There was a hint of humour in his voice which only heightened Tracey's anger. How the bastard had the front to smile in her face was beyond her comprehension. 'I'm Tracey Tempest,' she said, standing up, her back ram rod straight. 'My husband was Terry... Terry Tempest.'

Max nodded, and making his way around the desk, he took a seat, his large frame appearing too small for the chair.

Tracey waited for him to offer his condolences and when nothing came she involuntarily stiffened, not that she'd expected any different from him, it was because of him that Terry was dead after all.

'I know who you are.' Breaking her thoughts, Max gestured for her to take a seat, his voice gentle. 'We've met before.'

Tracey's eyes narrowed. To her knowledge she'd never laid her eyes upon him. If she had then she would have remembered, surely?

'I was at the funeral,' he volunteered when he sensed her

confusion.

As her heart began to beat faster, it took all of Tracey's strength not to turn on her heels and run from the office. He had to be sick she decided, sick in the head. Not content with just murdering Terry, he'd actually turned up at the funeral. What kind of man would even contemplate such a thing, let alone actually see it through? Had he got a kick out of being there, had he watched her break down and cry and felt nothing, not even a flicker of remorse?

'So...' As he leant back in the seat, Max's eyebrows rose a fraction. 'What is it I can do for you Mrs Tempest? Or can I call you Tracey? I'm guessing you're not here to buy a car?'

Tracey bristled, anger once again filling every inch of her being. 'Then you thought correctly.' Before she could lose her nerve, she opened her handbag, took out the documents and thumped them on the desk in front of him. 'I found these.'

Giving the paperwork a customary glance, Max looked up, quirked an eyebrow, and lifted his shoulders in a shrug. 'Is this meant to mean something to me?'

It took all of Tracey's strength not to swing for him, not to wipe the smug expression off his handsome face, and he was handsome, the type of man who was bound to turn heads wherever he went. Only not her head; she could see through the charade. In her eyes he was nothing more than the devil in disguise, an evil, cowardly bastard who deserved to rot. 'My husband sold you a number of cars.'

Max nodded. 'That's correct.'

For the briefest of moments Tracey faltered. The man had no shame. She'd fully expected him to lie, to deny all knowledge that he sold stolen cars. Her thoughts wandered to the vehicles on the forecourt – were they the cars Terry had acquired for him? An image of Kenny popped into her mind; he'd been happy enough to send her here alone, and she suddenly asked herself why that was. Was Kenny not worried about her safety? Regaining her composure, she stuck her chin in the air, defiance flickering in her eyes. 'And why did the arrangement end?' She tapped the papers with her index finger. 'You were both making a vast amount of money, so why suddenly stop?'

From across the desk, Max studied her before shrugging. 'It just did,' he answered nonchalantly. 'I assumed that Terry had taken his business elsewhere.'

Tracey screwed up her face. 'And you were happy with that, were you?' She didn't care that she was goading him, that he could lash out at her, that he could so easily kill her too. He was a big man and just one glance in his direction was enough to tell her that he had the strength to cause her some considerable damage. Only unlike Terry, who hadn't stood a chance of fighting back, she would claw the bastard's eyes out and scream blue bloody murder if he even so much as took a step in her direction.

Lounging back in the chair, Max shrugged again. 'It was business,' he said. 'Nothing more and nothing less. I didn't take it personally.' He paused for a moment and stroked the dark stubble across his jawline. 'Is there a purpose to this visit?' He glanced at the paperwork a second time and his forehead furrowed. 'Terry was paid for the cars; I didn't owe him any money if that's what you were wondering.'

Tracey's blood boiled. Was that why he thought she was here, to get money out of him? Over her dead body would she ever touch a penny that had passed through his hands. It was nothing more than blood money, and Terry's life had been worth more to her than a few lousy quid.

For a few moments they stared at one another. To her dismay Tracey looked away first. His hard stare unnerved her and as much as she didn't want to, she couldn't help but feel intimidated

by him. His expression was unreadable and he had a confidence
about him that bordered on arrogant, and seemed to seep out of
his very pores. There and then she wanted to kick herself. Why
hadn't she had the forethought to at least tell her sons where she
was going? What if Hardcastle attacked her, killed her and buried
her in a shallow grave? Other than Kenny, no one would even
know that she had come to see him. Surely Kenny wouldn't have
allowed her to walk into the lion's den without at least some kind
of backup. Perhaps he had even followed on behind her. Plucking
the paperwork from the desk, she stuffed the bank statements
haphazardly back into her handbag. 'You said that Terry had
taken his business elsewhere.'

Max nodded.

'Did he say where exactly?'

Raising his eyebrows, Max paused as though he was being
careful about how he answered. 'He didn't say,' he finally replied
his voice casual. Standing up, he walked across the office and
opened the door wide, signalling the end of their meeting.

Aware that she was being dismissed, Tracey's face was set like
thunder. She had never loathed anyone more than she did
Maxwell Hardcastle. Determined not to give him the satisfaction
of actually throwing her out of his office, she pushed past him
and stormed across the forecourt with as much dignity as she
could physically muster. By the time she reached her car her
mind was all over the place, and no matter how much she may
despise him, her interaction with Maxwell Hardcastle had left
her feeling even more confused than she already was. He hadn't
come across as the monster that Kenny had painted, and as for
her husband's best friend, a quick glance around her was enough
to tell her that Kenny hadn't had the foresight to come after her,
that he hadn't felt the need to protect her. The question was
though: why not?

6

Letting himself into his parents' house, Ricky glanced towards the hook beside the front door where his father had kept the car keys. Relieved to see that the keys were missing and that the car hadn't actually been stolen, he made his way through to the kitchen and flicked on the light switch. The stale stench of cigarette smoke still lingered and he contemplated throwing open a window to let in some air. Instead, he took a seat at the table and glanced down at the paperwork still scattered there. Jamie had been right; what exactly was their mum trying to achieve by going through her husband's documents? Picking up a bank statement, he began skimming through it. As far as he could make out, there was nothing there to set alarm bells ringing not that in all honesty he'd expected any different. His dad had only ever used his bank account for legitimate reasons, so that he had something to show the tax man or the old bill should they come knocking. For the majority of his business deals, Terry had used cash. Tucked away at the bottom of his dad's wardrobe was a key combination safe which contained at least eight hundred thousand pounds in used notes, plus two Rolex watches, and some gold jewellery.

'What are you doing here?'

The document slipped from Ricky's fingers and floated to the floor as he spun round. 'Jesus Christ Mum,' he complained as he bent down to scoop up the sheet of paper. 'What are you creeping up on me for?'

Tracey raised her eyebrows, her lips set into a thin line. 'I could ask you the same question.'

Ricky averted his gaze. As old as he was, his mum still had the ability to make him feel like a naughty school boy. 'I was worried about you,' he said, eyeing her warily, 'you weren't answering my calls.'

A long sigh escaped from Tracey's lips. She was sick to the back teeth of explaining herself to her sons; she was a grown woman for Christ's sake, not a child. Placing her handbag on the table, she kicked off her shoes, took a seat, then dragged her fingers through her hair, pulling the dark locks into a loose bun at the nape of her neck. 'I went to see Hardcastle.'

Ricky's eyes widened, the nerve in his jaw pulsating as he studied his mother with a measure of horror. 'Please tell me you didn't, that this is a joke.'

'Do I look like I'm laughing,' Tracey snapped back. 'I had to see the bastard with my own two eyes.'

The fine hairs on the back of Ricky's neck stood up on end as he got to his feet. He'd done enough pussy footing around his mother to last him a lifetime, and to put a finer point on things, he'd had an absolute gutful of her behaviour. She was becoming erratic, irrational and downright dangerous and if he was being truly honest with himself she was starting to frighten him and he didn't scare easily. As anger spread throughout his body, he had to grip on to the back of the chair to stop himself from taking her roughly by the shoulders and shaking some sense into her. 'Why the fuck would you go and see Hardcastle?' he bellowed, tapping the side of his head. 'Have you gone fucking mad; do you even know what kind of man he is?' He paused for breath, his eyes beseeching her for an answer. 'Hardcastle isn't the kind of man you mess with. He's got a rep mum, a highly warranted reputation; even Dad would have thought twice before contemplating pissing him off.'

Pursing her lips, Tracey chewed on the inside of her cheek in a bid to stop her own temper from boiling over. 'Of course I know what kind of man he is! He's an animal, a murderer. It was him; he killed your father.'

'He what?' There was disbelief in Ricky's voice. They had already been over this once and he'd stupidly assumed that he and Jamie had managed to get through to her, that they had been able to sway her away from Hardcastle being the killer.

Throwing up his arms in exasperation, he gave a low throaty laugh as though he could barely believe what he was hearing. 'You've lost it,' he said, shaking his head. 'Hardcastle knew Dad. They were pals, they did business together; how the fuck have you gone from that to Hardcastle being the shooter?'

Tracey stood her ground and leant her forearms on the table. 'Your father broke off the deal, and that,' she spat, 'was the reason Hardcastle killed him.' Reaching into her handbag, she pulled out the crumpled bank statements and waved them in the air. 'It's all here in black and white, and you said it yourself, selling the cars was a good earner. Did you really think that Hardcastle was going to take that lying down? He wanted revenge and my Terry paid the price with his life.'

'No Mum,' Ricky said, his voice a low growl. 'You're wrong.'

'I am not wrong.' Banging her fists down on the table, Tracey roared out the words. 'You want to know what's wrong, then I'll tell you what's wrong. *This* is fucking wrong.' She pointed a stiff finger towards him. 'That bastard is swanning about living the life of Riley while your poor father is six feet under and what have you done about it eh? What have either of you done? Sod all, that's what. It's like you don't even care! He was your father; he was a good man and he deserves justice.'

Breathing heavily, Ricky stared at his mother as though she'd grown a second head. Never had he ever imagined the day when she would speak to him with so much hatred. 'Mum,' he pleaded, changing tact. 'Please, just stop this, you're starting to sound like you've gone off your head.'

'I can't stop!' she screamed, her eyes blazing with fury. 'He even had the front to turn up at the funeral. I bet he got a kick out of that. And you've got the audacity to say that I'm not right up here,' she screeched, pointing to her temple. 'At least I'm not sick in the fucking head.'

Ricky closed his eyes. His temper was beginning to get the better of him and he willed himself to calm down, determined not to say or do anything that he may later regret. 'I know he was at the funeral,' he said through gritted teeth. 'Me and Jamie invited him.'

'You did what?' Sinking back in the seat, Tracey paled, her expression one of utter disgust. 'Oh, I see,' she sneered. 'Your poor father wasn't even cold in the ground, and already you were fraternising with the enemy, not that you or Jamie give a shit. In fact, I'll tell you what,' she spat, 'why don't we invite Hardcastle over for dinner and pretend that your father never even existed?'

A deathly silence followed and realising that she'd gone too far, Tracey bowed her head, her breath coming out in short, sharp bursts. Terry had always been close to their sons and they in return had looked up to their father. In that instant she knew her words would have stung and wished that she could take them back. Her big mouth had always been her downfall, especially when she lost her temper; she didn't have an off button, didn't know how to rein herself in. As for her two boys, they had been devastated when Terry had been gunned down. Never in a million years would they have ever entertained the notion of willingly putting themselves in the presence of the man responsible for their father's death. She had met Maxwell Hardcastle and as much as she had found him intimidating he hadn't come across as violent; in fact, he'd done nothing whatsoever to make her feel afraid of him, he hadn't threatened her, he hadn't even raised his voice towards her. But if it wasn't Maxwell, then who else could have murdered Terry, what other possible motive could there have been to want her husband dead?

Shaking his head, Ricky turned to walk out of the kitchen before spinning back around, his eyes hard. 'What exactly are you trying to achieve Mum?' he snarled. 'To alienate us from everyone who wants to help track down Dad's murderer? At the wake Hardcastle took me and Jamie aside and told us that if we needed help finding the bastard then he'd be there. No matter what time of day it was, all we had to do was give him a call.'

Her mind reeling, Tracey snapped her head up to look at her son. No, it couldn't be true. Why would Hardcastle offer his help? A niggling doubt began to creep into her mind and squeezing her eyes shut tight, she held her head in her hands. Had she made a mistake after all? She'd been so sure it was Hardcastle; the evidence pointed to him didn't it? Even Kenny had agreed that the man couldn't be trusted. A sickening thought suddenly hit her, had Kenny only told her what she'd wanted to hear, had he been placating her, had he called her sons as soon as she'd left the breakers yard and told them that she was deluded? As her cheeks flushed pink, shame engulfed her. How could she have been so wrong?

'Oh God.' Tears stung her eyes as she reached out to clutch her son's hand. 'I'm so sorry darling,' she said, looking up at him, her expression pained. 'I didn't mean what I said; if I could cut my wicked tongue out I would. You and Jamie idolised your father, you were his boys and he loved you, both of you.'

As she wept, Ricky pulled his mother into his arms and stroked her hair. Deep down he understood her need to point fingers or at least he thought he did. It wasn't as though the old bill were going to lift a finger to find his dad's murderer. The filth might have said all of the right things, might have even appeared sincere, but deep down he knew the truth, they were glad to see the back of Terry Tempest. His dad had had more run ins with the police than most people had had hot dinners, he would even joke that he was on their Christmas card list. But Terry had been a slippery fucker and had somehow managed to wheedle his way out of every charge they had attempted to throw at him, and God only knew how many times the old bill had tried to put him behind bars. It had been sheer luck, that and a good brief, which had been the cause of every case against him being flung out of court. He closed his eyes. 'It's going to be okay Mum,' he whispered, or at least he hoped it would, anyway.

* * *

'She did what?' There was a level of shock in Jamie's voice and as he shook his head, he let out a low laugh that was tinged with disbelief. 'You're kidding me ain't you?'

Ricky shook his head. 'I wish I was,' he answered with a sigh.

The two brothers were in their local boozer, The Roundhouse in Dagenham, and taking a sip of his lager, Ricky used the back of his hand to wipe away a layer of froth from his upper lip.

'She'd convinced herself that Hardcastle was the shooter,' he quickly explained.

Screwing up his face, Jamie sighed. 'I told you,' he stated, 'that she's lost the plot, but you wouldn't fucking listen to me, would you.'

Ricky eyed his brother over the rim of the pint glass, only thankful that Jamie hadn't been there to witness their mother's outburst. He had a nasty feeling that if he had then he would have had their mum carted off to the nearest psychiatric hospital and demand that she be locked up for the duration.

'What's she playing at?' Jamie continued. 'Ain't it bad enough that she's rifling through the old man's paperwork, let alone trying to make an enemy of Hardcastle?'

Ricky was thoughtful. Jamie was right; the last thing they needed was enemies. As it was, they already had one to contend with, the wanker who'd killed their dad.

Leaning in towards his brother, Jamie lowered his voice. 'Because right now bruv, we need Hardcastle and Kenny on our side. They're more than just faces; between them they've got a lot of sway, and they'll be able to demand answers. And let's face it,' he said with a quick glance around him. 'Right now, we don't know who we can and can't trust.'

As he followed his brother's gaze, Ricky nodded. Jamie had just hit the proverbial nail on the head. Other than each other, who exactly could they trust?

Across Dagenham, Max Hardcastle pulled his car into the car park of the Ship and Anchor public house. Taking a quick glance around him, he switched off the ignition and climbed out of the motor. It wasn't often that he ventured back to his old hunting ground; in fact, it would be fair to say that he avoided the place like the plague, not because he was afraid of any repercussions from the crime he'd committed as a teenager, but more so because he couldn't be arsed to deal with the hag that went along with it. He knew from experience that there was always someone, somewhere, who wanted to score a point, who wanted to goad him, or to be able to brag that they had brought him down, not that that was likely unless they resulted to dirty tactics or took him unawares.

Locking the car, he strode across the car park and pushed open the door to the boozer with a confident air. Instinctively, as soon as he stepped foot across the threshold, he knew that his presence had been duly noted. Not that he'd expected any different; people had long memories. They knew what he'd done and who he'd done it to, but what they didn't know was the reason why and Max was determined to keep it that way. As far as he was concerned it was his business and his alone; well, his and Terry's, considering his best mate had been there at the time the murder had been committed. And Terry hadn't been afraid to get his hands dirty either. In fact it had been Terry who'd dished out the final blow to Archie Rowling's head, the one which the prosecution claimed had killed him. Not that Max had ever mentioned Terry's name; what was the point in them both having a capture. Even at his trial Max had refused to utter a single word despite his brief's best efforts to try and make him explain the situation and admit that he hadn't acted alone. Even the promise that he'd have a more lenient custodial sentence bestowed upon him if he'd told the truth hadn't been enough to make him spill the beans. It was a secret he'd been determined to take to the grave. Not only had Archie Rowling made both his and his mother's life a misery, but he'd also beaten his mother black and blue and put her on the game, something which Max wasn't prepared to let slide. How could he? She was his mum at the end of the day, even if she had been blind to Archie's mistreatment of her.

At the bar he ordered himself a bottled beer, and after paying for the drink he slipped the change back into his trouser pocket. As he took a sip of the beer, his hard gaze wandered around the premises, on the lookout for anyone he recognised.

'Fuck me, what are you doing here?'

Max turned his head, recognition instantly registering across his face. 'Hello pal, long time no see.'

'Long time no see,' Eddie Winters exclaimed. 'Fuck me, it's been that long I thought you'd kicked the fucking bucket.'

Max chuckled; he could see Eddie's point. Other than when he'd attended Terry's funeral it had been years since he'd stepped foot on the manor. On his release from prison, he'd relocated to Southend-on-Sea, for a fresh start, somewhere his name was less likely to be known and to a certain degree his plan had worked. Of course, rumours had followed him around but all in all he'd not had too much trouble from the locals and as for those who'd attempted to push their luck and put the hard word on him he'd quickly put them in their place.

'What are you doing back here?' Eddie asked as he indicated for his two brothers, Charlie and Alfie, to join them.

Shaking the younger Winters brothers' hands, Max leant casually against the bar. 'I was in the area,' he answered, making sure to keep his answer vague. The truth was Tracey Tempest had left him feeling troubled. The fact Terry had gone into partnership with the Murphys then months later had been gunned down didn't sit right with him. Not that Max had been fully able to understand Terry's reasoning for going into business with them in the first place. He and Terry had had a good thing going on; the cars had been a nice little earner, and despite the fact he'd told Tracey that he hadn't taken the situation personally, the reality was that he'd been more than a little surprised when Terry had ended their partnership.

'I take it you heard about Terry?' Eddie asked, lowering his voice.

Max nodded. He'd been expecting the question. After all, it was no secret that he, Terry and Kenny had more than just knocked about together as kids, they'd been the best of pals. From an early age they'd spent their every waking moment together getting into scrapes or causing mischief. Scallywags, his mum had called them, and she'd been right. Was it any wonder they had turned out the way they had? They'd never been destined to live a nine-to-five life. It was only after his imprisonment that they'd drifted apart and lost contact for a while, not that he'd entirely blamed them. As the months had passed by they'd found less and less to talk about, and eventually their visits had become more and more sporadic until they had finally stopped visiting altogether. 'I went to the funeral.'

Eddie gave a shake of his head and blew out his cheeks. 'Bad business all around if you ask me.' He looked to his brothers who nodded in agreement. 'From what I heard, Terry had been in the wrong place at the wrong time, a stray bullet fired from the street.'

Max's eyebrows ever so slightly rose; he'd heard the same theory himself only in his mind he fully believed that Terry had been in exactly the right place at the right time. The shooting had been an execution, not a slip of the hand or a mistake. Taking a sip of his drink, Max cleared his throat. 'I heard Terry had gone into business with...' He clicked his fingers, pretending that the action would somehow jog his memory.

'The Murphys,' Charlie volunteered.

'That's right, the Murphys.' He watched as they screwed up their faces, only serving to reinforce his belief that the Murphy family were not well liked. 'Any truth to it?'

Alfie gave a chuckle. 'Now that,' he said, 'depends on who you ask.'

His forehead furrowing, Max gave a slight shake of his head, unsure of what the youngest of the brothers had meant by the remark.

'Put it this way,' Eddie said with a nod of his head towards the far side of the bar. 'Going into business with the Murphys came with its benefits, if you know what I mean.'

Turning his head, Max took note of a woman standing across from him at the bar. Tall, with a curvaceous figure, her thick blonde hair fell just below her shoulders, her expression hard, her lips set into what he suspected was a permanent scowl. From what he could see of the mystery woman she was the complete opposite to Terry's wife Tracey who despite her fiery temper was petite and had a vulnerability about her. 'He was playing away from home then.'

'When wasn't he?' Charlie chipped in. 'You know what he was like, he'd chase anything in a skirt. I even heard a rumour that he was going to give his missus the elbow and move in with the slapper.'

Max's eyebrows rose. He knew only too well what Terry had been like, but as for Terry leaving his wife, that was a new one. Terry had never given him any indication that he was planning to leave Tracey. He'd seemed happy; in fact, you could say he'd been as happy as a pig in shit.

'And as for her, Bianca Murphy...' Eddie winked, giving a nod of his head in Bianca's direction. 'Believe me pal, she's dropped more boxers than Mike Tyson and that's saying something.'

'Yeah,' Charlie sniggered, 'they don't call her BT for nothing, she's working her way through the phone book.' He raised his eyebrows, his expression one of disgust. 'I've even heard she's not averse to fooling around with her own brothers. I mean, look at the state of them, they're all fucking inbred, mate.'

Eddie waved his brother's comments away. 'Inbred or not, Terry was a fool to even entertain her. At the best of times, she's a trappy bitch much like her brothers.'

As the brothers laughed, Max forced himself to join in, but his mind was reeling. He'd known Terry well enough to know that he was no saint but for the life of him he couldn't see the attraction. Bianca Murphy was nothing special, and he himself wouldn't have given her a second glance, so why had Terry been willing to put his marriage on the line for the likes of a Murphy? Had she had some sort of hold over him, could she have been black-mailing him into a relationship? Downing his beer, he placed the empty bottle on the bar. 'What type of business are we talking about?' he asked, jerking his head in Bianca's direction.

The three brothers shook their heads. Their expressions alone were enough to tell Max that they didn't have a clue, that Terry had kept the nature of the business close to his chest. The question was: why?

'Fuck knows, maybe debt collecting,' Eddie volunteered with a shrug. 'Say what you want about the Murphys, but they're handy with their fists, her included.' He laughed, nodding towards Bianca. 'Fuck me, even I would have to think twice before taking her on.'

Max laughed aloud at the obvious joke. It was no secret that Eddie could have a ruck. In fact, only a fool or someone with a lot of clout would even contemplate causing beef with him. Deep in thought, Max took a second glance at the woman Terry had been fooling around with. Having seen first-hand just how fiery Tracey Tempest was, he wouldn't be surprised if she herself had found out about the affair and ordered the hit on her husband. Deciding the only avenue left open to him was to seek Kenny out and question him about his and Terry's business dealings with the Murphy family, he shook the brothers' hands and left the pub, eager to get away from the area, and more importantly away from the curious stares which seemed to follow his every movement.

* * *

The next morning Kenny banged his fists on the front door to Bianca's flat. As the seconds ticked by and she still hadn't answered he became more and more irate. After Terry's death it was imperative that he reinforced the business deal with the Murphys and even more importantly that they negotiated a price. After all, Terry had been his business partner, therefore he was entitled to his cut of the profits, wasn't he?

Lifting his fist, he'd been about to bang on the door again when it was suddenly flung open.

'Fuck me,' he exclaimed as he looked Bianca up and down. 'You look dog rough.'

Dressed in a short, well-washed black T-shirt that only just covered her backside, Bianca's hair stuck out in all directions, and traces of the makeup she had worn the previous day was smeared across her face, making her look almost clown like.

'Charming,' she remarked, pulling the door open wider and stepping aside. 'You don't look so hot yourself.'

Kenny ignored the remark, and walking through the flat, he made a beeline for the kitchen, wrinkling his nose as he did so. The place was a shit hole, not that he'd expected any different, Bianca hardly came across as the type of woman whose number one priority in life was to keep her home spick and span. She was more like a bloke in that respect; all she cared for was shagging and earning some dough. No wonder her and

Terry had got along so well; they had been cut from the same cloth.

Rinsing two grimy tea-stained mugs under the cold-water tap, Bianca flicked the switch for the kettle to boil, then took a seat at the table. She rubbed a wet wipe over her face, then tossing the used wipe in the general direction of the peddle bin, she lit a cigarette. 'To what do I owe this pleasure?' she asked, blowing out a thin stream of smoke.

Kenny afforded her a smile. Out of all the Murphys she was the only one with a bit of savvy, hence why he'd come here this morning rather than visit one of her brothers. 'Terry,' he began. He watched her eyes narrow and leant across the table towards her. 'Now that he's out of the picture we need to renegotiate our deal.'

She let out a hollow laugh then took a long drag on the cigarette all the while studying him. 'You really are a piece of work Kenny.' As she squinted through the curling cigarette smoke, Bianca's expression became menacing. 'I thought Terry was meant to be your best mate.'

'He was and I'm gutted that he's gone.' Spreading open his arms, Kenny leant back in the chair, a crafty expression filtering across his face. 'But business is business and seeing as Terry was my business partner, by rights I'm entitled to his cut.'

Bianca gave a second laugh. She didn't like Kenny and in fact had loathed him on sight. He was a slimy bastard, she didn't trust him as far as she could throw him and had told her brothers as much when Kenny had propositioned them. Not that her brothers had listened to a word she'd said; the temptation of earning easy money had been too good an opportunity to miss. Fair enough they were all earning a lot of dough, but it wasn't them who had to take all of the risks. It was her who had to put up with the women, she was the one who had to babysit the tarts until Shaun got off his backside and collected them. If anyone deserved a bigger cut then it was her. After all, it was her neck on the line. What if one of the whores escaped and led the old bill back to her flat? She was bound to have the book thrown at her, and serving time wasn't high up on her to-do list. What was the sentence for sexual exploitation and human trafficking? It had to be years, maybe even life. The mere thought was enough to make her inwardly shudder. She wasn't made for prison, couldn't bear the thought of being locked up for years on end.

'That wasn't the deal,' she told him, her voice becoming hard.

Anger flashed in Kenny's face; not that he'd expected her to just roll over and accept his demands. He opened his mouth to answer when she interrupted him, a wicked glint in her eyes.

'An old pal of yours and Terry's was in the boozer last night.'

Picking up on her smugness, Kenny narrowed his eyes into mere slits, his back involuntarily stiffening at her words. 'Who?' he demanded.

Bianca grinned and as she ground out the cigarette in an over-flowing ashtray, she took her time in answering, all the while basking in Kenny's discomfort. Right from the off she'd been astute enough to pick up on the fact that Kenny had been jealous of Terry and Hardcastle's friendship. She'd heard the sly digs and seen the sneer that creased Kenny's bloated face whenever Hard-castle's name had been brought up in conversation. Ever resourceful, she had stored the information away knowing full well that one day it would come in useful, that she would be able to use it as a yard stick, and more to the point as a way of getting one over on Kenny.

'Answer the fucking question.' Clenching his fists, Kenny snarled. 'Who was in the boozer?'

'Max Hardcastle.' She gave a nonchalant shrug, careful to keep the grin from her face. 'I was thinking that maybe he'd be interested in taking Terry's place. From what I've heard he's a hard fucker, and not the kind of man to take any shit from anyone, and let's face it, in this game that's exactly what we need.'

The blood drained from Kenny's face. Even when they'd been kids and had supposedly been the best of mates Kenny had secretly resented Max. And as for the old saying, two's company and three's a crowd, it had been him who'd felt left out. Terry and Hardcastle's closeness had made him feel as though he was nothing other than a spare wheel, the one who they allowed to tag along with them out of pity. And as for Hardcastle taking Terry's place on the deal, Max may have been a hard fucker but he also had morals. He'd go ballistic if he was to find out about the whores, let alone if he was to find out that the women in question were being forced into prostitution. He'd even served time for that very fact. Oh, he'd never actually admitted it out loud, but early on Kenny had guessed the truth – why else would Hardcastle have murdered the man his mother had been shacked up with? And it had been no secret that Hardcastle's mother had been on the game, he and Terry had overheard their own mothers talking about it. In fact, it had been him who'd let slip to Hardcastle during a particularly vicious argument that his mother was nothing more than a dirty dock Dolly.

'Well what do you reckon?' Cocking an eyebrow, Bianca gave another smug grin. 'Shall I proposition Hardcastle or should I leave it in your capable hands?'

Her words were the equivalent of a red rag to a bull, and scraping back the chair, Kenny lunged across the table, his hand curling round her throat. 'Look here you little slapper,' he hissed in her ear. 'You open your trap again and I'm seriously going to lose my rag.' He tightened his grip and took a moment of satisfaction to see her eyes almost bulge out of her head. 'Now you listen to what I'm about to say and listen good. I run this show and you and that fucking shambles that you call a family had better get that through your thick skulls. Terry's cut now comes directly to me, and one more mention of Hardcastle and I will personally end you. Are we clear on that?'

As her lips turned blue, Bianca desperately clawed at his hands. She was no pushover but even she knew when she was beat. She could barely breathe and as her lungs screamed for air, she actually wet herself. To her shame the hot urine trickled down her legs and pooled at her feet.

'Are we clear on that?' Kenny roared.

With great difficulty, Bianca managed to nod and as Kenny threw her away from him she gasped for breath, her fingers automatically rubbing at her neck where his nails had left indentations.

'Good.' Kenny grinned. Looking her up and down he gave a half laugh. 'What the fuck Terry saw in a skank like you I'll never understand.' As embarrassment flashed across her face, Kenny laughed even harder, a nasty little laugh that resonated around the small kitchen. 'And while you're at it, sort yourself out; you fucking stink.'

As he left the room, Bianca swiped a stray tear away from her cheek. She'd always had an inkling that Kenny was unhinged, that he was ruthless and a dangerous individual. Her heart thundered in her chest, her ears straining as his footsteps retreated down the hallway and as the front door slammed closed behind him it took every ounce of her willpower not to physically jump. For the first time in her life she could honestly say that she felt terrified.

7

With a heavy heart Tracey began tidying away the paperwork spread out across the kitchen table. Her sons had been right, she was doing more harm than good by scrutinising Terry's bank statements. And what exactly had she been hoping to find? A written confession from the man responsible for killing her husband? No, that would have been far too easy. No wonder her boys had looked at her as though she'd lost her mind. Her behaviour had scared them and it had scared her too. She'd been so focused on hunting down Terry's murderer that she hadn't given Ricky's or Jamie's concerns a second thought. In fact, she'd given her sons so little of her time that they may as well have not existed, and as for her little grandson Mason, he was the apple of her eye and yet to her shame even he had barely crossed her mind.

Her thoughts turned to Max Hardcastle and she inwardly cringed, her cheeks flushing a deep shade of pink. She could still hardly believe that she had willingly put herself in harm's way and stormed inside his office hellbent on having it out with the man. What on earth had she been thinking? If he was as dangerous as Ricky had stated then there was no way she could have stopped him from harming her too. The sheer size of the man should have been more than enough to alert her and anyone else with half a braincell for that matter to the fact that she was in over her head. The problem was, she hadn't been thinking, and if she was being even more honest with herself, she couldn't have given two hoots about her safety. Her actions had been the equivalent of a suicide mission; she'd been so caught up in grief that perhaps she too had wanted to die. She gave a shudder as she placed the last of Terry's bank statements into the shoebox and couldn't believe that she had been so selfish. She had always been a good mother, something she prided herself on, and yet she had willingly been prepared for her sons to lose both of their parents within a matter of weeks.

Hearing a key turn in the lock, Tracey slammed her eyes shut tight, forced a wide smile across her face then slowly turned round.

'Hello, my darlings,' she said with a note of trepidation in her voice.

As they entered the kitchen, Tracey watched as her sons' gazes darted to the cleared table before settling on her, their eyebrows raised questioningly. There and then she felt even more ashamed of herself, and giving a cautious smile, she gestured towards the shoe box containing her husband's documents and receipts. 'You were right,' she sighed. 'Searching through your dad's things isn't going to help us find his murderer, and it certainly isn't going to give us the answers we want.'

She watched as their broad shoulders relaxed and bit down on her bottom lip in an attempt to stop the tears from welling in her eyes. She had to stay strong, and more than anything she had to prove to her sons that she was capable of working with them rather than against them.

'It's for the best Mum.' Jamie smiled reassuringly. 'Dad wouldn't have wanted this.' He jerked his head towards the shoe box. 'He wouldn't have wanted you to put yourself in danger.'

Tracey nodded. For the majority of the time Terry had only ever been a good husband to her and throughout their marriage she had wanted for nothing. Take the house, for example: it was beautiful, and no expense had been spared when making it the show home that it was. The only thing he had never really given her was his time. Some days she had barely even seen him; he'd used their home as he would a hotel room, only coming home to sleep and shower. But even the knowledge that he would rather be out with his friends than spend any real quality time with her hadn't stopped her from loving him. And, even in death, the pull of him was strong; he was still the only man she would ever want.

A hard lump formed in Tracey's throat and she hastily swallowed it down. When she spoke her voice ever so slightly cracked. 'Just promise me,' she said, pulling herself up to her full height in a bid to regain a control of her emotions. 'That you will hunt this bastard down.' She saw the surreptitious glance they shared and taking a deep breath, continued. 'And I want you to promise that you will work with me, that together as a family we will see to it that your dad gets the justice he deserves.'

For the briefest of moments, she watched them falter, the muscles across their shoulder blades becoming rigid. The look in their eyes told her everything she needed to know, that they thoroughly believed that she had gone crazy, and who could blame them? Her behaviour over the past few weeks hadn't exactly been that of someone in control of their thoughts, or even their faculties.

'Promise me,' she urged them.

Reluctantly, Ricky and Jamie nodded. She was no fool and had a sneaking suspicion that they were only trying to placate her, that when the time came they would find every excuse under the sun to keep her in the dark.

'Good.' She exhaled through her nose, took a seat at the head of the table in what had been her husband's chair, then laced her fingers together. 'Now that that's settled, I want you to arrange a meeting with Hardcastle.'

In that instant their eyebrows shot up, surprise etched across their faces. There and then Tracey had to stop herself from laughing aloud.

'Don't worry,' she reassured them. 'I haven't completely lost my marbles. You said it yourself,' she said, pointing a finger towards her eldest son. 'We need allies, people on our side, someone who we can trust, and if your dad trusted Hardcastle then that's good enough for me.'

'Mum—' Ricky protested with a shake of his head.

Lifting her hand to cut her son off, Tracey leant forward. 'Arrange the meeting.' Her eyes flashed dangerously, daring either one of her sons to argue with her. Whether they liked it or not she was still their mum, and with Terry gone that meant she was now the head of the family. 'You're either with me or against me,' she warned, 'and believe me, I will fight you over this. Together we're stronger and together we can find this no-good murdering bastard.'

When they nodded, Tracey allowed herself to smile, her first real smile in weeks, and relaxing back into the chair, she finally felt as though she was proactively doing something to avenge Terry's death.

* * *

'Dad,' Shaun called out to his father.

Kenny ignored his son. In front of him, spread out across his desk, were several sheets of paper. As soon as he'd left Bianca Murphy's flat, he'd headed straight to the breakers yard and set to work, calculating how much cash was going to find its way into his money-grabbing hands now that he was entitled to Terry's cut. And from what he could make out he was looking at a small fortune, proving all along just how right he'd been: Terry and the bitch had been having him over. He rubbed his hands together with glee, then picked up a pen to make some notes. Maybe they should even up their game, invest in a second property to house the whores, and double their income? Besides, it was about time the Murphys began pulling their weight, they were paid enough wedge and in his eyes they did fuck all to warrant a cut of the profits. They were supposed to be heavies, yet all they did as far as he could tell was sit around boozing the day away.

'Dad!' Shaun's voice rose a notch, the unease he felt clearly noticeable in his stance as he peered through the barred window.

'What is it?' Kenny growled, looking up.

Not taking his eyes away from the yard, Shaun gestured to the car which had pulled onto the forecourt. 'Is that Hardcastle's motor?'

Cocking an eyebrow, Kenny tossed the pen onto the desk, pushed himself out of the chair and made his way towards the window. As he joined Shaun, Bianca Murphy sprang to his mind. Surely the slapper wasn't stupid enough to have gone against him and contacted Hardcastle? Or perhaps it had been Tracey? With a little bit of help from him she'd convinced herself that Hardcastle had murdered Terry. Had Tracey confronted him, was that why Hardcastle had turned up unannounced? Did he want answers as to why his name had been put in the frame?

A scowl creased Kenny's face as he watched a hulking figure step out of the car. He'd recognise Hardcastle anywhere, he wasn't exactly hard to miss. Standing at over six feet, Max was not only a big man, but he also had a muscular frame, and was more than capable of causing some considerable damage should he set his mind to it. Look how easily he'd battered to death the man who'd pimped out his mother, and he'd only been a teenager at the time. Even when they'd been kids, Hardcastle had been a vicious fucker and that, coupled with the years he'd spent locked up, was bound to have had an effect on him. Just how much pent-up rage did he have inside of him ready and waiting to be unleashed?

There and then, anger began to build within Kenny. It had to be Bianca; Tracey for all her talk didn't have it in her to have it out with Hardcastle. She would have crumpled at the first hint of trouble. Bianca on the other hand was a mouthy cow and he was going to kill the bitch stone dead when he got his hands on her. It was about time she was brought down a peg or two and without his former business partner around to protect her or smooth the situation over she was fair game as far as Kenny was concerned. Not to mention her and her brothers had far too much sway when it came to the business for his liking.

'What does he want?' Turning to look at his father, Shaun frowned.

'Do I look like I'm a mind reader?' Kenny barked back. Hastily he walked around the desk and swiped the paperwork into the desk drawer, hidden out of sight. The last thing he needed was for Hardcastle to see how much money was at stake, not that he expected Max to want to join the business at any time in the foreseeable future and, more to the point, Kenny wasn't prepared to share the profits. It was bad enough that Terry had tried to treat him like a mug, that he'd tried to swindle him out of cash, like fuck was he going to idly sit by and allow Hardcastle to do the same to him. 'Out.' He shoved his son non too gently towards the door, the harshness in his voice enough to warn Shaun not to argue back and to do as he was told.

Moments later, Max stepped into the office. 'Was that your lad?' he asked, jerking his thumb behind him.

As Kenny shook Max's hand he gestured for him to take a seat. 'Takes after his mother.' He grinned. 'She's a pain in my arse an' all. Kid's eh' – he winked – 'we must be fucking mad. All the little buggers ever do is bleed us dry. It's not like when we were kids; we had fuck all back then, nowadays it's all about the latest gadgets and designer clothes.'

Max chuckled as he made himself comfortable. Unlike his friends he had never really wanted children. He'd been in his mid-thirties by the time he'd been released from prison and settling down and raising a child had never been high up on his list of priorities. Not that he disliked children, because he didn't, he happened to like them, and perhaps if his life had taken a different course then he may well have followed on in his friends' footsteps and settled down and become a father. Perhaps he'd just never met the right woman, the one who he would want to raise a family with.

'So what can I do for you?' Kenny raised his eyebrows questioningly. 'It's not like you to venture onto the manor.'

Kenny had a point, Max conceded. Twice in as many days he'd been in the area, and considering he usually did everything in his power to avoid the place, that was saying something. Leaning forward he rested his forearms on his knees. 'The Murphys,' he said, watching Kenny's reaction closely. Out of the two men, Max had always been closer to Terry, and had considered him to be an open book. Kenny on the other hand, was harder to read. In fact he'd had a sneaking suspicion that Kenny had been the driving force behind his and Terry's partnership coming to a premature end, not that Terry had ever said as much; he hadn't needed to, Max had known him well enough to know that it hadn't been his idea to walk away from their deal.

'The Murphys?' There was a hint of caution in Kenny's voice which Max immediately picked up on. 'What are you interested in them for? The family are scum; you know that as well as I do.'

Max ever so slightly narrowed his eyes. If Kenny considered the family to be scum then why had he and Terry gone into business with them? 'I've heard one or two rumours that you and Terry were working with them.' He gave a casual shrug. 'Any truth to it?'

Clearing his throat, Kenny resisted the urge to wipe away the layer of cold sweat from his forehead. Just how much did Hardcastle know? Had he been told that women were currently being kept on the property against their will? No, he decided, if that had been the case Hardcastle would have stormed inside the office and immediately laid into him; there would have been no time for pleasantries, or idle chit chat. Making a conscious effort not to flick his gaze in the direction of the house, Kenny gave a shrug of his own. 'Yeah we did some business with them,' he reluctantly admitted.

Max sat up a little straighter and spread open his arms, his voice was suddenly hard. 'And you don't find it a little bit strange that Terry is now dead?'

Unsure of what Hardcastle was actually getting at, Kenny fidgeted in his seat. His heart was beating ten to a dozen, his palms felt clammy and he licked at his dry lips. Had Hardcastle guessed his part in Terry's murder? He had always been wary of the man; they may have been mates growing up, but a lot of years had passed since then and they were virtually strangers now. He had a nasty feeling that Hardcastle wouldn't let something like friendship get in the way of battering him to death if the need arose, or if he was to find out that it had been Kenny who'd orchestrated Terry's death. As he thought the question through, Kenny glanced around for a weapon he could use should Hardcastle decide to swing for him. His fingers curled round the pen that he'd carelessly tossed on to the desk; if he was left with no other choice he would stab it into Hardcastle's face, and if he was really lucky he might even be able to gouge out his eye.

'Come on,' Max urged. 'I know you and you're not stupid. Did it not cross your mind that Terry could have been murdered by those scumbags?'

Kenny's eyebrows shot up. To say that he was surprised was an understatement. Hastily he composed himself, careful to keep the smug grin from etching across his face. Right from the off he should have guessed that Hardcastle would point fingers towards the Murphys; why would he even suspect his involvement? 'I can't say that it crossed my mind,' he answered cautiously. 'But as we both know they can't be trusted and as you so rightly pointed out, they are the scum of the earth.'

Deep in thought, Max slumped back in the chair. 'What was the nature of the business? Was it debt collecting, protection rackets? I've heard that the Murphys are handy with their fists, so how did you put them to use?'

Kenny snorted. The Murphys may have had a rep, but as far as he was concerned they were fuck all for him to worry about. They were nothing other than sheep, and only came in useful when he needed some extra muscle, and even then he had to prise the ever-present cans of larger out of their fists first. Aware that Hardcastle was actually waiting for him to answer, Kenny opened his mouth only to be halted by the bleep of Hardcastle's mobile phone pinging a message.

He watched as Hardcastle fished the device from out of his jacket pocket and saw his eyebrows knot together as he read the message then hastily type out a reply before slipping the phone back into his pocket. 'So, was it debt collecting?' he asked again as he stood up.

Kenny nodded warily, hoping that he'd given Hardcastle just enough information to get him off his back.

'I thought as much,' Max stated as he made his way across the office. His hand on the door handle, he paused and turned back round. 'Any truth in the rumour that Terry was going to give his wife the elbow and shack up with Bianca Murphy?'

His eyes widening, Kenny burst out laughing. 'In her fucking dreams. She was an easy shag and nothing more than that. You know as well as I do what Terry was like,' he said, poking a finger forward. 'But for all his faults he loved his sons; there isn't a chance in hell that he would have wanted them to find out his marriage to Tracey wasn't worth the paper it was written on.'

Max nodded, somewhat surprised. He'd been under the impression that Terry had loved his wife, or at least, Terry had never given him any reason to think otherwise. 'Well keep your ears to the ground,' he said, pulling open the door. 'I'm gunning for this bastard, I owe Terry that much, and I won't rest easy until I've found him.'

'Of course.' Kenny smiled as he got to his feet. 'And the same goes for me. I want this no-good cunt found, and I can promise you now that I'm doing everything in my power to hunt the culprit down.'

Of course it was an empty promise and as Kenny watched Max go, the smile slid from his face, and it wasn't until Hardcastle had climbed into his car and driven out of the yard that he felt his heart once again return to its usual steady rhythm. Ever since Hardcastle's release from prison, Kenny had felt a familiar sense of unease whenever he had the misfortune to be in the man's presence. It was the way Hardcastle looked at him he decided, as though his steely grey eyes were able to bore into Kenny's very soul and pull out his deepest, darkest secrets. As though he'd somehow known that it had been him who'd grassed him up to the old bill all those years ago. And Hardcastle would have been right. It had been both him and Terry together who'd made the anonymous telephone call to the old bill informing them of Hardcastle's whereabouts. That had been the thing about Terry, even at a young age he'd known which side to hedge his bets on, and they had both known instinctively that it was only a matter of time until the filth had pieced together who was responsible for the murder of Hardcastle's mother's partner, and like fuck were they prepared to go down with him all because of their association. And the funny thing about it was that Terry and Hardcastle were supposed to be the best mates, and yet at the first hint of trouble Terry had so easily cut his losses, with a little bit of persuasion from Kenny of course.

In fact, as far as Kenny was concerned, Hardcastle had always been in the way, coming between Kenny and Terry even when they were kids. And as young as Kenny had been he'd known the score; they'd made that glaringly obvious. He'd seen their sly glances towards one another whenever he was near, he'd even heard Hardcastle's mumbled expletives whenever Kenny had knocked on Terry's front door. And despite all of this, Kenny had still wanted to be their mate, had still wanted to tag along with them. He'd liked the fact that they went out looking for trouble, that they could handle themselves, that they were feared by their peers. It had excited Kenny and made him want to be just like them – he'd wanted to wield that same power.

In the end it had been nothing other than jealousy and spite which had spurred Kenny on, and with Hardcastle out of the picture, Terry had been left with no other choice but to latch on to Kenny, even if it had only been out of guilt. Oh Terry had felt remorse for grassing up his supposed best mate up, and it had eaten away at him like a cancer, hence why they had eventually stopped visiting Max in prison. But in the end Kenny and Terry had become good mates, best mates even, and as the months and years had ticked by, Hardcastle had become nothing more than a distant memory. And that was exactly where the bastard should have stayed, a memory. But oh no, after his release from nick, Hardcastle had wanted to pick up where they'd left off and to Kenny's dismay he'd even wanted to go into business with them, or at least with Terry.

Retrieving the sheets of paper from the desk drawer, Kenny was thoughtful for a few moments. He'd already sowed the seeds of suspicion into Tracey's mind that Hardcastle had been the shooter; maybe now it was time to work his magic on Terry's sons. Just maybe with a little bit of input from him, they would avenge their father's death, hunt Hardcastle down, and get rid of him for once and for all. It wasn't as though anyone would actually miss Hardcastle; his old mum had died years ago, and he had no siblings.

Happier now that he had devised a plan of action, Kenny whistled a cheerful little tune. As far as he was concerned, Max Hardcastle's days were numbered. He only wished that he'd signed Hardcastle's death warrant years ago; that would have been one way of getting rid of him permanently.

8

———————

'She's fucking lost it,' Jamie hissed in his brother's ear.

Turning his head slightly, Ricky studied their mother out of the corner of his eye. For all intents and purposes, this was the calmest Tracey had been since their father's death.

'How do you know that she's not going to fly off the handle as soon as Hardcastle arrives?' Jamie continued to hiss. 'Maybe this little act she's putting on is just a ruse to get him here.'

Ricky screwed up his face. 'Fuck off Jamie,' he snapped. 'She's not dangerous.'

Jamie raised his eyebrows, and holding up his hands, he took a step away from his brother. 'Don't say I didn't warn you,' he stated.

Shaking his head, Ricky resumed the task of pouring himself a drink. With Jamie's words echoing through his mind, he gave the knife block set on the kitchen counter a quick glance, then hastily counted how many blades were present. Much to his relief none were missing, not that he'd thought there would be. As he'd already told his brother, their mum wasn't crazy she just wanted the same as they did, to know who had murdered her husband, and why.

A loud knock at the front door broke Ricky's reverie and with a flick of his head he indicated for Jamie to let Hardcastle in.

Moments later, Max entered the kitchen, his large frame filling the space. He shook both Ricky's and Jamie's hands then offered his outstretched hand to Tracey. 'Nice to see you again.' He smiled.

Hearing the hint of amusement in his voice, Tracey willed her cheeks not to blush pink as she took his large hand in hers. 'Take a seat.' She pulled her hand away and gestured towards a chair. 'And can I get you a drink? Tea, coffee?'

Max declined the offer of a beverage and after slipping off his jacket, he relaxed back into the chair, studying Ricky and Jamie as he did so. It was almost like looking at Terry all over again, they were his double, the spit out of his mouth, and he'd heard that they could handle themselves too, something else they had in common with their father. 'How can I help you?'

Ricky and Jamie shared a glance.

'At the funeral you said that you'd help find my dad's murderer,' Jamie volunteered. 'That all we had to do was give you a shout.'

Max nodded. 'That's right, and I meant every word,' he said sincerely. 'I've already been asking around, putting the feelers out.'

'And?' Tracey's breath caught in the back of her throat and as gooseflesh covered her skin she braced herself for what was about to come out of his mouth next. All they needed was a name and then she and her sons would be able to bring the murderer down.

'Well,' Max sighed. 'I've heard that Terry was working with the Murphy family.' He shot Tracey a glance in a bid to gauge her reaction. He still hadn't ruled out the fact that maybe she'd found out about the affair between Terry and Bianca and had put a hit on her husband. After all, she wouldn't be the first woman scorned to have maimed a cheating husband or partner.

'The Murphys?' Tracey exclaimed, her mouth falling slightly open. 'No.' She shook her head; it couldn't be true. She may not have had any knowledge of Max Hardcastle before her husband's death, but she'd definitely heard of the Murphy family. Fair enough she didn't know them personally. In fact, she didn't think she would recognise them if she were to pass them by in the street, but she had heard of them, everyone in the area had. They were well known and spoken about with a measure of both fear and mistrust.

'Nah, no way,' Jamie butted in. 'No fucking way. My dad wouldn't have had anything to do with the likes of them.'

Max spread open his arms. 'I've heard it from a reliable source; it was Kenny himself who told me,' he said, his voice gentle.

'But why?' Rubbing at his temples, Ricky could barely get his head around the fact that his dad would sink so low as to work with the Murphys. Everyone knew the family were scum and they were given a wide berth by the locals.

'Kenny said that him and your dad had used them to collect debts.' Max shrugged.

'Well that's bollocks for a start.' Screwing up his face, Jamie glanced towards his brother. 'Me and Ricky collect the debts, we've been doing it for years, ever since we left school.' He stabbed his forefinger in Max's direction, the anger in his voice tangible. 'And I can tell you now, I've never seen any of the Murphys hanging around. Dad never even mentioned them, not once.'

Holding up his hands in a bid to quieten the brothers down,

Max frowned. He'd heard that Terry was working with the Murphy family from two different sources, both reliable, one being the Winters brothers and the other Terry's own business partner. So how was it possible that Terry's own sons had had no knowledge of the business deal? Briefly it crossed Max's mind that perhaps Kenny had lied to him, but even that made no sense; why would he even need to? What Terry got up to was his business, it wasn't Max's place to judge him, and he wasn't exactly holier than thou, himself, was he? In fact, after his time banged up at her Majesty's pleasure, he still dabbled in illegal activities; it was who he was, and the only life he'd ever known, he was hardly going to stroll out of the nick and become a white-collar worker. In his mind the only good thing to have come out of his stint in prison was that he now had more connections than he'd had before being banged up.

'Something's not right about any of this.' Pulling out his car keys, Ricky tipped his head towards his brother. 'I think we need to have a chat with Kenny.'

'Too fucking right we do,' Jamie growled in agreement, anger flashing in his eyes.

Max got to his feet and, slipping on his jacket, he motioned towards the door. 'I'll keep asking around and if I hear of anything, you'll be the first to know.' He turned to give Tracey a smile. 'I'll see myself out.'

Tracey nodded in return and once Max left the house she turned her attention back to her sons. 'What the fuck is going on?' she exclaimed. 'Why would your dad have got himself mixed up with the likes of that family?'

Ricky chewed on the inside of his cheek. 'I don't know Mum,' he answered truthfully. 'But trust me, I'm going to find out.'

* * *

The Murphy family home was no better than a slum, not that
Bianca Murphy appeared to notice. Flung haphazardly beside the
front door were a pile of coats and jackets, the majority of which
were covered in dog hairs and slobber. Propped up against the
banister rail was an adult-sized bicycle, no doubt stolen if the
sawn through combination lock which still hung from the handle
bars was anything to go by, and dotted along the hallway amongst
the trainers and shoes which still sat where they had been kicked
off were carrier bags full of overflowing rubbish. Even the stale
stench of cigarette smoke which mingled with the unmistakable
scent of chip fat didn't seem to faze Bianca. After all, it was all
she'd ever known, it was the smell of home, or at least her
parents' home.

From the lounge she could hear her elder brothers screaming
and shouting at the television. They were so predictable. If they
weren't in the boozer then they were lounging on the sofa, a can
of cheap lager in one hand and a burning cigarette in the other.
Littered on the stained coffee table and surrounding floor would
be their betting slips, most of which would be screwed up into
tight little balls, their bets obviously lost.

None of the Murphys had ever had a legitimate job, Bianca
included. And even though they were making more than enough
money pimping out women, they also claimed benefits, both
housing and unemployment and her dad even claimed disability
benefit, not that there was anything wrong with him other than
being bone idle and allergic to work.

Bypassing the lounge, Bianca walked down the hallway
towards the kitchen. She heard her mother, Doris Murphy, before
she saw her, the usual shrill voice loud as she bellowed through
the open window at the youngest of Bianca's brothers to stop
winding the dogs up. Kevin made it his daily mission to whip the
two Rottweilers into a frenzy, until they were frothing at mouth,

their powerful jaws snapping open and closed as they leapt up into the air in an attempt to sink their teeth into a shredded rubber tyre that swung from a tree trunk. The dogs had been bought for protection, only Kevin didn't seem to have received the memo; he thoroughly believed the dogs' sole purpose was for his own perverted entertainment.

'Knock it off.' As she banged her fist on the glass window pane, Doris's face was set like thunder. From the corner of her lip a Benson & Hedges cigarette dangled precariously, the ash sprinkling on to the dirty dishes piled up in the sink. 'Kevin,' she screeched, 'I'm warning you.' Snatching an open can of cola off the kitchen counter, she launched it through the open window. 'That'll teach you,' she cackled as the brown liquid fizzed and sprayed, causing her son to jump out of its path. 'Now leave the bastard dogs alone.'

'About time he grew up, isn't it?' Bianca pursed her lips, watching as Kevin twisted one of the dog's collars in his fist, forcing the protesting animal into a sitting position. 'He behaves worse than a kid,' she complained.

Doris turned her head, her eyes narrowing on her daughter. 'Who's rattled your bleeding cage?'

'No one,' Bianca huffed, although strictly speaking that wasn't true. Kenny Kempton had rattled her; in fact, he'd done a lot more than rattle her, he'd left her feeling absolutely terrified.

'Are you sickening for something? You're as white as a bleeding sheet.'

Bianca reached up to touch her face, her fingers skimming over the angry red spots which dotted her chin. After Kenny had left the flat, she'd climbed into the bath and scrubbed herself clean. She hadn't even put any makeup on and in any normal circumstances wouldn't have been seen dead without wearing her trademark foundation that was at least three shades too dark for her. Even her damp hair hung limp just below her shoulders.

'Well…' Doris scowled. 'Are you ill?'

'Oh, leave it out Mum,' Bianca huffed.

Doris's eyes narrowed. 'You're not up the bleeding duff are you?'

'Mum!' Bianca's jaw dropped. 'Of course I'm not.' As she spoke, worry edged its way down her spine. She had been feeling more tired than usual lately, and her period was late, four weeks late to be precise. But that wasn't entirely unusual, her periods had always been irregular, but just that very morning she had felt nauseous, which again she supposed wasn't entirely surprising considering she'd sunk several bottles of white wine the previous evening. Besides, she and Terry had always been careful; she took the contraceptive pill, at least when she remembered to anyway. No, she decided, she couldn't be pregnant, she would know, wouldn't she? She would feel different, and would have certainly suspected that something was wrong long before her mother had planted the seed of suspicion into her mind. Chewing on her bottom lip, Bianca pushed the thought to the back of her mind. On the way home she would nip to the chemist shop and buy a pregnancy test just to put her mind at ease.

As she eyed her daughter, Doris tilted her head to one side. 'I take it you'd know who the father is this time if you were?'

Bianca's nostrils flared. 'Cheers for that Mum,' she answered sarcastically. Although she had to admit, her mum did have a point. Until she'd met Terry, she'd never been too choosy about who she went to bed with and more often than not, she hadn't even bothered to ask their names. As far as Bianca was concerned, the men were not only nameless but also faceless, and she highly doubted that she would even recognise the majority of them again. It wasn't as though she'd longed for them to romance her, so where was the harm in having some fun? No, all she had ever wanted from them was a quick shag with maybe a couple of drinks thrown in for good measure.

As she placed her hand on her abdomen, Bianca's heart sunk. Everything had changed when she'd met Terry; he'd whisked her off her feet, and she could hand on heart state that he was the only man she had ever truly loved. In fact, she'd loved him so much that she'd begged him to make their relationship official. She had a feeling that he'd been on the cusp of giving in to her too, that he'd known they had a good thing going on. If only Terry hadn't been married, then the world would have been their oyster. They could have lived comfortably, holidayed in exotic far away destinations, eaten out in the best restaurants and lived in a beautiful home together. Instead, Terry had treated her as though she were nothing more than his dirty little secret. He'd been afraid that his sons would find out about them, and even more afraid that his wife would find out about their affair, divorce him and bleed him dry in the process.

A thought suddenly hit Bianca. If she was pregnant with Terry's baby then the kid would be entitled to a cut of his wealth, wouldn't it? Even if the baby had been born out of wedlock? Not to mention, if she was indeed pregnant then she would be entitled to claim even more benefits. Maybe the council would even rehouse her? She quite fancied moving out of her poky flat and into a house with a garden. A smile edged its way across Bianca's face. Perhaps having a kid wouldn't be such a bad thing after all. 'Well if I am pregnant,' she told her mother, 'then at least you would know one grandchild; that lot in there could have fathered a hundred kids and you would be none the wiser,' she said, jerking her head towards the lounge where her brothers were still cheering on their horses.

Lifting her shoulders in a nonchalant shrug, Doris went back to looking out of the window.

The very notion that she could have Terry's child growing inside of her spurred Bianca on and, as she entered the lounge, her fear of Kenny Kempton hastily evaporated. She was no walkover, she was a Murphy, and she could also handle herself. The fact she had been raised with five older brothers was more than enough to tell her that. They had not only taught her how to fight but they'd also taught her to be afraid of no one and nothing. Kenny had just taken her unaware that was all; any other day and she would never have allowed him to get the better of her, she would have slammed a knife into the tosser's gut before he'd even dared raise a hand to her. Besides, if there was a possibility that she was going to become a mother and raise a child without its father then she would need all the money that she could get her hands on, wouldn't she? And that included Terry's cut of the profits. She was entitled to his money, it was her compensation, and she was determined that no one would stop her from having what was rightfully hers.

Stomping across the room, she came to stand in front of the wide screen television, blocking her brothers' view.

'Get out of the way,' they yelled at her as they craned their necks to resume watching the race.

Bianca stood her ground, and grabbing the remote control from the coffee table, she switched the television off and placed her hands on her ample hips.

'What the actual fuck B,' her eldest brother Michael growled. Slamming his can of lager down on the coffee table, he pulled in his long legs, his firm body suddenly taut as he prepared to launch himself off the sofa and wrestle the remote control out of her hands. 'I've got dough riding on that horse.'

'We have a problem.' Ignoring her brother, Bianca jutted her chin in the air, exposing the purple and black bruises that Kenny's fingers had left around her neck. Just as she'd known they would, her brothers fell silent. In fact, she could almost see the cogs turning in their heads as they tried to work out what it was they were actually looking at.

Moments later they leapt off the sofa and as her brothers begun to scream and holler, she had to stifle the urge to smirk. They were so predictable at times that it was actually laughable.

'Who did this to you?' Michael hissed, his tall frame towering above her, one hand gripping her by the forearm as he yanked her towards him so that he could get a better view of the damage Kenny had caused.

Bianca chose her words carefully. After all, she didn't want to lose face in front of her brothers. She had to prove to them that she was just as tough as they were. If not, they would walk all over her, and treat her as they did their mother, like a skivvy, whose only purpose in life was to be at their beck and call. 'I had words with Kenny Kempton.' She saw their faces cloud over, anger filling their eyes. 'He wants Terry's cut of the profits.'

Michael let out a raucous laugh. 'Well Kenny can go fucking swivel.' To emphasise his point, he lifted his middle finger in the air, much to the agreement of his brothers.

It was exactly what Bianca had expected him to say, and hearing the all too familiar sound of heavy panting, she turned to look in the direction of the doorway. The youngest of her brothers, Kevin, stood there, both fists gripping the dogs by their collars, and they were big animals, over one hundred and thirty pounds of sheer muscle.

'What's going on?' he asked, cocking his head to one side.

It was no secret that Kevin was wired differently. He had an edge about him, not to mention a temper that was both terrifying and impressive to witness. Even as a child there had been something different about him; he was cold hearted, and at times Bianca wondered if he even had a heart. She'd certainly never seen any evidence of one. By the age of fourteen he'd been seen by three different psychiatrists and yet none of them could actually pinpoint what was wrong with him.

He was just Kevin, the brother who felt no remorse for his actions. It was one of the reasons why they made him work at the brothel; no amount of crying or begging from the women would ever soften his heart towards them.

'Kenny Kempton wants Terry's cut of the profits,' she answered.

Kevin's eyes darkened. 'I told you,' he said, thrusting his head in his eldest brother's direction, 'that this would happen, that the bastard would try to have us over.'

For a few moments Michael was thoughtful. 'Fuck him,' he finally answered with a sneer. 'Do you really think Kempton would dare take us on?' He looked round at his siblings, one eyebrow cocked in the air. They were Murphys and their name alone was enough to instil terror in the community, and as a result they were given a wide berth; even the neighbours were too afraid to complain when the rubbish out in the front garden spilled over into theirs.

'So what do we do about this?' Bianca asked.

'For now we do nothing,' Michael replied. Waving away his brothers' protests, he lit a cigarette, and as the curling smoke wafted above his head he gave his sister a chilling smile. 'But believe me,' he said, 'I will be having words with Kempton over this. In fact, I'm looking forward to it.'

Bianca nodded. It was exactly what she had expected and as her hand slid down to her tummy she gave a smile of her own. Kenny Kempton wasn't going to know what had hit him.

9

Shaun Kempton had just been about to jump up into the van when he spotted Ricky and Jamie jogging across the forecourt towards him. There and then he felt his insides turn to liquid. He'd always been wary of the Tempest brothers, and although they had never physically lashed out at him, or given him any reason to fear them, he'd always sensed an underlying measure of menace about them. It was in their movements, the way they talked, and the way they watched everything around them.

'Oi, Shaunie,' Jamie called out.

Shaun groaned out loud; they knew he hated being called Shaunie.

'Where's your old man?'

Shaun's pulse quickened. His dad was over at the house dealing with the women before they were shipped out to the whore houses. Not that he could tell Ricky or Jamie this; they had absolutely no idea of what their dad had become involved with, and Shaun was determined that he wasn't going to be the one to tell them – it was more than his life was worth.

'I don't know, I haven't seen him.' The words came out in a

rush and as his cheeks flushed bright red, his hands ever so slightly trembled. Did they know what he'd done, that it had been him who'd murdered their father? Could they sense his guilt? To his relief they didn't pick up on his nervousness; instead, they appeared preoccupied as they made their way inside the office.

'Do me a favour,' Ricky said with a jerk of his head towards the door. 'Find your dad and tell him that we need to have a word with him.'

Shaun almost fell over his own two feet in his haste to get away from them. All along he'd known that this day would come. Say what you want about Ricky and Jamie but they weren't stupid and he'd told his dad as much at Terry's wake, not that his dad had listened to a word he'd said. And that right there was where the problem lay; Kenny didn't know the Tempest boys as well as he did. He still saw them as kids, when in reality they were far from it, they were men now and they had a lot of their father in them. They were as ruthless and as brutal as Terry had been, and sooner or later his dad was going to find that out the hard way.

Jumping back into the van, Shaun locked the doors as an extra safety precaution then took out his mobile phone. In reality, all he needed to do was holler for his dad and Kenny would have heard him, seeing as he was less than eight metres away, but the last thing either of them needed was to arouse Ricky's or Jamie's suspicions. As it was they believed that the house stood empty, other than perhaps storing some discarded scrap metal.

* * *

Switching off his mobile phone, Kenny groaned in irritation. He was sick to the back teeth of the Tempests. It was bad enough that he'd had Terry to contend with let alone his sons as well.

As far as Kenny was concerned, Ricky and Jamie were nothing but two jumped up little pricks who needed to be reminded that he was now their boss and that it was him who paid their wages. The fact that Ricky and Jamie were Terry's heirs was wiped from his mind. By rights, should something happen to Tracey then they would be entitled to Terry's share of the business, all of the businesses in fact, including the deal concerning the tarts.

A sly grin creased Kenny's face. Maybe he should bring the boys on board? If they were anything like their father then they would jump at the chance, and he had to admit the extra muscle would come in handy should there be any comebacks from the Murphys. All in all, it made sense, only it would also mean losing out on Terry's cut of the profits, something which Kenny wasn't prepared to do.

Entering the office, he offered up a wide grin – he had to play the game after all. 'Hello lads, what are you doing here?' He shook their hands, then took a seat behind the desk.

The two brothers turned to face him.

'The Murphys,' Jamie asked, 'is it true that our dad was dealing with them?'

Taken aback, Kenny narrowed his eyes. What the hell was going on? How did they even know about the Murphys? Had Hardcastle left the office and gone straight to Terry's sons and told them? Kenny hadn't even realised that they were on speaking terms, unless Hardcastle had gone to see Tracey? Yes, that made more sense. As he thought it over, Kenny almost laughed out loud. Max certainly hadn't wasted any time in cosying up to Terry's widow, not that he'd expected any different from him, Max had always been a sucker for a sob story. Kenny focused his attention back to Jamie. Out of the two brothers he'd always been a trappy little sod and was every inch his father's son. 'Your dad did do some business with them,' he sighed.

Both Ricky and Jamie screwed up their faces.

'But why?' Jamie continued, his face contorting with anger. 'Me and Ricky collect the debts, so why did my dad need them?'

Kenny paused. Hardcastle's visit had caught him off guard and as soon as the lie about debt collecting had left his mouth he'd wanted to kick himself. He hadn't been thinking straight, that was the problem. As of late he'd been snorting way too much coke, and it was messing with his head. Instead of making him sharper, it was making him reckless. Terry had put his sons to work as soon as they had left school, and over the years they had proved themselves to be more than capable. Tall and naturally well built, the two brothers were not averse to steaming in with their fists or boots should the need arise, and on top of that they didn't take any shit from anyone, so why would he or Terry have even needed to recruit the Murphys to work for them?

'Kenny,' Jamie said through gritted teeth. 'Answer the fucking question. Why did my dad recruit them?'

'I don't know,' Kenny spat. He watched as their eyebrows knotted together, confusion etched across their faces, and swiftly moved on to the second phase of his plan. 'All I know is that your dad had had some trouble; he'd been selling cars and wanted out of the deal. The situation ended up getting a bit heated and so he had a word with the Murphys for extra protection.'

Ricky and Jamie glanced towards one another; the shock they felt was mirrored in each other's eyes.

'My dad sold cars to Hardcastle,' Ricky said as he tilted his head to one side to study his dad's business partner.

Kenny nodded.

'So let me get this straight.' Rubbing at his temples, Ricky blew out his cheeks. 'My dad wanted out of the deal, and you're telling me that Hardcastle kicked off, that he threatened my dad?'

Careful not to let them see the crafty grin that threatened to crease his face, Kenny nodded, his expression remaining sombre. 'Put it this way, Hardcastle was gunning for your old man and trust me lads, a war was on the cards.'

'The sly fucker.' Clenching his fists, Jamie bristled. 'Are you trying to tell us that Hardcastle killed our dad?'

Kenny had wondered how long it would take for the penny to drop and as he answered it took every ounce of his strength not to laugh at them. Not only were they gullible but they were also as thick as shit, they had to be if they really believed that Hardcastle would have gunned Terry down. 'Now I didn't say that.' Kenny pointed his finger forward, his expression one of mock annoyance. 'All I'm saying is that there was trouble, and there was also a lot of money at stake. And let's face it, men have been murdered for a lot less.' He spread open his arms, allowing his words to sink in.

'The bastard,' Jamie roared. He turned to look at his brother. 'He won't get away with this.'

As far as Kenny was concerned, it was like music to his ears and as he relaxed back in the chair, he silently congratulated himself. 'I sincerely hope that he doesn't boys,' he said cheerfully.

Thirty minutes later, Ricky and Jamie were making their way back across the forecourt.

'Mum was right all along,' Jamie stated. 'We should have listened to her.' Hardcastle had fooled them all. Not only had they invited him to their dad's funeral, but they had also set up a meeting with him to discuss the murder. All along his mum had been right, she'd been convinced that Hardcastle was the shooter, but they had dismissed her, had treated her as though she had lost her mind.

Pausing beside the iron gate, Ricky turned to look over his shoulder, his gaze sweeping over the yard, office and then finally to the house. He still didn't get what his dad's attraction had been to the place; the yard was depressing, squalid, and not somewhere he wanted to spend his days, and yet Terry had loved being here, and look how much security he and Kenny had recently installed, even the derelict house had bars at the windows.

'Kenny was lying,' he blurted out suddenly.

'What?' Screwing up his face, Jamie snapped his head round. 'What are you talking about?'

Ricky jerked his thumb behind him. 'Do you really believe that dad would have needed the Murphys to fight his battles for him?'

When Jamie didn't answer, Ricky continued. 'Come on bruv,' he said. 'Think about it. If Dad had really needed help, then he would have had Kenny, me and you, and even Shaun on his side, although let's be honest, even on a good day Shaun's about as much use as a glass hammer. But my point is, why the fuck would Dad have needed to go to the Murphys, when he had all of us?'

Jamie scratched at his head as he thought it over. He could see his brother's point. His dad would have had more than enough muscle behind him, not that Terry hadn't been capable of taking care of his own business; he wouldn't have lasted five minutes in their world if he hadn't. 'Why would Kenny lie?'

'That,' Ricky said, giving the office one final glance, 'is exactly what I intend to find out.'

* * *

Tracey felt as though she was on tenterhooks while waiting for her sons to return; in fact, she couldn't sit still and alternated between staring out of the lounge window and then peering outside the front door, hoping that she would see Ricky's car pull up outside the house. They were close to finding out the truth, she knew they were, she could feel it in her gut.

Hearing a key turn in the lock, she raced out into the hallway. 'Well,' she demanded of her sons, 'why was your dad working with the Murphys?'

Tracey's gaze went between her sons. 'Well come on,' she spat, 'what's going on?'

'Kenny lied to us.' Pushing past his mum, Jamie slid off his jacket and tossed it on to a chair. 'He reckons that Dad went to the Murphys for protection.'

'He what?' Tracey's jaw dropped. 'Your dad would never have gone to the likes of that family for protection.' She stood a little straighter, her forehead furrowed. 'And why would he even need protection? Protection from who?'

'Exactly,' Ricky agreed. 'Dad wouldn't have needed protection; he had me and Jamie for a start.' He chewed on his bottom lip then jerked his head towards his brother. 'Fancy a trip over to Southend?'

Tracey's heart began to beat faster. 'Southend?' she asked, her eyes narrowing. She knew full well that Max Hardcastle lived in Southend. 'What's going on?' she demanded. 'What did Kenny say?'

'Nothing,' they answered in unison.

As soon as the word was out of their mouths, her sons averted their eyes. They were lying to her. All along Tracey had known that they would do this, that they would try to keep her in the dark. 'Don't lie to me,' she warned. 'And do not try to treat me like a fool.'

Ricky sighed. 'Kenny reckons that Dad had asked the Murphys for protection because he'd had a falling out with Max

Hardcastle. Apparently Dad had wanted out of their deal and Hardcastle had tried to put the hard word on him.'

Taken aback, Tracey narrowed her eyes, her mind in turmoil. Had she been right and it had been Hardcastle who'd murdered Terry after all? 'And... do you believe him?' Her breath caught in the back of her throat, and she placed her hand upon her chest as the enormity of the situation finally sank in. Had she allowed her husband's murderer to breeze into the house, to sit at the table, Terry's table?

Ricky shook his head. 'No.'

'But why would Kenny lie?' She recalled the conversation that she'd had with Kenny where he'd hinted at Hardcastle being the shooter too. In fact, he'd actively encouraged her to drive to Southend-on-Sea and have it out with Hardcastle, without giving her safety so much as a second thought. Had he known all along that Hardcastle was harmless, that he wouldn't have harmed her? Or could he have perhaps been sending her to her death? But why? Surely Kenny wouldn't have wanted to see her hurt. They had known one another for years. Kenny was like family; why would it even enter his mind to betray her?

'I don't know Mum, and that's the truth of it, but I'm going to find out.' He pulled out his car keys and jerked his head towards his brother, indicating that it was time for them to leave the house.

'Well you're not going alone.' As she slipped her handbag over her shoulder, there was a defiant gleam in Tracey's eyes. 'I'm coming with you.'

Ricky and Jamie shared a glance.

Pulling herself up to her full height, Tracey jutted out her chin. 'I do know how to handle myself,' she stated, 'and believe me, I am not scared of Max Hardcastle.'

'Fine.' Ricky gave his mother a hard stare. 'But try and behave yourself Mum. In fact, let me and Jamie do all of the talking.'

Tracey laughed out loud. Had her son really just said that? 'Just you remember who you're talking to,' she chastised them. 'And let me tell you something now, I was married to your father for thirty years, I'm not as green around the edges as you might think I am.'

Ricky caught his brother's eyes, and the look Jamie gave him in return said it all. Their mum was going to fuck everything up.

10

Patricia Tempest stubbed out her cigarette then made her way down the hallway. She patted her peroxide blonde hair into place before flinging the front door wide open.

'Kenny!' She beamed. 'Come on in, darling. It's good to see you.'

Stepping across the threshold, Kenny closed the front door behind him and followed Patricia into the lounge. He didn't wait to be asked to take a seat; he'd known Terry's mother long enough to know that she would have wanted him to treat her home as his own.

'How have you been keeping?' He reached out to clasp her hand and gave it a gentle squeeze.

'Oh, you know.' Patricia's gaze wandered towards the mantelpiece, her eyes falling on a photograph of her son. 'I miss him.' She sniffed. 'I suppose I always will.'

Kenny nodded. Terry had been Patricia's only child and so his death was bound to have hit her hard. 'And how about Tracey and the boys?' he asked innocently. 'Have they been to see you?'

Patricia pursed her lips. It was no secret that her and her

daughter-in-law had never got along. 'Of course I haven't seen her,' she spat. 'And as for Ricky and Jamie, I can count on one hand how many times they've been to see me, and even then they only stayed for ten minutes,' she complained. 'They've got too much of their mother in them, always have done. From day one Tracey set out to poison those boys against me, she didn't even like me visiting them when they were babies. Oh she might not have said anything to my face but I saw the sour look whenever I visited them. My Terry would turn in his grave if he knew how they've treated me; their own grandmother and they couldn't give a toss about me.'

Kenny shook his head, his expression one of mock sympathy. Not that he'd actually expected any different, Patricia could be a sanctimonious old bat at the best of times. Even Terry had only been able to spend short periods of time in his mother's company before wanting to wrap his hands round her throat and throttle her to death.

'Well, I expect she's been busy,' Kenny volunteered, his words loaded with meaning.

Patricia looked up, her eyes narrowed. 'What do you mean by that?'

Kenny sighed then made a point of shaking his head. 'It's not really my place to say anything.'

'No, go on,' Patricia urged him, her eyes lighting up at the thought of hearing some juicy gossip.

'Well...' He gave a sad shake of his head again. 'I've heard that she's been spending a lot of time with Max Hardcastle, and I know for a fact that she went to see him in Southend.'

Patricia's eyes widened and her mouth dropped open. 'She did bloody what?' she gasped. She'd never liked Max Hardcastle and in fact, despised him. She also fully blamed him for leading her son astray. Terry had been a good, decent boy until he'd become friendly with Hardcastle. And as for Max's mother, she'd been nothing other than a dirty whore, who'd sold her body down at the docks in Dagenham. And if that wasn't bad enough, when her son had committed a brutal murder she'd stood by him; she'd even had the front to hold her head up high in the street and stare down anyone who dared to say a bad word about him. The woman should have been ashamed of both herself and of her no-good murdering son.

Kenny held his hands up. 'You know me Pat,' he said, 'I'm not one to gossip or speak ill of people but it's only right that you know what she's been getting up to. And poor Terry's only been gone a few weeks, he's barely even cold in the ground.' He gave a crafty smirk. 'Makes you wonder what she was getting up to when Terry was alive doesn't it? I mean' – he leant forward in the chair and lowered his voice – 'I've never been able to see a resemblance between Terry and Jamie, myself, and at one point Terry did question whether or not Jamie was even his son.' It was a lie of course, Terry and Jamie were like two peas in a pod and as far as he was aware Tracey had only ever been faithful to her husband, unlike Terry who hadn't known the meaning of the word.

Astounded, Patricia glanced back at the mantelpiece. In her mind's eye she tried to conjure up her youngest grandson's face. She had always believed that Jamie and Terry had looked alike, or perhaps she'd only seen what she'd wanted to. One thing she did know was that Jamie's hair was a shade lighter than Terry's, and her Terry's genes had been strong. It stood to reason that his offspring should be a mirror image of him. 'The brazen cow,' she spat. 'And all this time she's treated my Terry like he was a fool.'

'It looks that way,' Kenny confirmed. Sinking back on the sofa, he eyed Patricia. 'And to think,' he said with a shake of his head, 'she inherited everything: the house, the businesses. I bet Hardcastle is loving that. Give it a few weeks and he'll be dining out on Terry's money.'

Patricia sat up a little straighter, fury setting in her eyes. 'Over my dead body will that no-good bastard see a penny of my Terry's money.' As she stabbed a finger forward, her lips were set into a straight line. 'You mark my words,' she said, 'I'll have it out with her, the bitch, him an' all if he's not too cowardly to face me.'

It was exactly what Kenny had been hoping for. He'd wanted a distraction and Patricia was exactly the right person to make sure that he had one. 'In fact,' he said, making sure to keep the sly grin from his face. 'It wouldn't surprise me if' – he lifted two fingers in the air making the shape of an imaginary gun – 'Hardcastle had been the shooter.'

The colour drained from Patricia's face and as she clutched at her heart, Kenny actually thought that she would keel over. 'No,' she gasped.

'Yep,' Kenny answered, his voice sincere. 'I've heard one or two rumours that put Hardcastle's name in the frame.'

'We have to call the police.' In a blind panic, Patricia looked around her as she tried to locate her mobile phone. 'They have to arrest him. Oh,' she spat, her face contorting with anger. 'I always knew he was a wrong'un. Over and over again I warned my Terry that sooner or later Hardcastle would be the death of him, I could feel it in here,' she said, stabbing her thumb into her chest. 'That bastard thrived on causing trouble and he dragged my boy along for the ride.'

'Hold on.' Putting out his hand and resting it on Patricia's arm, Kenny shook his head. 'You leave Hardcastle to me,' he said. 'Let's just say I won't allow him to get away with this. I'm going to destroy the fucker and believe me when I say this, Hardcastle isn't going to know what's hit him when I get my hands on him.'

As she digested Kenny's words, Patricia smiled. She'd pay

money to see Hardcastle brought to his knees just like her Terry had been so brutally brought down. 'Well you make sure you give that fucker a dig or two from me,' she said.

'Oh I will.' Kenny grinned. 'You can bet your life on that.'

* * *

It was almost dark by the time Tracey and her sons reached Max Hardcastle's car showroom in Southend-on-Sea. As they had driven along the motorway she'd been afraid that they would arrive too late and that the showroom would be locked up for the night. To her relief, the forecourt and office block were still lit up and she took a wild guess that Hardcastle was on the premises.

'Remember Mum,' Jamie said as they climbed out of the car. 'Let me and Ricky do the talking.'

Tracey bristled. Were they actually being serious? Did they honestly think that she would be able to keep her mouth shut? They should know her better than that; she'd never been the type of woman to keep her opinions to herself and certainly didn't intend to start now.

'Mum?' Jamie asked again, his tone becoming more urgent. 'We had a deal; you promised that you'd let us sort this out.'

'No,' Tracey answered, 'I promised you that I wouldn't lose my temper, and I won't. At the end of the day, I want the same as you do – to know what the hell is going on, because right now none of this is making any sense to me. We've got Kenny saying one thing and Hardcastle saying another. I just want the truth.'

Moments later, they were outside the office block and after rapping their knuckles on the door, they stepped aside as it was opened. Immediately they saw confusion spread across Max's face; he hadn't been expecting them and they hadn't called ahead, deciding that it would be better to take him by surprise so as to not give him the time to get his story straight.

'Come on in.' Hastily Max composed himself, and gesturing towards his office, he narrowed his eyes. 'What can I do for you?' he asked, tilting his head to one side as he studied them.

It was Tracey who answered and, ignoring the glare that her sons shot towards her, her voice didn't so much as waver as she spoke. 'Did you threaten my husband?'

Max's eyes narrowed even further. 'No.' He shook his head, bewildered.

'When Terry ended the deal with the cars,' she added, 'did you and him fall out, did you give him the impression that you wanted to kill him?'

Again, Max shook his head, and as he looked between them he shoved his hands deep into his trouser pockets. 'What the fuck is going on?' he snapped.

Tracey turned to look at her sons; she didn't know what or who they were meant to believe, but someone was definitely lying.

'We went to see Kenny,' Ricky explained. 'He was under the impression that my dad went to the Murphys for protection, because you'd kicked off when he backed away from your business deal.'

Max gave a laugh. 'Is this a joke?' he asked.

They shook their heads and seeing the seriousness in their faces, Max wiped his hand across his jaw. That certainly wasn't the version of events that he remembered. Fair enough he'd been disappointed that Terry had wanted to walk away from the deal, but he'd understood, and certainly hadn't kicked off, why would he? In fact, they had left on good terms, and he'd still considered Terry to be his mate.

'I don't understand this,' Tracey said as she slumped down into a chair.

'You and me both,' Max added as he followed suit and took a seat behind his desk. Clearing his throat, Max steepled his fingers. 'Look,' he said, 'I had nothing to gain in killing Terry. Now I don't expect you to believe me, but one look out there' – he jerked his thumb towards the forecourt – 'should be enough to tell you that I've got a lot of dough. Fair enough I was disappointed when Terry walked away; I'd wanted us to work together, we were mates, but I didn't need him, and my livelihood wasn't banking on him bringing me cars.'

'He's got a point,' Jamie said and Ricky nodded in agreement.

'So where do the Murphys fit into all of this?' Tracey asked.

They were all quiet for a few moments, and after what seemed an age Max spoke. 'I don't know,' he said, 'but I think it's about time we paid them a visit and got to the bottom of this, because I for one don't like my name being dragged through the mud. I've done fuck all wrong, and I won't be accused of shit that I have no knowledge of.'

It was a veiled threat, one which Tracey and her sons took on board. Just one look at Max Hardcastle was enough to tell her that if the mood took him he could be a very dangerous individual.

11

Patricia's face was set like thunder as she thumped her fist on the front door of her son's house, and as far as she was concerned, it was still Terry's house. It had been his hard-earned money which had paid for it, not Tracey's.

Flinging open the door, Tracey groaned. 'Fucking hell Pat,' she complained. 'Do you know what time it is?'

Patricia pursed her lips and as she pushed past her daughter-in-law, she flicked her eyes towards the staircase. Was Hardcastle up there, was he in her son's bed? 'Of course I know what time it is,' she hissed. 'It's just gone eight.' She turned to face Tracey, her forehead furrowed and her lips pinched. 'And why aren't you up and dressed yet?'

Tracey stifled a yawn and after a quick glance at her watch she answered, her voice still thick from sleep. 'I had a late night, and fancied a lie in.'

'I bet you bleeding well did,' Patricia retorted, disgust etched across her lined face. Just as she had always suspected, Tracey had no shame. Her son was barely cold in the ground and already his wife was up to no good.

Tracey padded barefoot down the hallway towards the kitchen. 'I expect you want a cup of tea,' she called over her shoulder.

Patricia's entire body bristled and as she followed her daughter-in-law into the kitchen, she tilted her chin up towards the ceiling. 'Is he here?'

'Who?' Turning round, Tracey frowned.

'Who she says?' Patricia gave a nasty chuckle. 'Your fancy man, who do you think I'm talking about? My God,' she cried, looking Tracey up and down, 'you didn't waste any time, did you? Not that I can say I'm entirely surprised. From my understanding you'd drop your knickers for anyone, him included,' she said, jerking her thumb behind her.

Tracey's jaw dropped open. 'What are you talking about?' she hissed.

Placing her hands on her hips, Patricia narrowed her eyes. 'I'm talking about Hardcastle,' she sneered. 'Is he here, is he in my Terry's bed?'

Tracey pulled her dressing gown tighter around her body as though the action would somehow ward off her mother-in-law's words. 'Of course, he isn't. Why the hell would you think that he would be here?'

Patricia wasn't about to be put off. The only reason she'd turned up on the doorstep so early was to catch Tracey out. 'I know all about you,' she said, stabbing her finger forward. 'I know what you were getting up to behind my son's back. And I've had it on good authority that my Terry even had doubts that Jamie was his son.'

'I always knew that you had a wicked tongue.' Shaking her head, Tracey slid her body onto a chair and grasped onto the dining table. 'But that's below the belt, even for you. Jamie is the spit of his father; you know that as well as I do.'

'I'm sure that he is.' Patricia smirked, feeling somewhat triumphant to see her daughter-in-law look so shaken. After all, she'd been caught bang to rights hadn't she? Patricia only wished she'd been given the ammunition years ago; it would have been one sure way to prise the woman away from her son. 'But the question is: who exactly is his father?'

'Terry is his father,' Tracey shouted back, her body trembling with rage. 'You'd have to be blind not to see the likeness, they were the image of one another, like two peas in a bleeding pod.'

Lifting her eyebrows, Patricia stared at her daughter-in-law. 'Well my Terry questioned the boy's parentage, so I'm guessing he must have been blind as well then.'

'Get out.' Leaping to her feet, Tracey grasped her mother-in-law by the arm and proceeded to drag her towards the front door. 'I should have done this years ago,' she bellowed. 'You're poisonous, always have been.'

As she was thrown outside the house, Patricia careered across the pavement before hastily regaining her balance. 'You've not heard the last from me,' she warned, thrusting her chin in the air. 'And you just wait until I tell Jamie that his father is not the man he thought he was. That you've lied to him his entire life. And you've got the front to stand there and say that I'm poisonous. At least my son knew who his father was.' It was a lie, not that Patricia would ever admit that fact out loud, least of all to Tracey. Terry had never met his father, and in fact had only ever been told his first name and that he had originated from Liverpool, and even then that had been a lie. The truth was Terry had been the result of a quick fumble behind the White Horse public house in Barking, and all Patricia had known of her son's father was that he'd been a handsome charmer, with a tall, athletic build.

Tracey slammed the front door closed and clutching her hand to her mouth, she retreated back into the house. The mere thought that Terry could have questioned whether or not Jamie was his son sickened her to the core. Her husband and sons were the image of one another, and she knew for a fact that throughout their marriage she had never so much as looked at another man, let alone allowed one to touch her. As a wave of nausea swept through her, she raced up the stairs and into the bathroom. Once there, she promptly sank to her knees and gripped the toilet bowel. After emptying the contents of her stomach, she sat back on her haunches, wiped the back of her hand across her lips and allowed hot, salty tears to slip freely down her cheeks. Her expression was a mask of concentration as she tried to think back over the years. Had Terry treated Jamie differently to his brother? Had she missed the signs that perhaps Terry had doubted Jamie was his biological son?

No, was her answer. Terry had loved the boys, both of them in equal measure; he'd never favoured Ricky nor had he ever given her any reason to believe that he'd wrongly thought she had been unfaithful to him. The knowledge did nothing to erase the knot of pain in her heart; just the mere notion that Terry had questioned the wedding vows she had made to him all but broke her.

* * *

Bianca Murphy guzzled down a glass of water, placed the empty glass on the kitchen worktop and then took a seat at the table. As she lit a cigarette, her fourth that morning alone, her gaze wandered to the home pregnancy test that she had placed on the table just moments earlier. She was pregnant, or at least that was what the testing wand indicated. No wonder she felt as sick as a dog.

For a few moments she sat just thinking. Could she really raise a child alone, and more to the point, did she even want to?

She had never considered herself to be overly maternal – oh, she guessed that one day she might have kids, it was inevitable she supposed, she just hadn't thought that that time would be *now*.

Her thoughts wandered to Terry. This baby was a part of him, his flesh and blood. In that moment she knew that she would see the pregnancy through, if for no other reason than that she had loved him and that she wanted to cling on to whatever she had left of him.

Stubbing out the cigarette, she began to apply her makeup, spreading the thick foundation over her cheeks. She glanced around the kitchen; the flat was no place to bring up a child. It was a dump; in fact, she had barely done anything with it since moving in other than give the lounge a lick of paint, and even then she had only half-heartedly painted one wall. The flooring was bare concrete, and at the windows she had hung cotton sheets in a bid to block out the sunlight. The only room in the flat that looked halfway decent was her bedroom, and even then her clothes were still being stored in black bin bags, and her one and only bedding set hadn't been washed in weeks. It wasn't as though she didn't have the money to make her home nice, because she did, she just couldn't be bothered; she hated the flat and could see no point in trying to make it homely.

Terry sprang to her mind again, or rather his wife did. A sneer creased Bianca's face. She'd bet her life on it that Tracey Tempest had a nice home. In fact, she knew that she did; she'd driven past the house enough times to know that it was stunning. Even the outside brickwork looked pristine, and as for the windows, they sparkled. Either side of the glossy black front door were large ceramic pots which housed topiary trees, and the driveway, which was large enough to house at least three cars, looked as though it was swept clean on a daily basis. It was more than obvious that Tracey took care of her home. No wonder Terry hadn't wanted to leave his marriage; look at what he would have been walking away from.

In that instant, anger began to surge through Bianca's veins. Why should her and Terry's child be raised in squalor while Tracey and her sons lived the life of Riley? Not that she felt any ill will towards Terry's sons because she didn't, they were a part of Terry too, and were her unborn child's siblings. No, it was Tracey who Bianca directed her anger towards, and it was all because of Terry's wife that she had been pushed into the background. After all, she too was grieving the death of her man, not that anyone had bothered to ask her how she was or how she was coping without him. It was as though the pain she felt at his loss didn't even matter, and why should it? She had been nothing other than his bit on the side.

A wicked smile tugged at the corners of Bianca's lips. As far as she was concerned, she was entitled to as much as Tracey was, if not even more considering that she was pregnant with his baby. Her child would be entitled to a cut of his or her father's wealth, and Bianca was determined that her and Terry's child wouldn't go without, that it wouldn't become another of Terry's dirty little secrets. If need be she would shout her child's parentage from the rooftops and would do so with a smile across her face, if for no other reason than to prove she had meant something to Terry, that he had been hers and that they had loved one another, regardless of the fact he had already had a wife. What was a piece of paper anyway? Terry had certainly never taken his wedding vows seriously; he would never have climbed into Bianca's bed night after night if his wife had meant anything to him.

After applying her mascara, Bianca lifted the mirror and inspected her appearance. She looked much more like her old self, and after lighting yet another cigarette, she stood up and took one last look around the kitchen. Yes, she decided, her child would have everything its heart desired, and if Tracey didn't like it, then Tracey could go fuck herself, because Bianca was prepared to take her for every penny she had.

* * *

'Mum?' Jamie called out.

As she heard the front door close behind her sons, Tracey's breath caught in the back of her throat. Had Patricia already spewed her vicious, twisted lies into Jamie's ear? From the kitchen below, Tracey could hear them rummaging around in the fridge and gave a half laugh tinged somewhat with relief. They appeared to be in high spirits, and from what she could make out they certainly didn't sound as though Patricia had got to them. 'I'm coming,' she called down the stairs.

Moments later, she entered the kitchen and as they turned to face her, she gave them a warm smile. Perhaps she should warn her youngest son about his grandmother's visit and explain to him that it was nothing but lies, not that she actually expected Jamie to believe Patricia. He knew himself how alike he and his father were; not only had they been almost identical when it came to looks, but they had also shared the same temperament and mannerisms. It was ridiculous that Patricia would have even questioned Jamie's parentage. Out of her two sons, it was Jamie who was the mirror image of his father, so much so that at times it almost took her breath away how alike they were; it was almost like looking at Terry when he'd been the same age.

'Are you ready?' Ricky glanced at his watch. 'Hardcastle said that he would meet us at the boozer.'

Realising that the moment was lost, Tracey ran her fingers through her dark hair and nodded. Dressed in a fitted black suit with a leopard print satin shirt underneath, she collected her handbag, then slipped on her black high heels.

As they left the house, it didn't occur to Tracey to wonder how her mother-in-law had even come up with the notion that Jamie wasn't Terry's son or how Patricia had even known that she had been in recent contact with Max Hardcastle.

* * *

The Ship and Anchor public house was heaving with customers as Max, Tracey, Ricky and Jamie stepped inside. Over in the far corner a band was playing, and Tracey instantly recognised the song: it was a poor rendition of a Chas & Dave hit: 'Ain't No Pleasing You'. The band was so loud that Tracey could barely hear herself think.

They followed Max towards the bar, and looking around her, Tracey was more than aware of the attention that their arrival had created.

'What can I get you?' Max shouted towards her.

Tracey looked up. 'A white wine, please,' she shouted back. As he turned back to the bar to order their drinks, she couldn't help but feel more than a little bit self-conscious. 'People are staring at us,' she said, tugging on her eldest son's arm, her cheeks flushing pink.

Ricky looked around him and gave a light laugh. 'What did you expect Mum?' He jerked his head towards Max. 'They know shit is about to go down.'

Tracey swallowed deeply and taking note of the faces staring back at her, she averted her gaze. Not for a single moment had she expected them to be involved in any kind of trouble. Their sole purpose for coming here tonight was to simply have a chat with the Murphy family, wasn't it? They wanted answers and as far as she was aware nothing more than that; she certainly wasn't anticipating an altercation between them.

With the drinks handed out, Max took a gulp of his larger, his steely grey eyes scanning the bar. After a few beats, he discreetly lifted his chin towards the far side of the pub.

As her sons turned their heads, Tracey followed suit and craned her neck to get a better view of the bar. Even in her heels she could barely see above the crowd.

'Is it them?' she asked.

Max nodded.

Tracey's heart was in her mouth, and toying with the wine glass in her hand she nervously ran her fingers across the beads of condensation that coated the glass, smearing them into obliteration, before lifting the glass to her lips and swallowing down a mouthful of the alcohol.

'What are we waiting for?' Jamie asked.

Hearing the impatience in her son's voice, Tracey turned her head. Jamie had a point: what exactly were they waiting for?

Max lifted his eyebrows. 'You're your old man's son all right.' He chuckled out loud. The Terry he'd known from old would have steamed in with his fists, inflicting as much damage as he possibly could before asking questions. It had been one of his biggest downfalls, hence why they had ended up getting into so many scrapes. Max had an inkling that Terry's youngest son was of the same mindset, unlike his elder brother who was more of a thinker, and whose actions would be meticulously planned down to the smallest of details before striking out. Instinctively he knew that out of the two brothers it would be Ricky who people would be more wary of. It stood to reason; the thinkers were dangerous, they took no prisoners, and played the game to win.

Draining his drink, Max placed the empty glass on the bar

then jerked his head once again towards the far side of the pub, indicating for them to follow him.

'You're the Murphys, am I right?'

About to take a gulp of her wine, Bianca snapped her head round.

'Who wants to know?' her eldest brother Michael answered, his voice loud and menacing.

Bianca looked around her, noted that her brothers were suddenly alert, then turned her attention back to the man who'd asked the question. Max Hardcastle. Of course she recognised him, she'd seen him just days earlier, not that she'd known who he was at the time; it was only once he'd left the pub that she'd heard the whispers about him. And he was a big fucker she'd give him that, good looking too. Dressed in a black shirt and dark denim jeans, even from where she was standing, Bianca could see that he had an air of arrogance about him, a confidence that was more than enough to alert her to the fact that he knew how to handle himself. But Bianca wasn't overly concerned; her brothers were hard fuckers too. Take Kevin for example, he was a bona fide nutcase.

She took note of Hardcastle's hard stare then looked past him to the two men accompanying him. There and then her heart almost stopped beating. Terry's sons. There could be no mistaking who they were; they were the image of their father: same height, same build, same handsome faces. Her gaze then went to the woman standing slightly behind them and she felt an instant knot of anger form in her gut. Tracey.

'I said, who wants to know?' Michael repeated with a sneer. Naturally aggressive, he clenched his fists into tight balls, more than prepared to lash out should the need arise, not that he'd ever needed much of an excuse in the past to batter someone half to death.

'Max Hardcastle.'

To Bianca's surprise Michael ever so slightly blanched. It was so slight that she doubted anyone other than her would have even noticed and looking from her brother to Hardcastle, she narrowed her eyes. What the hell was going on? And more to the point, why hadn't her brother smashed his pint glass into Hardcastle's face already? Did Hardcastle really weald that much power that even her brother was prepared to back down from him?

'What do you want?' As he lowered his arms to his sides, a hint of trepidation could be heard in Michael's voice.

Bianca stared at her eldest brother. And as Michael took a tentative step away from Hardcastle, Bianca's eyebrows were pinched together in confusion. They were Murphys and in any normal circumstances, no one would have dared even approach them, at least not if they had any sense anyway. Their surname was notorious and went hand in hand with trouble. Her brothers, and herself included, were the real deal; they could take care of themselves and were not known to back down from a fight.

'A word,' Max said. He gestured towards a secluded table. 'I'm guessing that you won't want your business aired in front of all and sundry?' He motioned around the busy pub to emphasise his point.

Dumbstruck, Bianca watched as Michael did as he was bid. She couldn't get her head around any of this, and it also didn't escape her notice how quiet the pub had become, as though the majority of punters knew that a brawl was on the cards. After all, her family were legendary on the Dagenham council estate, and it didn't take much for one of them to kick off. Even the slightest of slurs, or a wrong look in their direction, was enough to ensure that at least one of them erupted with fury on a weekly basis. She glanced across to the bar staff and noted that they too were watching the interaction unfold with interest, no doubt their fingers ready and poised to phone the old bill should the situation get out of hand.

She turned her attention back to Terry's wife and a smirk played out across Bianca's lips. She was about to blow the bitch's life wide apart and it would serve her right too. Tracey had come between her and her man, and despite what anyone might say Terry *had* been her man, he'd told her so enough times. They'd had a chemistry that had taken Bianca's breath away and it would have only been a matter of time until Terry had given his wife the elbow. As she reached down to gently caress her still flat tummy, she fought the urge to laugh out loud. She couldn't wait to see Tracey's face when she told her that she was carrying Terry's child. But that was Bianca all over, she loved nothing more than to cause aggro. Her mum had often remarked that she could start a fight in an empty room and it was true she could, she thrived off it; so much so, that she often went out of her way just to piss people off – it was a particular trait of hers.

As she looked Tracey up and down, jealously consumed Bianca, not that there was anything for her to be jealous of, or at least this was what Bianca tried to convince herself. Tracey may have been a looker, but she was old, much older than Bianca. Was it any wonder that Terry had looked for a younger model?

* * *

Tracey looked around her. Her throat felt dry and she nervously licked at her dry lips. She didn't even care about her own safety; it was the safety of her sons which concerned her the most. Not that Ricky or Jamie needed her protection; they weren't children any more, they were men But still the knowledge did nothing to erase her fears, and from what she could see of the Murphy family they looked rough, not to mention deranged.

Her gaze fell upon a woman standing at the bar and taking note of her smirk, Tracey narrowed her eyes. She'd seen her before, Tracey was sure of it, but where that was she couldn't remember.

Tearing her gaze away from the woman, Tracey turned back to look at Max. His face was white with anger and as he bumped back the chair and stood up, he placed his hands on the table and leant forward so that his and Murphy's faces were within touching distance. She couldn't hear what was being said but could tell by his stance and the way that the muscles across his shoulder blades suddenly became tense, that he wasn't happy. In fact, he looked downright furious and unless she was very much mistaken about ready to tear Murphy's head clean off his shoulders. Moments later, he straightened up, then after a few last words stormed out of the pub, leaving Tracey and her sons with no other choice but to follow on behind.

* * *

Bianca was more than enraged. 'What the fuck, Michael?' she bellowed as her brother made his way back to the bar. 'Why didn't you smash him in the face?'

Michael picked up his pint glass and guzzled the beer down. Wiping the back of his hand across his lips, he belched loudly then slammed the empty glass down on the bar. 'Same again,' he called out to the barmaid.

Bianca watched her brother warily. 'Michael,' she hissed, 'what is going on?'

Turning his gaze on her, Michael's eyes were hard. 'Max Hardcastle,' he said with a raise of his eyebrows.

'And?' Bianca demanded. 'What about him?'

As he paid for his drink, Michael slipped his change into his trouser pocket, then turned his head. 'Max Hardcastle is aggro that we can do without. Let me put it this way,' he said, leaning in towards his sister. 'The bloke is a nutter and trust me, he makes Terry look like a pussy cat in comparison.' A slow smile edged its way across his face, and he nodded towards the exit. 'And he may just be the answer to our prayers.'

Confused, Bianca frowned.

'It's no secret that Hardcastle served a lump,' Michael explained further. 'He has a penchant for topping pimps and being the nice sort of bloke I am I just happened to let slip about Kempton's involvement with the whores. So you see little sister...' Michael grinned as he slung his arm across Bianca's shoulder. 'All thanks to my quick thinking, Kempton is going to be taken care of, and that means both his and Terry's cut of the profits will now work its way into our hands.' He gave a wry laugh. 'We're gonna be rolling in dough.'

Tipping her head back, Bianca chuckled out loud. 'Michael, you clever bastard.' She planted a kiss on her brother's cheek, then picking up her wine glass, she swallowed the liquid down in one large gulp. 'I think this calls for a celebration, don't you?'

Michael didn't need asking twice, and puffing out his chest, he clicked his fingers towards the bar staff and indicated for another round of drinks. Too right they were going to celebrate. After all, as his sister had so rightly pointed out, he was clever; in fact, he was more than clever, he was a fucking genius.

* * *

As they made their way across the car park, Tracey had to practically run to keep up with Max's long strides. 'What's going on?' she asked.

Max's nostrils were flared, his jaw was clenched and every muscle in his body rigid. Turning his back on her, he unlocked his car. He didn't trust himself to answer; how could he when he felt so angry that he could practically taste the fury as it pumped though his veins?

Looking from her sons then back to Max, Tracey threw up her arms. 'Well he must have said something, you were speaking to him for long enough, and I'm guessing it was a bit more than idle chit chat.'

'He said nothing.' As soon as the words left his mouth, Max inwardly groaned. He hadn't intended to sound so harsh, and as she took a step away from him, he wanted to kick himself for losing control. He'd never been in the habit of taking his anger out on a woman before, and certainly didn't intend to start now. 'He didn't say anything of importance, so let's just leave it at that, okay?'

Jamie screwed up his face, and turning to look over his shoulder at the pub, he snarled. 'Nah,' he said. 'Something's not right about any of this; my dad wouldn't have entertained the Murphys, let alone ask them for protection.'

Max shot a glance towards the two brothers. 'They're as clueless as we are.'

'Yeah but...'

'I said leave it,' Max interrupted. His voice brooked no arguments and his steely grey eyes were hard.

Jamie opened his mouth to answer but as he caught his brother's eye, Ricky gave a slight shake of his head in a warning for Jamie to calm down and more importantly to keep schtum. They needed to keep Max onside. It was bad enough that their mother had almost fucked everything up, let alone Jamie shoving his size-ten boots in to drive the final nail in the coffin. The last thing any of them wanted was for Max to turn his back on them, especially not now when they were so close to finding out the truth.

Thankful that his brother had taken the hint, Ricky chewed on the inside of his cheek thinking the situation over, before blowing out his cheeks. 'So, we're back to square one then?'

As he nodded, Max averted his eyes. The truth was, Michael Murphy had been more than forthcoming. In fact, he'd told him things about Terry that sickened Max to his very core, things that he would never have believed even possible of his old friend, and to a certain degree still didn't want to believe.

Glancing back to the pub, Max snaked his tongue across his teeth, his fists involuntarily clenching at his sides. He needed to have a word with Kenny and fast, before he ended up losing his rag, charging back inside the pub and causing some serious damage, starting with the Murphy family.

12

Tracey was deep in thought. After her sons had dropped her off home, she'd poured herself out a large glass of wine then sat in the lounge mulling over the night's events. Max had lied to them; she was sure of it. Something had been said in the pub, something that he wasn't telling them; the question was: what?

Setting her glass down on the coffee table, she picked up her mobile phone, went to the search bar and typed in Hardcastle Limited. Within seconds, a link to the car showroom flashed up on the screen. Several telephone numbers were listed, and hovering her finger over the dial button, Tracey bit down on her lip, unsure if she was doing the right thing by calling him.

She had to know what was going on she decided, and taking a deep breath, she pressed dial.

* * *

Max was stalking the length of his lounge; a combination of anger and disgust in equal measures rippled through his veins. He'd known Terry for years, and had considered him to be a mate, a good mate, so how the fuck hadn't he known that he sold women, that he'd used and abused them for his own gain?

His mobile phone began to ring, and glancing down at the device, an unknown number flashed up on the screen. He'd been about to let the call ring off when curiosity got the better of him.

'Yeah,' he barked into the phone.

Hearing a female voice on the other end of the line, he inwardly groaned and ran his hand through his light brown hair, wishing more than ever that he'd declined the call. The last person he wanted to speak to was Terry's widow. Briefly it crossed Max's mind whether Tracey had known what her husband had been getting up to, how he'd earned his living? Instinct told him that she was clueless. After all, she'd had no idea that Terry had been unfaithful throughout their marriage, or at least this was what he presumed, so what was the betting that Terry had also kept her in the dark when it came to his business interests?

He could hear the pleading in her voice and reluctantly nodded. 'I'll be there within the hour,' he told her. He then switched off the call, dug out his car keys, and promptly left his apartment.

* * *

Before Max had even climbed out of his car Tracey had flung open the front door, and as he walked towards her, she was reminded once again of his size. Not only was he tall, but he also had an athletic body; his shoulders were broad, and his hands were the equivalent of shovels. Not forgetting he was dangerous; he'd already proven that fact by brutally murdering a man. Only he had never given her the impression that she was in any danger from him, even when she had stormed into his office ready to confront him over Terry's murder. She hadn't been afraid, not really, and she suddenly asked herself why not? Why hadn't she felt threatened by him, why did he make her feel safe whenever she was in his presence?

'Thank you for coming.' She led the way into the kitchen and gestured for him to take a seat. 'Can I get you a drink?' she asked, opening the fridge and taking out a bottle of wine.

For the briefest of moments Max hesitated before nodding.

After refilling her glass, Tracey took a second glass out of the overhead cupboard and filled it. Passing it across, she took a seat at the table and tucked her legs underneath her.

'I know that something was said, in the pub I mean, between you and Murphy.' She tucked a lock of dark hair behind her ear and watched him warily over the rim of her glass. 'Please, just be honest with me and tell me. No matter how bad it is I have a right to know. Terry was my husband.' She gave a small smile and looked around the kitchen. 'I already know that he was no angel, and despite what he thought of me, I'm not a complete fool. I now know for a fact he wouldn't have been able to afford all of this selling a few cars or running a debt collection agency. He paid for the house outright, and as for the renovations, the final bill for the kitchen alone came to more than what most men earn in a year.'

Max sighed, averted his eyes, sucked in his bottom lip, then lifting the glass to his lips, swallowed down a mouthful of the wine, if for no other reason than to put off the inevitable. Where was he supposed to even begin? Terry had been a fool; he'd had a beautiful wife, a stunning home, two strapping, loyal sons, and yet they hadn't been enough for him. Being the greedy bastard he was, he'd still wanted more.

'I need to have a word with Kenny,' he finally answered. 'I need to know the facts first, before I...' He left the remainder of the sentence to hang in the air, not wanting to say the words out loud, because once he'd said them he could never take them back, and as angry as he was he didn't want to be the one to bring Tracey's world crashing down around her; she had already been through hell and back and he didn't want to add to her heartache.

Tracey's forehead furrowed, her expression one of bewilderment. 'Facts about what?' she asked.

Hearing the confusion in her voice, Max looked down and sighed, debating within himself just how much information he should give away. In hindsight, maybe he should have taken Ricky and Jamie aside and left it in their capable hands to break the bad news to their mother. Surely it would have been better coming from them. As it was, he and Terry's widow were strangers. It wasn't until the funeral that he had even clapped his eyes upon her, and it suddenly occurred to him to wonder why that was; why had Terry never introduced him to his wife? Why all the secrecy? And more to the point, what had he been so afraid of? Granted, he'd assumed that they would be introduced to one another at some point, he just hadn't thought it would take Terry's death to make that happen. Fair enough, he and Terry hadn't seen each other for years, but Max had still classed Terry as a mate, and he'd trusted him. And when Max had first been sent down, other than when his mother had visited him, Terry had been his only link to the outside world. Terry's visits were one of the only few times that Max could actually find it in himself to smile, until of course those visits became less and less frequent and he'd had to learn to stand on his own two feet.

Perhaps Terry had done him a favour in the long run. His absence had forced Max to forge new alliances with people who he could trust on the inside. Then on his release from prison he and Terry had picked up their friendship, they may have been older and somewhat wiser but their conversations had been easy, comfortable even, it was almost as though they had never been apart.

After what seemed an age, Max looked up. 'I was told one or two things and...' His grey eyes roamed over her face, searching for any clues that she already knew what he was about to say, that perhaps she'd known her husband sold women, perhaps she'd even been involved, although he highly doubted this was the case. 'I was told that Terry and Kenny were running a...' He swallowed deeply and glanced away, not wanting to say the words out loud.

'Running a what?' As she smiled, Tracey tilted her head slightly, forcing Max to look at her.

Max sighed, and slumping back in the chair, he gave a shrug. 'Terry and Kenny were running a brothel, and the women in their employment, and believe me I use that term loosely, are forced into prostitution. They're trafficked into the country and held against their will, treated no better than animals.'

Tracey's blood ran cold. Jumping up from the chair, she retreated to the far side of the kitchen all the while vehemently shaking her head. 'No,' she gasped, her face turning a deathly shade of white. 'No, my Terry would never have been involved in something like that. He was a good man, he'd been...' Her voice trailed off and she slammed her hand over her mouth as the enormity of his words finally hit her.

Max rubbed his hand over his jaw. He'd expected her to deny any wrongdoing on Terry's part, and why wouldn't she? He himself had been just as shocked at the revelation; a large part of him still didn't believe that Terry could be capable of something so heinous. 'The Murphys were never used for protection, neither did they collect debts. They're in partnership with Kenny and Terry, have been for months.'

'I said no.' As she gripped on to the kitchen worktop, Tracey's legs buckled from underneath her. She didn't believe it, would never believe it in fact, not her Terry. He may have been a rogue, but he'd had a good heart, he'd been a family man, and she had loved him with every ounce of her being. If he'd been a monster then she would have known, she would have sensed it, somehow.

Max made to stand up.

'Stay away from me.' Tracey held her hand up in a warning, her eyes blazing with fury. 'I will not have anyone bad mouth my husband, especially not you. You killed a man in cold blood, and you've got the front to sit there and make my Terry out to be a wrong'un. Well let me tell you now, he was worth ten of you.'

Studying the glass in his hand as though it were the most fascinating thing he'd ever seen, Max inwardly cringed at her words. It was true he had killed a man, and he knew for a fact that despite what he'd told the parole board he had never felt any kind of remorse over his actions, and why should he? As far as he was concerned the no-good ponce his mother had been shacked up with had deserved everything he had coming to him, and despite the prison sentence that he'd served, Max wouldn't hesitate in killing the ponce all over again. But for all his faults, and he was the first to hold his hand up and admit that he had many, one thing that he had never done was earn a living off women, women who were forced day after day to give their bodies to men. He had morals and when it came to women those morals were of a high standard, always had been and always would be. Fair enough since his release from prison he'd more than made up for the lost time he'd spent locked up, but he had never given the ladies in his life any false pretences, he'd made it clear from the start that he wasn't interested in a relationship or settling down and the majority of women he'd dated had been more than happy with their arrangement.

Tracey's shoulders heaved and, as silent tears slipped down

her face, she gripped on to the work top even tighter. As much as she didn't want to admit it to herself, instinctively she knew that there could be a hint of truth to the information Max had been given. In the months leading up to his death Terry had changed; he'd become distant, and if the truth were told she had rarely seen him, and when he had bothered to come home he'd barely wanted to touch her. Night after night he'd made his excuses to stay away from her, that he was too tired, or that he'd had a stressful day. It had even crossed her mind that perhaps he'd met another woman. It wouldn't have been the first time. She'd had her suspicions in the past that he'd been up to no good, and he hadn't exactly been discreet; the lipstick stains on his collars had been a dead giveaway, not that she had ever confronted him. She may have regarded herself as a strong woman but when it came to Terry she'd been like putty in his hands, and deep down she had been terrified that there could be some truth to her suspicions, and that he had met someone else, someone that he cared about, maybe even loved. She couldn't bear the thought of losing him; he'd been her whole life and was the only man she had ever wanted. But now, with the knowledge that Terry had pimped out women, innocent women, she felt sick to her stomach, ashamed even. She'd longed for Terry to touch her, for their marriage to get back on track and all the while he had been more concerned with earning immorally off women. Had he even gone one step further and slept with those women? It would certainly explain why before his death he hadn't wanted to be intimate with her.

She didn't hear Max get out of his seat and it wasn't until his arms were wrapped around her shoulders that she buried her head into his chest and sobbed her heart out. Her marriage had clearly been a sham; not only had Terry lied, and kept secrets from her but he'd also betrayed her trust. 'I didn't know,' she cried. 'I swear before God I didn't know.'

'I know,' Max soothed. 'Believe me darling, no one knew; Terry covered his tracks well.'

Tracey shook her head, and slamming her eyes shut tight, she cried even harder. Her sons would be devastated, they were bound to be. Terry and the boys had been close and the boys had worshipped him. In that instant her eyes snapped open wide and she took a sharp intake of breath.

'No,' she cried. 'Please God, no.' Could the boys be involved too? Were her handsome sons capable of forcing women into prostitution like their father had been? 'The boys,' she croaked out.

Max frowned. 'What about them?'

Pulling herself out his arms, Tracey walked across the kitchen, and as she swiped the tears away from her cheeks, the tiny hairs on the back of her neck stook up on end. 'Are my boys involved?'

Max screwed up his face. It hadn't even crossed his mind that Terry's sons could be involved, and Michael Murphy had made no mention of them. Surely he would have said something, considering they were present when he and Michael had had their chat. Before he could open his mouth to answer, Tracey charged out of the kitchen. Moments later she returned, shrugging on her jacket.

'If they're involved in any of this, I will kill them stone dead,' she stated as she rummaged through her handbag looking for her car keys.

Despite her words Max could see the anguish written across Tracey's face. 'How much have you had to drink?' he asked, eyeing the near-empty wine bottle on the table.

Tracey looked up and as she followed his gaze she groaned out loud. She'd had at least four glasses and that was before Max had even arrived.

'Come on,' Max said, pulling out his car keys. 'I'll drive.'

Tracey hesitated. 'I'll be fine,' she lied. 'It's not that far and, besides, I don't want to put you out.'

'You're not.' Lifting his chin in the air, Max gestured towards the front door. 'Let's get one thing straight,' he said, giving a small smile to take the edge off his words. 'Terry may have been your husband, but he was also my mate and I can tell you now that I intend to get to the bottom of this.'

Tracey nodded her appreciation, it was on the tip of her tongue to ask him if he too suspected her sons were involved. It was only the fact that she didn't want to hear his answer, that she didn't want him to confirm her worst fears, that forced her to keep her mouth firmly closed. To her dismay she realised that there was every chance that her sons *were* involved and the mere thought was enough to make her feel physically sick.

* * *

'I was on a promise tonight,' Jamie groaned as he entered his brother's house. 'That little blonde bird who works behind the bar' – he winked – 'has been giving me the come on for weeks. I ended up looking like a right prat when I had to bail on her.'

Ricky laughed out loud. It was no secret that his brother had a penchant for blondes. 'You're slacking bruv,' he told him. 'It's not like you to hold off, you normally dive straight in head first.'

Jamie grinned. 'I'm keeping her on her toes.'

In any normal circumstances, when he wanted something he went all out in attack mode just to get it. He'd put on the charm, even throw in some cheesy chat up lines, if the end result was him getting his end away. Only he hadn't been feeling it lately. Fair enough, the barmaid was a stunner and she was also exactly the type of bird he usually went for. The problem was, it was all just too easy and he was bored. He liked the thrill of the chase and wanted a challenge; he was sick to the back teeth of women who dropped their knickers for him at the drop of a hat.

'What's all this about anyway?' he asked, changing the subject. Dropping a kiss on Kayla's cheek, Jamie turned back to face his brother. 'Do you reckon Hardcastle has said something? You know as well as I do,' he said, pointing his finger forward, 'that something was said in that boozer, something about the old man.'

Shrugging, Ricky shoved his hands into his pockets. He'd been under the same impression as Jamie, that Hardcastle had been told more than he was letting on. 'Fuck knows,' he said, looking over his shoulder as the doorbell rang, 'but I guess we're about to find out,' he added, lifting his eyebrows.

On seeing his mother's expression, the smile instantly slipped from Ricky's face and as he led her and Max into the lounge, he flicked his gaze towards his girlfriend. 'Babe, why don't you get us all some drinks?' he said, jerking his head towards the kitchen.

Kayla looked warily around her, and astute enough to pick up on the tension, she gave a nod, glad of an excuse to get out of the way. 'I'll put the kettle on.'

As soon as her future daughter-in-law had left the room, Tracey flew at her sons, slapping whichever part of their bodies she could lay her hands on. 'Did you know?' she screeched at them. Her breath came out in short bursts, and her body trembled with rage. 'Did you know what your father was getting up to?'

Pushing his mother away from him, Ricky's hand automatically reached up to touch his face. His cheek felt hot to his touch and was still smarting from the slap. 'Jesus fucking Christ, Mum,' he yelled. 'What the fuck are you playing at?'

'What am I playing at?' Shaking her head, Tracey was incredulous. 'Believe me, this is no game. I know,' she spat, her eyes blazing with anger. 'I know about the women.'

'What women?' Ricky asked, shooting a glance towards Max. 'What are you talking about?'

Tracey could barely look at her sons; she was too afraid that she would see the guilt written all over their faces. Until today she would never have believed that her boys could be cruel, that they could give so little thought to another human being. 'Tell them.' She crossed her arms over her chest, her lips set into a thin line. 'Tell them exactly what Murphy told you.'

Ricky narrowed his eyes and, tearing his gaze away from his mother, he turned to look at Max.

'Maybe now isn't the right time.' Max motioned towards the kitchen where Kayla was making the tea. 'Maybe this should be done in private.'

Giving her eldest son a cold stare, Tracey jutted her chin in the air. 'No.' Her gaze went to the door. 'If they're up to their necks in any of this then Kayla has a right to know what kind of man she lives with.'

Ricky's eyes narrowed even further and, shooting a glance in the direction of the kitchen, he swallowed deeply. 'What the fuck is this about?' he demanded.

Before Max could open his mouth to speak, Tracey rounded on her son. 'You tell me!' she cried, tears welling up in her eyes. 'Did you know that your father was running a prostitution ring?' she asked, pointing beyond the front door. 'That those poor women are trafficked into the country and held against their will?'

Jamie gave a quizzical laugh. 'Leave it out,' he snorted. 'As if Dad would be involved in something like that.'

Tracey gave her son a cold stare; it was enough to tell him that this was no time for laughing, that she was deadly serious and that she wanted answers from them.

As he looked around him, the colour slipped from Jamie's face. 'Mum,' he implored. 'The Murphys are scum, you know they are. They can't be trusted; they'll say and do anything to cause hag. They get off on it; they're not fucking right up here,' he said, tapping his temple to emphasise his point.

'It sounded kosher to me,' Max volunteered. 'And according to Murphy, your dad and Kenny were the brains behind the outfit.'

'He's lying. My old man would never have kept women against their will; he was no fucking pimp.'

Tracey snapped her head back round to look at her youngest son, the sincerity and hurt in his voice startling her. On the drive over to Ricky's house she'd prayed over and over that her boys were innocent, that Terry wouldn't have dragged their sons into his sordid world, and just maybe from their startled reactions he hadn't.

'Tell them,' Jamie roared at his brother, his eyes hard. 'Tell them that this is bollocks.'

Ricky's mind was reeling and as he slumped onto the sofa, he held his head between his hands. 'You'd believe the Murphys over Dad, over your own flesh and blood?' he asked as he looked up at his mother, his tone accusing.

Before Tracey had the chance to open her mouth, Ricky got to his feet, his voice becoming chillingly calm. 'Don't bother answering,' he growled. 'The fact you're even here tells me everything I need to know. And trust me, I'm going to kill the no-good lying bastards over this.'

Fear edged its way down Tracey's spine and her mouth dropped open. 'No,' she cried.

'What do you mean no?' Ricky screwed up his face. 'This is what you wanted, wasn't it?' He stabbed his finger towards her.

'Why else would you have come here, accusing our dad of trafficking women. You knew exactly what our reaction would be. Did you honestly think that we would let that cunt of a family get away with bad mouthing him or spewing fucking lies about him? He was our dad,' he roared.

'No,' Tracey cried a second time as she attempted to tug on her son's arm. She knew enough about the Murphys to know that they were dangerous, that they were unhinged; she'd even heard a rumour that one of the brothers had escaped from a psychiatric unit, that he trained dogs to maul anyone who looked at him the wrong way. 'I don't want you anywhere near that family,' she pleaded with him.

Batting his mother away from him, Ricky gave a nasty chuckle. No wonder his dad had kept her in the dark throughout their marriage; she had no idea of what her husband and sons were capable of.

'Like I said,' he sneered, 'I'm going to kill them.' Walking across the room, he reached behind the television stand and pulled out a baseball bat then turned to look at his brother. 'Are you with me bruv?'

Not needing to be asked twice, Jamie nodded, and taking the makeshift weapon from his brother, he slapped the wooden bat against his palm, testing the weight of it.

'Do something, stop them,' Tracey beseeched Max, her eyes wide and panic stricken.

Max eyed Terry's sons. If they were anything like their father then he knew it would be pointless to try and stop them or rein them in. Terry had been a law unto himself and would have had the Murphy family wiped out within the blink of an eye and then viewed the massacre as just another day's hard graft; he certainly wouldn't have felt any remorse, nor would he have lost any sleep over the murders he'd committed.

'Please. They're my babies,' she cried. 'They're all that I have left.'

Her tears were Max's undoing, but that was him all over, he'd always been a sucker when it came to women, especially when they turned on the waterworks. 'Wait.' He held out his arms, his large frame blocking the doorway. 'The Murphys can wait.'

'Nah.' Jamie made to shove past. 'They're going down.'

'I get that you're angry,' Max answered. 'You're hot tempered like your old man.' He glanced down at his knuckles that still bore the faded scars from the fights he and Terry had got into as kids. 'But your dad should have taught you better than this. The first rule in this game is that you get your facts straight before diving in headfirst; makes the clean-up that little bit easier,' he said, lowering his voice, his gaze going between them. 'And the last thing you need is to bring unwanted attention to yourselves, trust me, I've been there and done it,' he told them. 'You don't want to go down for the likes of a Murphy.' Sensing that the mention of their father had the desired effect, Max lowered his arms to his sides. 'We talk to Kenny first,' he told them. 'We play this clever, and once we have the facts, we make a plan and strike out.'

Hearing the truth in Max's words, both Ricky and Jamie reluctantly nodded. He was right they supposed; the Murphys could keep; it wasn't as though they were going anywhere.

'Right then.' Rubbing his hands together, Max gave a smile then glanced down at his watch. It was late, not that that actually mattered in the grand scheme of things. From what he knew of Kenny he was a creature of habit and should be fairly easy to find, not that he intended for Terry's sons to be there when he did eventually catch up with his old friend. 'Kenny's son,' Max said.

'Who, Shaun?' Jamie asked, rolling his eyes.

Max nodded. 'That's right, Shaun. Find him for me and bring

him to your dad's yard.'

Screwing up their faces, both Ricky and Jamie groaned. Despite the fact their fathers were business partners, they had never considered Kenny's son to be a mate. They didn't actually have any particular beef with him, Shaun had never given them any reason to, but there had always been something off about him, something they couldn't quite put their fingers on.

Max glanced at his watch again. 'Well come on,' he started, gesturing to the front door. 'Time's ticking.'

As they did as they were bid and headed outside the house, Max turned to look at Tracey. Relief was etched across her face, and he gave a small smile. 'I'll keep them busy for as long as I can, but...' He looked briefly down at his feet, before looking back up. 'You know as well as I do that I can only keep them under control for so long. They've got too much of Terry inside of them to be any different and at some point those tempers of theirs are going to erupt and then there'll be no stopping them.'

Tracey nodded, the relief she had felt replaced once more with fear. Turning her head, she saw Kayla standing in the doorway to the kitchen, her skin ashen and her eyes wide and filled with terror. There and then her heart went out to the young woman, and stretching out her arm, she took Kayla's cold hand in hers, blinking back her tears as she did so. She had to remain strong. Strong for her sons, for Kayla, and for her grandson. They needed her, and as much as her own heart was breaking at Terry's betrayal, she knew instinctively that she had to look out for her family, that she had to keep them safe, that she had to be the voice of reason. Whether they liked it or not, when the time came, which it would, and her sons had finally learnt the truth and pieced together that their father had not been the man they thought he was, they would crumple, then they would want revenge and God help anyone who stood in their way.

13

On the drive towards Elm Park, Ricky and Jamie were quiet, both lost in their own thoughts. Finally, Ricky cleared his throat.

'Are you all right?' he asked, giving his brother a sidelong glance.

Still staring out of the window, Jamie nodded. It was a lie; of course he wasn't all right. His stomach was tied up in knots, and as he clenched then unclenched his fists in quick succession he wanted to lash out, to take his anger out on something or someone. He wanted to punch and kick out until his knuckles were a bloody mess, and his muscles ached, and more importantly until he was spent, and his anger had subsided. 'I can't believe this,' he said, turning his head and screwing up his face. 'Dad wasn't a pimp, and you know he fucking wasn't.'

Ricky nodded. He didn't need his brother to tell him that their dad was clear of any wrongdoings, he already knew that he was innocent, and no one would be able to convince him otherwise. Their dad had been a diamond; fair enough, he had his moments but didn't everyone? And underneath his tough exterior he'd been a family man; look how much he'd doted on his grandson

Mason. And as for Kayla, his dad had welcomed her into the family with open arms. An image of his girlfriend entered his mind and he quickly pushed it away. What if Kayla had been one of those women who'd been trafficked, what if she'd been forced to give her body to men? It didn't bear thinking about, and swallowing down his repulsion, Ricky flicked the switch for the indicator as they approached the turn off to where Kenny lived.

'I don't want Mum involved in any of this,' he blurted out. 'This is getting out of hand now, what with the Murphys and...' His hands tightened around the steering wheel, the familiar sense of anger once again spreading throughout his body. 'I'm going to kill them over this, every last one of them, and that's a fucking promise.'

Jamie raised his eyebrows. It went without saying; of course they would have it out with the Murphys, but as for their mum not getting involved, he had a sneaking suspicion that she wasn't going to be happy. 'Are you going to be the one to tell her then bruv? Because I can tell you now, she won't take it lying down.'

Ricky shrugged. He could see Jamie's point. Their mum had never backed down from anything in her life. Maybe Hardcastle could have a word with her; she clearly listened to him and despite their shaky start they appeared to get on well, maybe a little bit too well for Ricky's liking. Narrowing his eyes, he pushed the dark thoughts that had suddenly popped into his head to the back of his mind. Nah, his mum would never look at Hardcastle as anything other than her husband's friend, would she? And besides, to his knowledge they had never actually spent any time alone, certainly not enough time to get to know one another on a personal level, perhaps other than tonight. He opened his mouth to express his concerns when Jamie interrupted his thought process.

'Do you think Shaun knows about any of this?'

Pressing his foot on the brake, Ricky looked up at Kenny's house, gave it the once over then shook his head. 'I doubt it,' he answered. 'You know what the little tosser is like; he's scared of his own shadow. Why do you think they keep him holed up at the yard?' Momentarily, Ricky's forehead furrowed. Come to think of it, other than perhaps walk the guard dogs every now and then that Kenny and his dad had used for added security, what exactly did Shaun do? He knew for a fact that he didn't collect the debts and yet he'd never once heard his old man complain that Shaun wasn't pulling his weight. He gave a shrug, climbed out of the car, and then jerked his head towards the front door. 'After you bruv.' He grinned.

As he followed his brother down the pathway, Ricky understood Max's reasoning behind bringing Shaun to the yard; they were going to use him as leverage, a sure way of ensuring that Kenny opened his mouth and told them exactly what was going on. And as far as Ricky was concerned, he didn't care if they had to drag Shaun kicking and screaming from the house, he would be coming with them whether he wanted to or not.

Max stepped outside his car, leant his forearms on top of the metal door frame then shook his head. Just as he'd known he would be, Kenny was a creature of habit. Despite the late hour, he'd rightly guessed that Kenny would still be at the yard, and the fact a light was still on in the office was enough to tell him that his instincts had been correct.

Slamming the door closed, he pulled up the collar of his jacket, crossed over the street then made his way across the forecourt. Talk about a sitting duck; even the gates had been left wide open and as for the dogs that he could hear barking in the distance, he took a wild guess that they were chained up, therefore meaning that they were no actual threat to him, or anyone else for that matter should someone decide to take a late-night walk around the yard.

Within a matter of moments, he'd reached the office and without hesitation he pulled down on the door handle. The scene before him made him groan out loud.

'Seriously mate,' he said, screwing up his face.

Shock resonated across Kenny's bloated face and as he hastily wiped traces of white power away from his nostrils, he noisily cleared his throat. 'Been a tough few weeks,' he said by way of explaining the cocaine laid out on the table before him.

Max shook his head and, watching as Kenny hastily shoved a hand mirror and what looked like a bank card and a rolled-up twenty-pound note into the desk drawer, he closed the office door and made his way inside. 'I thought you'd given that shit up?'

Kenny shrugged. 'Needs must and like I said it's been—'

'Yeah, a tough few weeks.' Still shaking his head, Max finished off the sentence, then taking a seat, he leant back in the chair and studied his old friend. Had they always been this distant with one another or had his imprisonment spelt the end of their friendship? Not that he and Kenny had been particularly close to begin with; in fact, he'd only ever considered Kenny to be a hanger on, someone they allowed to tag along with them whenever they were bored. He'd actually been quite surprised to learn that during his absence Terry and Kenny had become business partners.

It was Kenny who spoke first and after clearing his throat a second time he offered up a weak smile. 'To what do I owe the pleasure?' He spread open his arms, his grin intensifying. 'I mean, this is the second time you've visited me in as many days. Next, you'll be telling me that you're thinking of moving back to the manor; you can't seem to keep away from the place.'

Max raised his eyebrows before giving a laugh. It was true, he couldn't seem to stay away. 'It's just a flying visit.'

Hiding his relief, Kenny shifted his weight. The last thing he needed was Hardcastle living on his doorstep. 'I heard you were in the Ship and Anchor tonight?'

Max's eyes widened; news obviously travelled fast. 'Yeah I was.' He leant forward and rested his forearms on his knees. 'Had a nice little chat with the Murphys, the eldest one I think it was,' he said with a laugh. 'Mind you, they all look the same to me; they've all got that same shifty look about them if you know what I mean?'

Kenny nodded; he knew exactly what he meant. You could see it in their beady little eyes that they couldn't be trusted, that they wouldn't think twice about screwing someone over, much the same as Kenny himself, not that he would ever compare himself to the Murphys, mind.

'And believe me, it was interesting.' Standing up, Max moved across to the barred window, then turned round, crossed his arms over his chest and leant casually against the wall. 'Was very interesting in fact.'

Kenny's mouth became suddenly dry and he nervously licked at his lips. Had the Murphys guessed that he'd been behind Terry's murder? Nothing would surprise him where Bianca was concerned; she'd been obsessed with Terry and had actually believed his cock and bull story that he would leave Tracey for her; it would have been laughable if it wasn't so pathetic.

'In fact, I was told one or two things about you and Terry that shocked me. And you know me,' Max said, flashing a grin, 'I don't shock easily. But do you want to know what the worst part about all of this is, the part that I can't get my head around?' He tapped his temple, his voice beginning to rise. 'How I didn't suss any of this out before now, nor why it took a fucking Murphy to have to fill me in on what my so-called pals had been getting up to behind my back.'

Swallowing deeply, Kenny blinked rapidly. The minute Hardcastle had begun sniffing around, poking his nose into his and Terry's business, he should have known that this day would come. Hardcastle was like a dog with a bone once he'd sunk his teeth into something.

'It was all Terry's idea,' he said, the words tumbling out of his mouth in a rush. 'You know what he was like, he'd screw anything with a pulse and he wanted the tarts on tap. I wanted nothing to do with it and I swear to you it was a one off.' He held up his hands as though trying to ward Max off. 'I don't know what the Murphys have told you but...' He looked around him as he tried to desperately think of an explanation; something, anything that would get him off the hook. 'You know as well as I do that they can't be trusted.'

Max shook his head and gave a bitter laugh. The kind of laugh that chilled Kenny to his very core. 'Do I look like I've got mug written across my forehead?' He pushed himself away from the wall, feeling nothing but satisfaction to see Kenny flinch away from him. 'I did time for killing a cunt just like you, so what makes you think that I won't do it again? All that stands between me killing you is our so-called friendship, and even that I don't think is rock solid. You didn't even bother to visit me when I was inside; yeah fair enough you might have been there for me the first few months but what about after that eh? Where were you, eh?' he shouted. 'Where were you and Terry?'

Kenny opened his mouth to answer before quickly snapping it closed again, his eyes narrowing as he studied his old friend. This wasn't even about the whores, it was about Hardcastle feeling hard done by. Well, as the old saying went, if you can't do the time, then don't do the crime. Lifting his shoulders in a shrug, Kenny sighed. 'You can't blame us,' he said with a wry grin. 'We weren't the ones banged up. That was on you mate, you were the one who lost control of yourself, you were the one who killed your step dad.'

'He wasn't my fucking step dad,' Max growled.

A smirk tugged at the corners of Kenny's lips; he felt like he was fifteen all over again. God he'd missed this, missed winding Hardcastle up. It was no secret that Max had detested his mother's boyfriend on sight. After all, he'd made his displeasure known to him and Terry more than once over the years, and that was before he'd even found out that the ponce had forced his mother into prostitution. But that was the thing about Max, he'd always been so predictable, and right from the off Kenny had known exactly how to rile him up, it had almost become a sport to him. 'Step dad or not,' he gloated, 'you should never have killed the ponce.'

Lunging forward, Max grasped the front of Kenny's shirt and pulled him close, so close that their noses were almost touching. 'Yeah and why did I top him?' he growled. 'Come on,' he roared, 'you've got a lot to say for yourself, so answer the fucking question. Why did I kill the cunt?'

'I don't know.' As he gasped for breath, the colour drained from Kenny's face, and beads of cold sweat broke out across his forehead. Terrified, he clamped his buttocks tightly together, sending up a silent prayer that he wouldn't actually shit himself out of fear. He'd clearly let his guard down and forgotten just how dangerous Hardcastle could be.

'Yeah, you do,' Max snarled. 'It was because of you that I killed him, because of you and that big fucking trap of yours. You'd been goading me for weeks; what was it you called my mum?' He tilted his head to one side as he pretended to try and recall the slur Kenny had used. 'Yeah that was it, a dock Dolly, a fucking dock Dolly. That was my mum you were talking about, you arrogant piece of shit.' Throwing Kenny away from him, Max was so incensed that he could feel the rage pounding through his veins. At the side of his jaw a nerve ticked, a sure sign that it was taking everything in his power to regain control of his temper, and more importantly not to actually follow through with his threat and kill Kenny with his bare hands. 'So don't you fucking dare sit there trying to mug me off. Do you actually think I'm stupid, that I haven't got the nous to know what's been going on?'

'Of course I don't.' Kenny vigorously shook his head. To say he was terrified would be an understatement; he'd been a loose cannon as a kid and all these years later he was still a dangerous fucker. A coward through and through, Kenny had only ever picked his battles wisely, the majority of his victims too weak to ever fight him back, unlike Hardcastle who had been afraid of no one and who had gone out of his way to cause trouble with those whose reputations matched his own. 'I was trying to protect Tracey.'

'Do what?' Reeling away from the desk, Max straightened up. 'What do you mean by that? What's Tracey got to do with any of this?'

'It's this place.' Gesturing around him, Kenny used the cuff of his sleeve to wipe the sweat away from his forehead, and as he watched Max's gaze go around the office, the smirk filtered back across his face. 'With Terry gone, she owns half the business in fact.' He left the words to hang heavy in the air as he waited for the penny to drop.

'What are you trying to say?' Placing his hands on the desk, Max leant forward again, his steely grey eyes boring into Kenny's.

Leaning back ever so slightly, Kenny smiled. 'Exactly what I said; she owns half, and if the old bill were to find out about some of Terry's business interests, namely the prostitutes, well...' He lifted his shoulders and gave a sad shake of his head. 'Let me put it this way, I hope for her sake that she likes porridge. And as for you, you were sentenced to life, that means you're still on licence doesn't it?'

Max narrowed his eyes, his expression hard. As much as he didn't want him to be, Kenny was right; he was on licence, would always be on licence, it was part of his life sentence.

'I mean you've hardly lived your life on the straight and narrow since your release from nick have you?' Kenny said, tilting his head to one side, a crafty glint in his eyes. 'And I don't think the courts would be too happy if they were to find out about the cars you and Terry sold, the majority of which were stolen, might I add. No.' He shook his head, smirking. 'Your feet wouldn't even touch the fucking floor as they dragged your arse back to prison.'

Grasping onto Kenny's shirt, Max pulled back his fist. 'You no-good—'

Before he could land the punch, the office door swung wide open and Ricky and Jamie pushed a clearly terrified Shaun through the door.

'Dad,' Shaun cried as he took in the scene before him.

Gingerly, Kenny opened one eye, and seeing his son standing in the middle of the office, he took note of Shaun's flushed cheeks, and the way his body trembled as he tried to pull himself free from Jamie's grasp. In that instant Kenny felt his bowels inadvertently loosen. Had Shaun opened his mouth? Had he told the brothers that it had been him who'd killed their father? Nothing would surprise him; he should never have used his son to execute the murder. Shaun was a liability, he wasn't made for their world, he'd crack under pressure, and Kenny knew the Tempest boys would use brute force to get the answers they wanted, regardless of the fact that Shaun was his son. 'What's going on?' he asked, trepidation clearly audible in his voice. 'Why have you brought Shaun here?'

'I could ask you the same thing.' Looking from Kenny to Max, Jamie screwed up his face. 'What the fuck is going on here?' he exclaimed.

'Nothing,' Max growled. Releasing his grip, he shoved Kenny away from him, the hard look in his eyes enough to tell his so-called old friend that they weren't done, not by a long chalk. 'Me and Kenny were just having a nice, friendly chat, and believe me,' he said, gesturing towards the door for the brothers to follow him out, 'it was interesting.'

Unsure of what was going on, Kenny narrowed his eyes. Was Hardcastle actually walking away and leaving him unscathed without so much as getting in at least one quick jab to his face or ribs? He let out a disbelieving laugh. Talk about piss and wind; Hardcastle had clearly lost his touch. He supposed that serving a lump could do that to a man. The Max he'd known before would have wiped the floor with him, and not stopped until he was a broken, bloodied mess.

'Dad?'

Kenny turned to look at his son. The persistent whine in Shaun's voice irritated the life out of him. How the fuck had he managed to produce a kid with no backbone, while Terry had sired two sons who were afraid of no one? 'What?' he groaned as he rubbed a hand over his face.

'Do you think that they know?' Shaun's bottom lip wobbled, and much to Kenny's annoyance he looked as though he was about to burst into tears.

Getting out of his seat, Kenny clipped his son around his ear. 'They won't if you keep your mouth shut,' he spat.

Yeah, his son was a liability all right, and he had a nasty

feeling that Shaun wouldn't only talk but that he'd sing like a canary should the Tempest boys even look at him the wrong way, let alone should they actually lay a finger on him. It was a sobering thought and for the first time since his son's birth he actually felt ashamed of his boy, ashamed that he'd turned out to be such a weak individual. Perhaps it was all his own fault. Perhaps he hadn't been there enough for Shaun while he was growing up, and he should have been. He only had himself to blame for his absence; the truth was he'd been too busy building his empire rather than wanting to spend any quality time with his family. Perhaps the private school had been Shaun's undoing. Terry had warned him that Shaun would turn out soft, but at the time Kenny hadn't wanted to listen; he'd been more interested in boasting that his son could speak Latin. Or perhaps Shaun was too much like his mother; she was a snivelling wreck too, always whingeing and crying about something or other. Anyone would think that she was hard done by the way she carried on, when in reality she lived the life of Riley and had never done a day's work in her life. She had more money than she could spend, but still she moped around the house. Well, he'd indulged her too much and given her everything that her heart had ever desired. He should have put more babies in her belly, that would have sorted her right out, would have given her something to concentrate on rather than sit around wallowing in self-pity day after day.

'Yeah but what if they do?' Shaun continued to whine.

His lips curling up in disgust, Kenny turned away from his only child to look out the window, watching as Hardcastle and Terry's sons made their way across the forecourt to where they had parked their cars. What with Hardcastle sniffing around, Kenny decided that it made sense to bring Ricky and Jamie on board, even if it meant that he would have to give them a cut of Terry's profits – just enough to keep them quiet. In the long run it had to be a lot safer than having Hardcastle on his back, and let's face it, Max was hardly going to take out Terry's boys, was he? He'd loved Terry like a brother; it stood to reason that he would view his best mate's boys in the same light. The thought was enough to make Kenny laugh out loud. It was a pity really that Hardcastle had never found out the truth – the truth being that Terry had committed the ultimate betrayal, that he had been the sole reason why Max had served a lump in the first place. Still, Kenny decided, there was plenty of time to let that slip. In fact, he couldn't wait to see the look on Hardcastle's face when he finally spilled the beans and blew his world wide apart.

'We need to move those tarts,' Kenny said, jerking his thumb towards the house. 'Get on the blower to Bianca Murphy and tell her to expect a delivery.'

* * *

'Well?' Ricky asked as they walked across the forecourt. 'What did Kenny have to say about the Murphys?'

Max paused, and as he clenched his fist he looked over his shoulder at the office, wishing now that he'd cracked Kenny on the jaw while he'd had the chance. It was nothing less than what the bastard deserved. Taking a quick glance at his watch, he nodded towards the cars. 'I'll explain everything,' he said with a sigh, 'but your mum needs to hear this as well.'

Intrigued, Ricky and Jamie both nodded, and sharing a surreptitious glance, they raised their eyebrows.

'I thought you were going to whack Kenny one when we walked in,' Jamie said, changing the subject.

Max gave a hollow laugh and as he unlocked his car door, he looked up to give the office one final hard stare. 'Believe me,' he answered. 'I wish that I had.'

14

Without saying a word, Tracey listened intently to everything that Max had to say. Even when her sons had screamed and hollered blue murder, she didn't interrupt them, deciding to let them get it all out of their system. The fact Kenny had hinted that their father had not only been involved with the prostitution ring but that he'd also been the mastermind behind it was bound to devastate them. Not only had they loved their dad but they had respected him too. They'd been proud of Terry and had been proud to call themselves his sons.

Once they had quietened down, she finally spoke. 'Kenny's right. As Terry's widow, the businesses do belong to me now, or at least Terry's share of the businesses do anyway.' Taking a deep breath, she braced herself for the outburst that she knew was going to come. 'So why don't I work at the yard and gather information on him?' She held up her hand in a bid to quash their protests. 'I need to know just how much your father was involved, if he was even involved. For all we know, Kenny could be lying and Terry knew nothing about the prostitutes,' she hastily added, seeing the fury once again flitter across her sons' faces.

'Like fuck you are,' Jamie bellowed, his cheeks turning bright red. 'I'm not having this, I'm not having you anywhere near Kenny, it's not safe.'

Tracey resisted the urge to laugh out loud. She'd known Kenny almost as long as she'd known Terry, and he was no threat to her. Fair enough, she didn't entirely trust him any more, but at the same time she certainly wasn't afraid of him either. Holding her ground, she cocked her head to one side to look at Max. 'It's the only route left open to us. I have to know if Terry really was involved, and if the Murphys were connected to my Terry's death, then they'll slip up. One of them is bound to give the game away.'

'Are you actually being serious?' Ricky growled. 'You actually want to put yourself in danger? You would be mixing with the Murphys, Mum, and as for Kenny, I don't trust him, not now.'

For the briefest of moments, Tracey faltered. Of course she didn't want to put herself in danger, but what other option did she have? Terry may have betrayed her trust but he had been her husband and she'd vowed to make his murderer pay. And she had also promised her sons that their father would have the justice he deserved and she intended to keep that promise.

'You're taking a big risk,' Max finally chimed in, 'and for what? Kenny will be on his guard; he isn't going to divulge any information, especially not to you.'

Ricky's eyebrows shot up, his mind ticking over. 'He's right, Mum,' he said, motioning towards Max, 'Kenny will tell you sweet fuck all, but what about me and Jamie? We already work for the business. It'll be easier for us to find out what's been going on, and if Dad was involved, then it could be a link to who murdered him.'

Tracey was about to protest when Max interrupted her.

'They could be on to something, and like Ricky said, they already work for the business.' Rubbing his thumb across his bottom lip, Max shrugged. 'They've got a better chance of getting information out of Kenny than either you or me would, and with a bit of luck, Kenny won't even suspect what they are up to – why would he?'

As she reluctantly agreed, Tracey sighed. 'I don't like this,' she said, looking between her sons. 'As big as you are, you're still my babies.'

Both Ricky and Jamie rolled their eyes; they were hardly babies any more. The fact they were Terry Tempest's sons meant that they had reputations of their own, not that they expected their mum to know this, nor did they actually want her to know. Like their dad had always said, ignorance was bliss, and when it came to their mum the less she knew the better as far as they were concerned.

'We'll be careful,' Ricky told her as he shot a glance towards his brother.

'Yeah,' Jamie chimed in. 'You know us Mum,' he said, slinging his arm around her shoulder. 'We're not stupid; we can handle this.'

Nodding, Tracey hugged her son to her. All she could do was hope and pray that that was actually true.

Georgiana Cazacu's ears were straining. The room where she and three other women were being held was in darkness, with only the moonlight that streamed through the barred windows giving them any form of light. Not that there was very much for her to see. Other than a double divan bed pushed against one wall, a threadbare carpet, and a stained toilet bowl sitting beside a cracked washbasin that was caked with ground-in dirt, the room was bare.

A short while earlier, she'd heard the distinctive rumble of tyres from somewhere outside the property and had felt her heart begin to beat faster and a prickle of fear run down the length of her spine. During the day it wasn't unusual to hear comings and goings and other than when the men holding them captive brought them food and water, they had been left alone. But once darkness descended, an eerie quietness took over the property and surrounding area. Until tonight that was. Unlike the other nights, tonight there had been some activity. Not only had she heard the familiar rumble of tyres and the sound of car doors being opened and closed but she had also heard voices, male voices. They had been too far away for her to make out what was being said, but she had still heard them.

A sudden movement from inside the house made the hairs across Georgiana's arms stand up on end. Her body tense, she counted the heavy footfalls climb the staircase. Shoving the other women awake, she scrambled off the bed and motioned towards the door.

Sensing Georgiana's sudden panic, the three women cowered, and moments later a light switched on, temporarily blinding their vision, making the three women on the bed scream out in fright.

'Come on,' the man bellowed, taking a step towards them, 'you're moving.'

English may not have been Georgiana's first language, but she knew enough to understand what was going on. They were about to be transported and she had a pretty good idea that now was the time that they would be put to work, that their bodies would be used and abused. The mere thought was enough to make her want to cry out loud at the injustice of it all. She had fully believed that she was coming to England to work as a nanny and it was only once her passport had been confiscated that the true nature of what that work would entail became apparent to her. There was no nannying job, there were no children. Of course, she'd heard about women being trafficked for the sex industry but had never in a million years believed that she would become one of those women. She was no fool; a little too trusting perhaps, but certainly no idiot. And she had trusted. The job had seemed legitimate; she had even been shown photographs of where she would live, of the children, of their parents, and even the family pets. And she had been so excited to leave her home in Romania for a new life, that she had been blinded by the lies.

'I said move,' the man roared again.

Georgiana resisted the urge to flinch. She was afraid of this man; he had a wickedness in him, she could see it in his eyes, unlike the younger man who often brought them their food.

'No.' Despite the fear she felt, her voice was loud. Tilting her chin upwards, her eyes held a note of defiance. 'We are not...' She grappled to find the right word, and suddenly remembered the children she had believed she was to care for. 'We are not toys; we do not belong to you.' She thumped her fist against her chest. 'We are human beings, not your playthings.'

Fury edged its way down the man's body and as he twisted his lips into a snarl, he balled his fist at his side. 'Move.'

Georgiana swallowed deeply and glanced across to the women who were still cowering on the bed. The fear written across their faces all but broke her. Her heart ached; she wanted to go home, and more than anything she wanted to see her family, she wanted to hold her mum in her arms, she wanted to hear her younger siblings laugh as they told her jokes that she had heard a hundred times before.

'No.' As she shook her head, her long blonde hair flew around her face. She may have been small in stature, but she wasn't a coward. She knew what was right and what was wrong, and knew how people should and shouldn't be treated. 'We are not your toys.'

* * *

It was more than enough to make Kenny see red, and as his fist shot out, he caught the woman on the side of her face. She fell to the floor in a crumpled heap and the women on the bed screamed.

'Shut up,' Kenny roared as he dragged them off the bed then pushed them towards Shaun. 'Put them in the van,' he ordered, 'and make it quick.'

Once Shaun had led the terrified women out of the room, Kenny looked down at the woman who had spoken out. Her right eye was already beginning to swell and unless he was very much mistaken, she would have a shiner come the next morning. He'd hit her hard, as hard as he would have lashed out at a man, not that Kenny was overly concerned – the bitch had deserved it. No one, and he meant no one, spoke to him with disrespect and got away with it and the bitch lying sprawled out on the floor had better understand that before he ended up embedding it into her skull with his fists.

Crouching down beside her, he gripped her jaw tightly. 'In future, when I say move, that means you move, have you got that?' he asked, stabbing his forefinger into her the side of head. Her terror was tangible, and he took great pleasure in watching her try to squirm away from him. 'In fact, if I tell you to strip butt naked and jump off the roof, then you do just that. You belong to me, have you got that? No one else but me.'

The young woman stared up at him, her blue eyes wide and fearful.

'I said have you got that?' Kenny roared a second time.

The woman nodded and tears filled her eyes. And as Kenny dragged her up off the floor and shoved her none too gently through the door and into the hallway, she let out a whelp of fear.

'Because believe me,' Kenny growled in her ear. 'I'm going to enjoy bringing you down a peg or two.' In fact, he couldn't wait to put her to work in the very same brothel where they often sent Kevin Murphy and his two Rottweilers to work. The thought of the nutcase babysitting the big-mouthed bitch almost made Kenny laugh out loud.

* * *

Bianca took one look at the woman's swollen and bruised face and rolled her eyes in annoyance. She was already angry at the fact Kenny thought he could drop the tarts off whenever he felt like it, as though she was at his beck and call, as though she didn't have a life of her own to contend with.

'What the fuck happened to her?' she asked, jerking her thumb towards the little blonde woman as she was pushed into the lounge with the rest of the women.

Kenny turned his head, his hard expression falling on Bianca. 'She had a bit too much to say for herself,' he answered, his words loaded with meaning.

Taking the veiled threat on board, Bianca lifted her eyebrows towards the ceiling, her dislike of Kenny once again rushing to the fore. Well, all thanks to her brother Michael having a chat with Max Hardcastle, Kenny's days were numbered, not that she would let on just yet. Kenny was going to find out soon enough and the mere thought was enough to make her smile, not that she would of course, she didn't want Kenny to get wind of his impending fate, and more importantly she didn't want to give the old bastard the chance of wheedling his way out of the predicament he was soon going to find himself in. 'How am I supposed to put her to work looking like that? She looks like she's been hit by the back end of a bloody bus.'

Kenny laughed out loud. Bianca was a fine one to talk about looking like the back end of a bus. 'I'm sure you'll think of something. In fact, I want her put to work straight away.'

Bianca narrowed her eyes. The brothel was notorious for trouble, the majority of the clientele either buzzing off their heads, pissed, or spoiling for a fight, hence why her brother Kevin was often sent to work there. Studying the young blonde's retreating back as she was led into the lounge, it didn't take a genius to work out that the woman wouldn't last five minutes in there. Although well proportioned, she was tiny, and far too pretty not to become one of the star attractions. 'I'll see what I can do,' Bianca sighed.

It was Kenny's turn to narrow his eyes. 'This isn't up for a debate,' he told her, 'it's a fucking order. The bitch had the cheek to actually try and give me lip. Me,' he said, poking a stiff finger into his chest. 'Like I'm some kind of fucking mug.'

Holding up her hands, Bianca backed away; it was on the tip of her tongue to tell him that she agreed with the woman. Kenny was a mug, he proved that every time he opened his mouth. Keeping her lips firmly sealed, she gave a nod of her head. The last thing she needed was to get into a slanging match with him. 'Whatever you say,' she answered sarcastically.

Unsure whether or not she was taking the piss out of him, Kenny narrowed his eyes even further. 'Tell your brother to expect me within the next few days,' he said as he glanced at his watch. 'The deal needs finalising.'

Bianca smiled sweetly. 'I will do.' Not that there would be any further deals; Kenny would be long dead before then. All they needed was for Hardcastle to pay Kenny a visit, sort the fucker out and then they would be running the prostitution racket. The thought was enough to make Bianca want to laugh out loud. Turning abruptly away from Kenny before he had the chance to see the hint of a smirk play out across her lips, Bianca entered the lounge, her voice loud. 'Now it might not be the Ritz,' she said, pronouncing each word slowly as though she were speaking to a child. 'But believe me' – she nodded around the room, her gaze falling upon the bare concrete floor then the cotton sheets hanging at the windows – 'this is a whole lot better than where any of you lot will be going.' She chuckled.

As he heard Bianca laugh, Kenny shook his head. The brothel was a darn sight cleaner than the shithole Bianca Murphy called home. Wrinkling his nose, he was once again both amazed and disgusted in equal measures by the fact Terry had willingly jumped into Bianca's bed. What was the betting that the soapy cow hadn't even changed the bed sheets once in all the time she'd lived here? The mere thought was enough to make him want to gag.

15

A few days later, Jamie was all smiles as he entered the office situated at his father's yard, albeit a smile which was forced and didn't quite reach his eyes.

'You all right Kenny?' he asked as he flopped down on to a chair, his voice slightly louder than usual.

'Yeah,' Kenny answered dismissively, barely even looking up from the paperwork on his desk.

A few moments later, Ricky entered the office, and giving Kenny a surreptitious glance, he lifted his eyebrows towards his brother before sitting down beside him and kicking out his legs to make himself more comfortable. 'You all right Kenny?'

'Is there a fucking echo in here?' As he looked up, Kenny's irritated gaze went between the two brothers. He narrowed his eyes, suspicious. 'What are you so fucking cheerful for anyway?' he asked, glancing down at his watch. It had only just turned nine; in any normal circumstance, Terry's sons didn't put in an appearance until at least ten or eleven, the lazy little bastards that they were.

Jamie gave a nervous laugh before glancing across to his

brother. 'We can be happy can't we? Fucking hell, what do you want us to do,' he asked, 'walk around looking miserable all day?'

Kenny's eyebrows ever so slightly rose. Even before Terry's death his sons were never this happy, especially not in the mornings when they usually only communicated through grunts and a series of expletives all thanks to a raging hangover or because they had been up half the night doing God knows what. 'Just makes a change that's all,' he said with a wry grin. 'You must have had a good night then, eh lads. Get lucky did you?' he added with a wink before looking back down at the paperwork on his desk.

Not so long ago Ricky would have laughed out loud at Kenny's words, but that was before he'd found out that his father and his business partner were supposedly nothing other than low-life pimps who were responsible for women being trafficked into the country, then presumably held against their will to be used by all and sundry. Or at least this was the version of events the Murphys and Max Hardcastle wanted them to believe. For all he and Jamie knew, it could be lies, and Ricky held on to the sliver of hope that his dad was innocent. Nonetheless, whether it was true or not, the hidden innuendo behind Kenny's words now seemed seedy, dirty even, and he couldn't help but form a mental image of Kayla in his mind's eye. If it was true and his dad and Kenny were running a prostitution racket, had they ever looked at Kayla inappropriately, had they ever sized her up with the intention of wanting to pimp her out too? The mere thought that his father could have looked at Kayla as anything other than the mother of his grandson was enough to make Ricky see red. Clenching his fists, he wanted to charge out of his seat, drag Kenny over the desk and then batter the life out of him with his bare hands. Instead, he gritted his teeth and breathed heavily through his flared nostrils, forcing himself to calm down. He had to keep a clear head; if they wanted to get information out of Kenny then it was imperative that he didn't suspect his or Jamie's repulsion.

With a slight nod of his head in Kenny's direction, Jamie indicated for his brother to say something, anything, just as long as it was enough to get Kenny talking.

Taking the hint on board, Ricky swallowed down his anger. It was no mean feat and as he cleared his throat, he gripped onto the armrests so tightly that his knuckles turned white. 'My old man, eh?' he said, forcing a smile.

Kenny looked up again. 'What about him?' he asked, screwing up his face.

Ricky spread open his arms. 'You know exactly what' – he winked – 'the women. Although I've got to admit,' he said, giving an incredulous shake of his head, 'I wasn't expecting it. I mean, I know my old man was no angel, but prostitution, I didn't think that was his game.'

As both Ricky and Jamie looked towards Kenny expectantly, a heavy silence fell over the office and for the briefest of moments they thought that Kenny was going to leap out of his seat, lash out at them and then proceed to tell them to fuck off. To their surprise he did none of those things. Instead, he leant back in the chair, steepled his fingers in front of his chest and studied them, as if weighing up whether he could trust them or not.

'What can I say?' Kenny finally answered with a hint of caution. 'Your dad was a boy all right.'

Ricky snaked his tongue across his teeth, his heart instantly sinking down to his stomach. It was all the confirmation he needed and if he hadn't heard it from Kenny's own mouth he would never have believed that his dad could have been capable of something so abhorrent. In that instant, disgust tore through him, and as he took in Kenny's smug expression it took all of his strength not to swing back his arm and knock his dad's business partner to the floor in one fell swoop.

Sensing his brother's rage, Jamie gave a hollow laugh. 'Yeah,' he quickly answered as he silently willed Ricky to calm the fuck down, before he consequently blew apart their plan to get information from Kenny. 'I just don't get why he didn't bring us in on it. I mean' – he motioned towards his elder brother – 'didn't he trust us or something?'

Kenny was thoughtful for a few moments. He'd lost count of how many times he'd suggested that Terry's boys were brought on board, but Terry being Terry wouldn't hear of it. Oh it was all right for Shaun to be embroiled in the prostitution business but not Terry's precious boys. Bitterness surged through Kenny, and as he looked the brothers over he was reminded once again of their combined strength. They could come in handy against the Murphys and with Terry out of the picture, he needed the added muscle. It would be the final two finger salute to his old business partner, and should the filth come knocking, well, he'd make sure that Terry's boys were the first in line to take the rap. Terry would have understood; he'd known all about saving his own skin and he'd done the exact same thing when it had come to Hardcastle and the murder he'd helped him to commit. The knowledge that Terry and Hardcastle's friendship hadn't been as rock solid as everyone had been led to believe was like a balm to Kenny and he thrived on knowing that he held something over Hardcastle.

'Kenny.'

Jamie's voice broke Kenny's reverie and he blinked rapidly, refocusing his gaze back on Terry's boys. 'What?'

The two brothers shared a glance.

'My dad,' Jamie probed. 'Didn't he trust us?'

Kenny waved his hand in the air dismissively. 'You know what your dad was like,' he said with a dramatic sigh, 'he didn't trust anyone.' In that instant he saw the hurt in their eyes and fought the urge not to laugh out loud. Terry may have been blessed with sons who were capable of a tear up, but beyond the muscle Ricky and Jamie were as thick as shit. At least Shaun had a good head on his shoulders and was capable of using his brain, when and if he needed to, unlike these two louts in front of him. It was laughable really. Terry had been so proud of his sons, and yet when it had come down to the crunch Ricky and Jamie barely even knew who their father was, at least not the real Terry. Oh they saw the side of him he wanted them to see, the tough man who ruled the manor with an iron fist, but they never saw the other side of him, the womaniser, the grass.

* * *

Ten minutes later, Ricky and Jamie made their way out of the office. Their strides were long as they marched across the forecourt, and the muscles across their broad shoulders tense.

For a few moments neither of them spoke; the realisation that their father had been as guilty as sin lay heavy in their hearts.

'This is a waste of our time,' Ricky complained. 'Max was right, Kenny isn't going to talk. We're never going to find out who killed Dad.'

Grasping his brother by the arm, Jamie pulled Ricky to a halt beside him. 'Listen,' he said as he glanced back over his shoulder at the office. 'Let me have another crack at him.'

As he followed his brother's gaze, Ricky shook his head. What was the point? Kenny wasn't going to say anything, they both knew that; he may be a lot of things but Kenny wasn't stupid, he would never do or say anything to implicate himself, especially not in front of them, anyway. 'We'd be better off going for Shaun;

that sly bastard knows something,' he said, stabbing his finger
towards his brother. 'I know he does, I can feel it in my gut.'

Chewing on his bottom lip, Jamie shrugged. Now he stopped
and thought about it, Ricky was right. Shaun was at the office a
lot more than they were; he was bound to know something or at
the very least have an inkling as to who could have killed their
dad. And if the Murphys were involved then surely Shaun would
know.

'Come on bruv,' Jamie implored. 'Let me at least try; what
have we got to lose, eh?'

Reluctantly Ricky agreed, not that he thought his brother
would get very far. 'I'll be in the motor,' he said, nodding towards
where he'd parked his car. 'You've got ten minutes.'

Jamie gave a wide grin. 'Trust me' – he winked with an air of
confidence – 'that's all I'm going to need.'

As Jamie walked into the office, he could see that Kenny was
more than surprised to see him back so soon. Closing the door
behind him, he walked across the linoleum floor, perched his
backside on the corner of the desk, then making a great show of
pretending to check that no one else was within earshot of their
conversation, he spoke, his voice low, as though he and Kenny
were conspirators.

'These women,' he said, glancing back towards the door.
'What are they like?'

Kenny gave a hearty chuckle. He'd always known that Terry's
youngest son was a chip off the old block. Ricky may have looked
like Terry but that was where the similarities ended, he wasn't hot
headed and didn't have Terry's quick temper. There and then he
wanted to berate himself; he should have told Patricia it was

Ricky who Terry had had his doubts about fathering, it would have made more sense. It still amazed him that Patricia had fallen for his lies so easily, but then he supposed she was too clouded by her hatred for her daughter-in-law to see what was right underneath her nose. She'd always wanted a yard stick to beat Tracey with and now she finally had one, only it was too late, Terry was already dead and buried; she had no way of ever prising her son out of his wife's arms.

'They're tasty,' Kenny answered as he brought his cupped hands up to his chest by way of demonstrating the women's breasts. 'And game as well, let me tell you.'

Jamie's eyes lit up. 'I'm guessing,' he said as he flicked a biro pen across the desk, 'with my dad gone, you're going to need a new business partner.'

Kenny laughed even harder. He should have known all along that Terry's sons would want in on the deal. They weren't completely daft, they knew there was money to be made, and a lot of it. 'And let me guess,' he answered. 'You think you've got what it takes to be my new partner?'

Jamie nodded. 'I am my dad's son, after all. So what do you reckon?' he asked, lowering his voice a fraction further. 'Because between me and you, I want to get in on the action. Fuck what Ricky thinks, that prick is too far up Kayla's arse to even look at another bird, but me' – he poked himself in the chest – 'I'm not fussy. Pussy is pussy as far as I'm concerned and as long as a bird is putting out, then I'm game, and if there's money to be made, then happy fucking days.' It was all lies of course, but he was just about willing to say and do anything so long as it would gain Kenny's trust.

Kenny laughed again and, glancing towards the closed office door, he brought his head closer to Jamie's. 'I'll tell you what,' he said with a wink. 'Let me have a think about it.'

Standing up, Jamie forced a smile. 'Where are the women anyway?' He made a point of looking out of the window and surveying the yard. 'I mean,' he said, turning back to look at Kenny. 'They don't work from here, do they?'

'Of course they fucking don't.' Kenny waved his hand dismissively. 'We ship them off to the house.'

Sucking in his bottom lip, Jamie nodded, his mind working overdrive. What house? Since when had his dad owned any other property than the yard and the house where his parents had lived, the same house he and Ricky had grown up in?

* * *

As promised, within ten minutes, Jamie was climbing into his brother's car.

'Well,' Ricky asked, 'was it a waste of time?'

'Not quite.' Jamie shook his head and stared out of the windscreen. 'What do you know about Dad owning another property?'

Snapping his head round to look at his brother, Ricky screwed up his face. 'What?'

'I said, what do you know about Dad owning another house?' Jamie asked again.

Confused, Ricky shook his head. 'I don't know what you're talking about, I don't know anything about any house.'

'That's where they are; the women I mean.' Jamie turned to look at his brother. 'They've been shipped off to a house. Dad wasn't only a pimp,' he said, screwing up his face, 'he and Kenny actually own a brothel.'

Ricky's heart dropped and as he punched the steering wheel, he took a series of deep breaths in a bid to calm himself down. It couldn't be true, and more than anything he didn't want it to be true. If his dad had actually owned a brothel then that meant it hadn't been a one off as Kenny had led Max to believe. His dad had been a trafficker; he'd bought and sold women as though they were nothing more than cattle. 'How did you get Kenny to talk?' Ricky asked.

Jamie shrugged, his cheeks turning pink. 'It doesn't matter,' he answered, feeling somewhat ashamed of the things he'd had to say to get Kenny to open up. 'All that matters is that we know the truth. Dad was up to his eyeballs in all of this.' He swallowed and, averting his gaze away from his brother, he squeezed his eyes shut tight. He still couldn't get his head around it; he'd idolised his dad, he'd looked up to him, he'd loved him, and all along he'd never known him at all; he may as well have been a stranger.

'We'll have to tear apart Mum and Dad's house,' Ricky growled, breaking his brother's thoughts. 'There has to be evidence, deeds to a property, electricity bills, maybe even a mortgage. He turned to look at his brother, the horror he felt mirrored in Jamie's face. 'There has to be something.'

'Yeah,' Jamie answered as he rubbed his hand over the stubble covering his jawline, but before they even contemplated searching through their Dad's belongings, they had to break the bad news to their mum first. She was bound to be as devastated as they were, if not even more so. After all, she'd not only loved and trusted him but she'd also shared a bed with him.

As if reading his brother's thoughts, Ricky put the car into gear, pushed his foot on the accelerator and then glanced sideways. 'We'll tell Mum together, bruv.'

Nodding, Jamie didn't answer. What was he even meant to say?

* * *

Tracey's heart hammered wildly in her chest and as she felt the colour drain from her face, she clutched on to her son's hands for dear life. She couldn't get her head around what she was being told. Her mind felt numb and her body heavy as though her legs were unable to support her and she was in danger of crashing to the floor at any given moment.

She'd been fully prepared to forgive Terry of any wrongdoings and had even believed Kenny when he'd told Max that the prostitution racket had been a one off. She'd wanted to believe in her husband so much that she'd held on to Kenny's explanation. Right or wrong it had even in a roundabout way made sense to her. Terry had been a grafter, he had the gift of the gab and could sell the shirt off a man's back; perhaps he'd even been a silent partner in the whole sordid affair, maybe he hadn't even known or been made aware of what his latest business adventure entailed, or perhaps Kenny could have even coerced him into selling women? The bottom line was that she'd convinced herself that Terry could never be so evil – she'd known him hadn't she? She'd loved him, she had even born his sons. How could she have not known that underneath the charm and the handsome façade he was a monster?

Tears slipped down her cheeks and she let them fall freely, unashamed that her boys were witnessing her grief, a grief that was so raw she had only felt the likes of it once before and that had been the day when Terry had been gunned down.

For what seemed like an age they sat in silence, all three of them doing their best to come to terms with Terry's betrayal. Finally, Tracey wiped the tears from her eyes, and when she spoke, the lump lodged in her throat made her voice sound hoarse.

'Do you really think that your dad...' She paused momentarily and closed her eyes. Terry was tainted and she didn't want her boys to be associated to him in any way, shape, or form, and certainly didn't want her boys to become just as tainted, and all because they had the misfortune of having Terry's blood run through their veins. 'Do you think that *he*,' she spat, accentuating the word, 'could have stored the deeds to the property here?'

Ricky nodded. 'They have to be here, and other than the office, where else would he have stashed them?'

Tracey could see her eldest son's logic. 'Right then,' she said, getting to her feet. 'Let's tear this house apart.'

Both Ricky and Jamie followed suit and stood up.

'Are you okay Mum?' Jamie asked, full of concern.

Giving a weak smile, Tracey nodded, and hugging her son to her, she rested her head on his chest. 'I will be, darling,' she answered, her voice ever so slightly quivering.

As he and his brother shared a glance, Jamie hugged his mother back. She was lying to them, she had to be. Perhaps it was the shock; maybe after they had left, and the house was once again quiet, she would fall apart?

'I'm okay.' Sensing her sons' concern, Tracey pulled herself up to her full height. 'No more crying,' she told them. 'I think your father has had more tears from me, from all of us, than he ever deserved, don't you?'

Reluctantly, they nodded, and as much as they hated to admit it, their mum had just hit the proverbial nail on the head. Their dad had definitely had more tears from both his wife and his sons than he'd deserved.

'Right, come on then.' Releasing her arms from around her son, Tracey placed her hands on her hips, her face a mask of concentration. 'I'll tackle the bedroom,' she told them. 'Ricky you take the kitchen, and Jamie you get up in the loft and sort through the boxes of paperwork up there.'

* * *

Two hours later, they regrouped and much to their dismay they had come up empty handed. There was nothing in the house relating to houses, flats or indeed any property that Terry may have owned other that the breakers yard and the house where he and his wife had lived.

'Well that's it then,' Jamie sighed. 'He must have stored them at the yard.'

'Bollocks,' Ricky muttered under his breath. 'How the fuck are we meant to get our hands on them now?'

For a few moments they were all quiet.

'It's simple,' Jamie piped up. 'We just barge in there and ransack the gaff; it's not like Kenny will be able to stop us, is it?'

'What and give him the heads up on the situation, let slip that we suspect the Murphys of having a hand in Dad's murder?' Ricky said, shaking his head. 'You know as well as I do that even if we do find something, Kenny will go to ground; he's as sly as they come, always has been.'

Thinking it over, Jamie screwed up his face in concentration. 'I've got it,' he said with a click of his fingers. 'Kenny already thinks that he can trust me, well at least to a certain degree anyway; I'll just play along with him until I get the chance to have a shifty around the office. I mean, he has to leave there at some point doesn't he? He might even let something slip about Dad.'

'That sounds dangerous to me,' Tracey interrupted. 'What if he catches you? And for all we know, Kenny may not have any idea of who killed your dad.'

Jamie rolled his eyes. 'Leave it out Mum, this is Kenny we're talking about. I could take him out with one hand tied behind my back. Tell her,' he said to his brother.

Ricky was thoughtful. 'He's got a point,' he said. 'But...' his voice trailed off and he shook his head. 'What about the Murphys? This isn't just about Kenny, and yeah fair enough, I don't doubt for a second that you could take Kenny out, but you can't take on everyone. Mum's right, this could get dangerous.'

'Then I'll play along with the Murphys as well. Kenny already thinks that I'm as sick as they are up here,' Jamie said, tapping the side of his head. 'Trust me, this will be a piece of piss. I can do this, you know I can.'

As much as he didn't like it, Ricky didn't doubt his brother in the slightest. Jamie had always had a lot to say for himself and in Ricky's eyes that was exactly where the problem lay. Jamie had a big mouth, and if he lost his temper then he'd lash out regardless of whether he had back up or not. He thought he was invincible, and fair enough he wasn't afraid to steam in with his fists or boots, but up against the Murphys and Kenny, he wouldn't stand a chance.

'C'mon bruv,' Jamie urged his brother.

'All right,' Ricky said, holding up his hands. 'But if at any time you don't feel safe then you give me or Max a call, have you got that?'

Jamie resisted the urge to laugh or come back with a sarcastic quip. At the end of the day, his brother was looking out for him, and he appreciated it. 'You'll be the first to hear from me if they cotton on to what I'm up to.'

'Right then.' Blowing out his cheeks, Ricky gave another shake of his head. 'I'll get on the blower to Hardcastle and fill him in, but I mean it bruv, at the first sign of trouble—'

'Yeah, yeah,' Jamie interrupted him. 'I get it, I give you or Hardcastle a call, so that you can come swooping in to rescue me.'

Narrowing his eyes, Ricky gave his brother a hard stare. 'This isn't a joke Jamie, if this goes wrong you'll be outnumbered; you need to remember that bruv.'

Jamie sighed. Ricky was right, he wouldn't just be outnumbered, he'd be extremely outnumbered and from what he knew of the Murphys they were dirty bastards. They didn't fight one on one, they fought together as a family, it was what made them so dangerous. 'I'll be careful,' he promised.

Satisfied, Ricky left the room to make the call to Max.

'I'm still not sure about this.' Biting down on her lip, Tracey was once more on the verge of tears. 'What if something goes wrong?'

'Mum,' Jamie reassured her. 'I'll be all right, and you heard what Ricky said for yourself. If I need help all I have to do is call. I'll tread carefully anyway, it'll probably take me a few days to even set the ball in motion. I need to make sure that Kenny trusts me first.'

As much as she didn't like it, Tracey nodded. She didn't really have any other choice in the matter. Jamie had already made up his mind, and nothing she or Ricky said or did would be able to alter that. Just as his father had been, her youngest son could be a stubborn bugger when the mood took him.

16

The next day, Ricky and Jamie were in the office waiting for Kenny to give them a list of debts to be collected.

Outwardly, they behaved as they usually did, and even grumbled out loud when they noted that one of the debts they were due to collect was at least a two-hour drive there and back.

Sitting behind the desk, Kenny smirked. He loved the fact that he had Terry's sons dangling on a piece of string, that they were nothing but his puppets. In other words when he said jump they asked how high, and the fact that he paid their wages was enough of a guarantee to make sure that they continued to do his bidding.

'This is going to take us all fucking day,' Ricky complained.

'And?' Kenny retorted. 'You get paid for it, don't you?' He stabbed his finger forward, his voice becoming serious. 'And you get paid a hefty wedge as well, might I add. When I was your age I had to graft my bollocks off, and for what eh, I'll tell you for fucking what, for pennies that's what.'

Rolling his eyes, Ricky let out a half laugh; he'd heard the exact same thing from his dad over the years. As he turned back to look out the window, it was on the tip of his tongue to ask what

Shaun did to earn his wages, because he sure as hell didn't drive halfway across the country chasing debts. He continued to watch as Shaun reversed the transit van into the yard and narrowed his eyes. That was another thing he'd observed: why exactly did Shaun need a van, and more to the point what did he use it for? It wasn't used for collecting scrap metal, he knew that much, considering the yard was only a front for his dad's and Kenny's real business interests, and it wasn't used to transport the dogs either.

'Well get on with it,' Kenny growled. 'Those debts won't collect themselves.'

Tearing his hard stare away from the van, Ricky got to his feet. 'Come on,' he said to his brother through gritted teeth, 'we might as well get this over and done with.'

Jamie jerked his head towards the door. 'Just give me a few minutes,' he said. 'I'll be out in a bit.'

Once Ricky had left the office, Jamie turned to face Kenny with a wide grin spread across his face. 'Well,' he asked, 'have you thought about my proposition? When can I get in on the action?'

Kenny leant back in the chair, his forehead furrowed as he studied Jamie. 'Bit keen aren't you?'

His smile faltering, Jamie shrugged. Had he inadvertently fucked everything up by coming across as too eager? The last thing he wanted to do was make Kenny suspicious. At the best of times his dad's business partner could be a shrewd fucker who didn't trust easily, which was probably the reason why he and his old man had got along so well. Terry had trusted no one either, although Jamie had to admit he hadn't for a single moment thought that that sentiment would stretch to his own flesh and blood.

'Of course I'm keen,' he finally answered. 'I've got a nose for business' – he tapped the side of his nose – 'and I don't want to collect debts for the rest of my life. Ricky might be happy plod-ding along, doing the same old shit day in and day out, but not me. I want more than that.'

Laughing out loud, Kenny picked up his cigarette packet from the desk and plucked out two cigarettes. Passing one across to Jamie, Kenny lit up, sucked the smoke deep into his lungs then noisily blew a thin stream of smoke up into the air. 'And there was me thinking that that cock of yours was all you thought about.'

Jamie laughed, although he had to admit it sounded hollow to his ears. 'Yeah, well' – he spread open his arms, a cocky grin making its way across his face – 'if it was handed to me on a plate I wouldn't say no. There's got to be some perks to the job, hasn't there? And I'm guessing me getting my end away as often as I want has to be one of them.'

Kenny chuckled even harder. Oh he definitely had Terry's boys exactly where he wanted them, or at least he had Jamie where he wanted him. The same couldn't be said for Ricky, at least not yet anyway, not that Kenny was overly concerned. After all, Ricky was a hot-blooded male and he knew enough about the two brothers to know that fucking and fighting was all they were good for, much like their father had been at the same age.

'Like I said, let me think about it.' He gave a nonchalant wave of his hand, bringing the conversation to an end.

It wasn't exactly the answer Jamie had been hoping for but at the same time it wasn't a flat-out refusal either. Getting to his feet, Jamie made his way over to the door. 'Well don't leave me hanging for too long,' he said, turning his head to flash a wide smile. 'I'm looking forward to getting stuck in.' He winked. 'And I mean that in every sense of the word.'

As he walked towards his brother's car, the smile slipped from Jamie's face. He chewed on the inside of his cheek, and in the pit of his stomach, worry began to gnaw away at him. He couldn't help but think that he'd inadvertently given the game away. After all, Kenny wasn't stupid, he was bound to put two and two together, come up with three, and suspect that they were in cahoots with Hardcastle. They hadn't exactly been discreet had they? No, it had been him and Ricky who'd hauled Shaun to the yard at Max's request.

Climbing into Ricky's car, Jamie flopped on to the seat, his body sagging.

'Well?' Ricky asked.

Jamie shrugged and as he glanced over at the office, he rested his forearm on the window frame and sucked in his bottom lip. 'I've got a nasty feeling that this is going to be a lot harder than we first thought.'

'What do you mean?' Following his brother's gaze, Ricky studied the office.

'I don't know.' Jamie shrugged again, deflated. 'I've just got this feeling, in here I mean,' he said, pointing to his stomach, 'that he's on to us.'

As Kenny watched Jamie go, he leant back in the chair and laughed out loud. Terry's youngest son was a chip off the old block all right, and as much as he resented the notion of having to pay Jamie a cut of Terry's profits, a part of him knew that it made sense, a lot of sense to be precise. He wanted the Murphy family cut out of the business deal and if he brought in Terry's sons then theoretically speaking he could kill two birds with one stone. Not only could he sever ties with Bianca and her brothers but he could also pay Ricky and Jamie next to nothing for doing practically the same service that the Murphys had provided. It was a win-win situation as far as he was concerned.

A sly grin etched its way across Kenny's face. He'd break Jamie in gently he decided, see if he had what it took to work the business, and more to the point, see if he really did have his father's blood pumping through his veins.

Warming to the idea, he pulled open the desk drawer, all the while mulling over the next phase of his plan. He'd introduce Jamie to the brothel, let him have his pick of the women, and then once he'd had his fun, he'd set him to work. With a bit of luck, Jamie would prove himself to be even more ruthless than his old man had been.

Happier now that he had a plan of action, Kenny took out the mirror and rolled-up bank note from the drawer, then began cutting a copious amount of cocaine. Oblivious to the fact he was using more and more and becoming reliant on the drug, Kenny expertly snorted the coke in quick succession. Not that he would ever admit to having a problem; only mugs became addicts and as far as he was concerned, he was no mug. Noisily he cleared his throat, then wiping the excess traces of white powder away from his nostrils, he slumped back in the chair.

A large part of him wanted to make Jamie wait for his answer, to make him sweat. Yet the businessman in him knew that he had to strike out while the iron was hot and bring Jamie on board while he was so eager to get stuck in.

Reaching for his mobile phone, Kenny scrolled down his contact list, then brought the device up to his ear. He'd put the boy out of his misery he decided, and once he had Jamie exactly where he wanted him, it would be all the more satisfying to keep him under his control.

* * *

'I still don't like this,' Ricky stated later that evening as he, Jamie, Tracey and Max gathered in the lounge of Tracey's home.

Throwing up his arms, Jamie rolled his eyes in irritation. 'C'mon bruv,' he said. 'How many times do we have to go over this? I know what I'm doing; I'm not stupid.'

Ricky groaned. Jamie may not be stupid but he was impulsive and headstrong, which in his opinion made for a dangerous combination. Jamie wouldn't back down from a fight and that was half the problem; he didn't know when to say enough was enough, nor would he care about his own safety. No, Jamie would see red, kick off, and before he knew it he would be heavily outnumbered, with no chance of walking away unscathed.

'Tell him will you, Mum, for fuck's sake,' Jamie said, nodding towards his brother. 'I'm not going to fuck this up.'

'It's not about you fucking it up,' Ricky shouted back. 'It's about you staying one step ahead of Kenny and the Murphys and more to the point you being able to keep your mouth shut long enough to stay alive should they figure out that you suspect them.'

Jamie laughed. 'Leave it out,' he chastised. 'Do you really think I'm bothered about Kenny? I could take him out with one arm tied behind my back and as for the Murphys, they're fuck all for me to worry about; you know as well as I do that they're all mouth and no trousers.'

Ricky narrowed his eyes. 'You do realise that one of them escaped from a psychiatric hospital? Kevin Murphy is a complete and utter lunatic, he wouldn't think twice about slicing you up, he's notorious for it.'

'Says who?' Jamie asked, laughing even harder. 'Don't tell me you actually believe all of that crap? The Murphys put that rumour out there themselves; they think it gives them an edge, a reason for people to be even more cautious of them. Jesus Christ,'

Jamie said, slapping the palm of his hand against his forehead. 'Have a word with him will you Mum.'

Tracey sighed. She had to admit she was in agreement with Ricky. She didn't want either of them anywhere near Kenny or the Murphy family. It was bad enough that they still worked for the business chasing debts, let alone them entering into the world of trafficking and prostitution. The mere thought made her feel sick to her stomach. What if Jamie was walking into a trap, or what if the police were watching Kenny and the Murphys with the intention of collecting intel on them? Turning her head, she lifted her eyebrows towards Max, silently beseeching him to help her out and tell Jamie that the plan he'd concocted was ridiculous, that he was needlessly putting himself in danger.

Max glanced towards Jamie and, taking note of the determined look on his face, he decided to give him the benefit of the doubt. 'He's right, he isn't stupid, he knows what he's doing.'

Jamie gave a triumphant grin and, digging out his car keys from his jacket pocket, he began to make his way towards the hallway when Ricky caught hold of his arm, bringing him to a halt beside him.

'You don't have to do this alone,' Ricky said, his voice low. 'Do you want me to come with you?'

'What and have you hold my hand for me while you're at it?' Jamie answered with a sarcastic laugh. 'I'm not a kid any more,' he said, gesturing towards himself. 'Unless it's escaped your notice bruv, I'm all grown up now. I know how to look after myself, and not only can I legally drive a car, and get served booze, but I can even cross the road all by myself.' He chuckled.

Ricky screwed up his face; it hadn't been what he'd meant at all. He knew that Jamie could take care of himself. After all, he'd seen his brother in action and it hadn't been pretty. Jamie could have a tear up and there was no denying that fact, but despite

knowing that Jamie was no walk over he was still his younger
brother and always would be; he was entitled to worry about him.
They were close, and they looked out for one another. Their dad
had drummed it into them as soon as they were old enough to
walk and talk that they had to learn to be one another's greatest
allies, that there were too many bastards out there with chips on
their shoulders looking to cause aggro and take them down.

His laughter dying down, Jamie shook his head. 'I can handle
it bruv,' he said, clasping his brother on the shoulder.

'Well just be careful,' Ricky told him. 'And take this with you.'
From his back pocket Ricky produced a flick knife. 'Just in case
things get out of hand.'

Resisting the urge not to come back with a sarcastic comment,
Jamie nodded and slipped the blade into his pocket, more so to
placate his brother than anything else, not that he suspected he
would need to use it.

Moments later, he climbed into his car, switched on the ignition, flicked the indicator, then pulled out on to the road. As he
drove through the dark streets towards his dad and Kenny's yard
he was deep in thought. He would never have admitted it out
loud in front of his brother, Max, or even his mum, but he was
feeling nervous. It was the unknown he supposed; he'd never
even contemplated visiting a prostitute let alone actually going
through with it and using the services of one, and the fact that
those women were trafficked into the country against their will
didn't sit right with him, would never sit right with him. Fair
enough, if a woman wanted to sell her body for money then good
luck to her, he was the last person on earth to ever judge a
person's choices – let's face it, he was hardly a saint himself was
he – but when those choices were taken away from them and
women were being controlled by fear and threats of harm, it was
a different matter entirely, one that he wanted nothing to do with.

He just hoped and prayed that his anger and repulsion didn't make him lash out tonight. As it was, he already wanted to tear Kenny's head clean off his shoulders.

* * *

Within ten minutes, Jamie was pulling up outside the yard, and as he switched off the ignition he watched as Kenny exited the office, locked up, then made his way over to the car. Winding down the window Jamie forced himself to relax then smiled a greeting.

'You okay, son?' Kenny asked as he leant his forearms on the car roof and looked through the open gap.

Jamie bristled at Kenny's choice of address. He wasn't his son and never would be. 'Yeah,' he answered. 'Why wouldn't I be?'

Kenny ignored the question and, flashing a grin, there was a craftiness in his eyes. 'Look at you,' he said, 'you're chomping at the fucking bit.' Straightening up, he dragged his hand through his greying hair and beamed even wider. 'Don't you worry son, you'll be balls deep before you know it.'

The crude comment made Jamie want to pull back his fist and knock Kenny to the ground. There wasn't a chance in hell that he would lay a finger on any of the women, let alone do anything else with them. Kenny was only planning to show him round the brothel, and introduce him officially to the Murphys, wasn't he?

'Right then,' Kenny said, slapping the car roof. 'Follow on behind me.' He made to walk towards his own car then turned abruptly round and retraced his steps. 'One more thing.' He leant forward again and studied Jamie, his expression becoming suddenly serious. 'Watch out for Kevin Murphy; he's a mouthy cunt, and not right up here,' he said, pointing to his temple. 'Start as you mean to go on; if you show him weakness then he'll use it to his full advantage, believe me when I say this, he's got a screw loose and those mutts he drags around with him are just as fucking deranged. Oh, and while we're on the subject of dogs, here's a word of warning for you, don't stand too close to them; the vicious buggers would take your fucking hand off as soon as look at you.'

Jamie nodded, taking the warning on board, and as Kenny made his way to his car, Jamie rolled up the window and started the ignition. Across his forehead a layer of cold sweat formed, and using the back of his hand, he hastily wiped it away.

Flicking the indicator, he pulled away from the kerb, and bit down on his lip, wishing that he'd had the forethought to ask Kenny where they were actually going so that he could give Ricky a heads up. Eyeing his mobile phone on the passenger seat, Jamie snatched it up, contemplating whether or not he should give his brother a call anyway so that he could at least give him a general location, should the need arise, and he or Max needed to come search for him.

Against his better judgement, he tossed the phone back on to the seat. He'd end up looking like a right prat if he had to call his brother for help especially when it wasn't even warranted, and even more so after his big speech about being able to handle himself. Tapping his fingers on the steering wheel, he switched on the car radio, hoping for a distraction, or at least something to help calm his nerves. It was no use and switching the radio back off, he concentrated on the road ahead. As the signs for Ilford came into view, he glanced around him, taking in his surroundings. Immediately he recognised where he was and as Kenny slowed his car down to turn off the high road and into a side street, Jamie followed, all the while frowning. He'd been here once before; he was sure of it. A couple of months before his death his dad had said that he'd needed to collect something

from a mate, and while Jamie waited in the car for him his dad
had got out and entered a house.

At the time Jamie had thought nothing of it; his dad had been
in and out of the property within minutes, and it had been so
unnoteworthy that they had never mentioned it again. He
couldn't even recall asking his dad what it was he'd needed to
collect. At the time he'd taken a wild guess that it was money, and
his dad hadn't been carrying anything, at least nothing obvious
anyway, to make him think otherwise.

Pushing his foot down on the brake, Jamie looked across at a
house, the very same house where his father had said that his
mate had lived. The mere thought that he'd been just feet away
from the women his father had forced into prostitution sickened
Jamie to the core, even if he had been oblivious to what was going
on at the time.

He couldn't help but feel as though he should have somehow
known what was going on, that perhaps he should have guessed
that something was off. The rational part of his brain told him he
couldn't have possibly known; it wasn't as though the house had a
neon sign above the door telling all and sundry that it was a
brothel, neither were there any stereotypical red lights lighting
up the windows.

From the outside, the house was nondescript and looked no
different from the neighbouring houses. It was a semi-detached
property and he noted that there was a side gate that led to the
rear of the house. And other than a sign informing visitors of the
fact there were dogs roaming loose on the premises, there was
nothing to alert him to what the property was being used for.
Even the thick net curtains hanging at the windows looked fairly
clean, and as for the small garden at the front of the property,
although it didn't appear to be particularly well cared for, it
wasn't what he would call overly unkempt either.

As Kenny opened the car door and climbed out, Jamie hastily mirrored the action.

'Is this it?' Jamie asked as he joined Kenny outside the house.

Kenny smiled, his bloated face looking grotesque under the street lamp.

It also didn't escape Jamie's notice that Kenny's nostrils held traces of white powder. He'd never been into taking coke himself and couldn't quite see the attraction. Give him a blunt any day of the week and he was as happy as a pig in shit, but as for the hard stuff, nah that wasn't his game, even though he knew his dad had participated every once in a while, another thing his mum was oblivious to.

Slipping his key into the lock, Kenny grinned even harder. 'What do you mean, is this it?' He chuckled. 'What were you expecting, the Ritz?'

'Nah of course not.' Shoving his hands into his pockets, Jamie's fingertips skimmed over the knife as he looked up at the house. 'I just thought it would have been more obvious as to what it is, that's all.'

Kenny shook his head. 'What and end up with the filth on the doorstep? No.' He winked. 'Discretion is the name of the game, son.'

'Yeah, but what about the neighbours?' Jamie asked, motioning to the neighbouring properties. 'They must know what's going on; they could grass you up to the old bill.'

Kenny gave a hearty chuckle. 'Don't worry about them,' he said. 'They know well enough to keep their traps shut. Me and your dad put the hard word on them when we bought the gaff, and believe me, if they want their kneecaps to stay intact then it's in their best interests to turn a blind eye.' Pushing the door open wide, he indicated for Jamie to step across the threshold.

The smell was the first thing that Jamie noticed; stale sweat mingled with overpowering cheap perfume, mixed with the underlying stench of ground-in dirt. As for the inside of the house, it would be fair to say that it had seen better days. The paint work was chipped and peeling, and the linoleum flooring under their feet sticky and covered in a layer of grime.

As he made to step forward, a low guttural growl halted him in his tracks; it was enough to make the tiny hairs on the back of Jamie's neck stand up on end.

'Oi Murphy,' Kenny shouted out as he slammed the front door closed, his voice filled with irritation. 'Keep your fucking mutt under control.'

Jamie swallowed deeply and as he looked towards the far end of the hallway he spotted the dog. It was no ordinary dog; no, this was what he could only describe as a beast. With its body rigid, teeth bared, and ears flat against its large, muscular head, long tendrils of slobber hung from the corners of its snarled lips. Seconds later a second dog appeared, equally as large and from what Jamie could make out from the deep, throaty growl it emitted, equally as angry.

'Murphy,' Kenny called out again.

'What?' a gruff voice called back from the rear of the property.

Doing nothing to hide his agitation, Kenny walked forward as though he didn't have a care in the world, his footsteps loud across the linoleum floor. 'I thought I told you to keep these mutts chained up.'

Stepping into the hallway, Kevin Murphy placed his tall, wiry body between the dogs. He gave Kenny a hard stare then let out a sharp whistle. The dogs' tails immediately dropped between their legs and as they looked up at their master they whined before turning around and sloping off back to where they had come from.

Jamie's heart pounded in his chest. He'd never been afraid of dogs, and as a kid had spent a lot of time with the German Shepherds his dad kept at the yard, but he had to admit, for the briefest of moments he'd thought that his number was well and truly up, that he would end up being mauled to death, and that, he concluded, would just about be his luck.

'Who's this?'

Jamie snapped his head up, his gaze taking in who he could only assume was Kevin Murphy.

With dark hair that was cropped close to his scarred head, Kevin's hard, beady eyes scrutinised Jamie as he looked him up and down.

Even with the distance between them, Jamie could see the madness in Kevin's eyes. His body language bordered on nonchalant, and as Kevin leant casually against the wall, from the corner of his thin lips an unlit joint dangled.

'Terry's boy.' Kenny waved his hand dismissively in Jamie's direction. 'He's here to learn the ropes.'

For a few moments, Kevin didn't answer, and striking a match, he cupped his hand around the flame and brought it up to his lips. 'I wasn't told about this,' he said in a low growl. As he took a deep toke, the sweet scent of cannabis filled the air. 'Does Michael know you've brought him on board?' he asked as he lazily picked a flake of tobacco off his tongue.

Kenny's back stiffened, his expression becoming murderous. 'I don't need Michael's permission,' he snapped. 'I run this show and it's about time you lot understood that.'

Kevin shrugged, the hint of a smirk playing out across his lips; it was so slight that Jamie doubted that Kenny would have even picked up on it, but he had, and as a result a wave of unease swept through him.

'From my understanding, we don't work for you.' Pushing himself away from the wall, Kevin took a step forward, his wiry body suddenly taut. 'We're partners,' he said with a wry smile that didn't quite reach his eyes. 'And that, Kenny my old son, means that before you even think about bringing anyone else in on our deal you run it through my family first.'

Kenny tilted his chin in the air, his mouth opening and closing in rapid succession. Not wanting to lose face, he gestured towards Jamie. 'He's Terry's son,' he hastily added. 'It's his given right to take over Terry's share of the business.'

Kevin chuckled and leaning slightly forward, he sniffed the air. 'Ah, do you smell that?'

Kenny narrowed his eyes.

'It's the smell of bullshit,' Kevin said, roaring with laughter. 'Either that or it's your arsehole flapping.' The laughter died as quickly as it began, Kevin's expression once again devoid of any emotion. 'So which is it?' he asked, his hard stare going between both Kenny and Jamie.

Watching the exchange, Jamie involuntarily clenched his fists at his sides. He'd heard the rumours about Kevin Murphy, and until now had believed them to be just that, rumours. Now he wasn't so sure. Murphy was devoid of emotion, even his beady little eyes were hard and cold, and unless Jamie was very much mistaken, he looked as though he was capable of causing them some serious harm.

Despite the urge to take a step backwards, Jamie stood his ground. All the while, Kenny's warning echoed in his mind. He couldn't show weakness, couldn't show Murphy that his presence unnerved him, even though it clearly did. 'Are we going to stand here all night?' he barked out, 'because as lovely as this is, I'm a busy man and don't have time for this bollocks.'

Kevin slowly turned his head. 'I didn't like your old man,' he stated, matter-of-factly.

Jamie rolled his eyes in annoyance. At that precise moment in time, that made both of them, not that he was prepared to let Kevin in on that little titbit. 'Yeah, well I'm not my old man,' he replied. 'And like I said, I don't have time for all of this shit, so either show me the ropes or fuck off out of it.'

His forehead furrowing, Kevin took a menacing step forward.

'Enough.' Putting out his arms, Kenny shook his head. 'Just unlock the fucking door,' he snapped. 'The quicker I show him round' – he jerked his thumb towards Jamie – 'the quicker we can get out of this shit hole.'

Kevin pushed past them and pulled out a bunch of keys from his back pocket. His hard gaze remained firmly locked on Jamie's as he unlocked a door just inches away from where they were standing.

Returning the stare, Jamie brought himself up to his full height and puffed out his chest. They had only been in each other's presence for a few minutes and already Murphy had rubbed him up the wrong way.

'See, it wasn't so fucking difficult was it,' Kenny stated with a shake of his head as he led the way into the room.

The sight which met Jamie was almost enough to make him want to turn on his heels and run. His eyes widening, he took an involuntary step backwards, colliding with Kevin Murphy's hard body.

Along one wall was a sofa, and underneath the bay window a second smaller sofa. Peeling wallpaper covered the walls, and covering the floor was a worn brown carpet, so threadbare in places that Jamie could see the bare floorboards underneath. Women in various stages of undress turned their heads to look at them, their expressions blank, their movements almost sluggish as though they had either been drugged or had given up on life. But it was their eyes which Jamie was drawn to; there wasn't only a sadness there, but also a sense of helplessness, as though they had resigned themselves to the fact that all hope was lost, that from now on this was to be their life, and that this hell hole and the seedy world of prostitution and everything that it entailed was all they would ever have to look forward to.

'Pick one.' Waving his hand towards the women, Kenny lifted his eyebrows, his expression one of pure glee.

'What?' Jamie snapped his head round to look at Kenny, horror resonating across his handsome face.

Kenny chuckled out loud. 'I said pick one,' he said again as he leant in towards Jamie so that their heads were almost touching. 'This was what you wanted, wasn't it?' he asked, his voice low. 'You wanted the perks that come along with the job.'

Jamie shook his head and, taking note of the look both Kenny and Kevin gave him, he gave a half laugh then cleared his throat. 'As much as I'd love to mate, it's getting a bit late,' he said, glancing down at his watch. 'I should be getting off.' Of course, it was a lie, it had only just turned 9 p.m.

Kenny chuckled even harder. 'It's never too late to get laid. Go on, pick one,' he coaxed, full of camaraderie.

Aware that he was being intently watched by both Kenny and Kevin, Jamie took a deep breath, his gaze sweeping over the women. 'I dunno,' he tried again. 'I mean, we've got a busy day tomorrow, and like I already said, it's getting late.' He glanced once more at his watch to emphasise his point. 'Maybe we should do this another night.'

Kenny's body became rigid, his steely eyes narrowed. 'Pick one,' he said, spitting out each word with menace.

Jamie swallowed. All he wanted to do was leave the house and never come back. He could barely bring himself to look at the women and as shame washed over him, his cheeks flushed pink. He felt so repulsed by what was being offered to him that he could actually taste bitter, acrid bile rise up in his throat.

'Don't you fucking dare show me up in front of this lunatic,' Kenny hissed in his ear. 'Now fucking pick one before I take the choice out of your hands and pick one for you.'

Jamie nodded, weighing up his options. He could either stand his ground, refuse the offer, walk out of the house and end up blowing the plan wide apart or he could give Kenny what he wanted and play along. It wasn't as though he had to physically take anyone to bed was it. His gaze roamed over the women again and finally settled on a blonde woman. Seated the furthest away from him, she was so petite, that that she was almost hidden out of sight. He pointed his finger forward. 'That one.'

On seeing who Jamie had picked out, Kenny laughed out loud. It was the very same bitch who'd had the audacity to try and mug him off. 'She's got a big mouth on her this one,' he warned as he yanked her roughly to her feet and shoved her forward. 'She likes it rough, so make sure that you take your time with her. In fact,' he said, spreading open his arms, 'take as long as you need.'

17

Tracey glanced at her watch for the third time in as many minutes. She couldn't settle, couldn't stop herself from worrying. Why hadn't she put her foot down and told Jamie to stay away from Kenny and the Murphys? Fair enough, Jamie was a grown man, but as she had already stated, he was still her baby, and always would be, and no matter how big he was she would still worry about him; it was part and parcel of being a parent.

'Mum.' Sitting down beside his mother, Ricky clasped her tiny hand in his. 'He'll be okay.'

'Will he?' Tracey choked out, her voice a lot higher than it usually was. 'This is Jamie we're talking about; you know what he's like, one wrong word and all hell will break loose, and then what, eh?' Oh, she was under no delusions when it came to her youngest son, she knew him well enough to know that he had a quick temper, and that it wouldn't take much for him to erupt.

'Of course he'll be okay,' Ricky answered with a half laugh to try and ease her concern. 'Like he said himself, he's a big boy now, Mum.'

Tracey nodded, although it did nothing to erase her fear. Getting to her feet she began to pace the length of the lounge. 'Your phone is on, isn't it?' she asked, giving the coffee table where Ricky had placed the device a sidelong glance.

'It's on,' Ricky reassured her as he picked up his phone to double check that he'd had no missed calls from his brother.

Glancing at her watch again, Tracey continued to pace. 'Shouldn't he be back by now?' she asked, turning to look at Max.

Max checked the time on his watch; Jamie had been gone less than an hour. 'You're going to wear that carpet out,' he said as he watched her pace. 'Why don't you try and calm down, have a drink or something.'

'Calm down,' Tracey hissed. 'This is my son we're talking about.'

Holding up his hands, Max retreated to the far side of the lounge, deciding to keep his own counsel. Who was he to interfere when it came to a mother and her son. Look at his own mum; she'd stood by him, even though she could have wiped her hands off him. And who would have blamed her if she'd done precisely that? He certainly wouldn't have. After all, his mates had abandoned him, so what was stopping his mum from doing the same? It had near enough killed his mother to see her only child sent down. She'd never even had the chance to see him released from prison, having passed away five years before he'd regained his freedom. It was a guilt that he carried with him, and he couldn't help but believe his actions had somehow contributed to her death. Had he inadvertently been responsible for putting his own mother into an early grave? He would never know the answer to his question, and a part of him didn't want to know. It was far easier to blame himself, and his biggest regret would always be the fact that she had died alone and he hadn't been by her side as she took her last breaths.

Tracey perched her backside on the edge of the sofa, her knee jerking uncontrollably up and down. Maybe Max was right and she should have a drink; she was sure that there was still some wine leftover in the fridge, or maybe she should have a cigarette, perhaps it would help calm her nerves, and now more than ever she could do with a nicotine hit, something to take her mind off her youngest son. No, she quickly decided, she hadn't touched a cigarette in days and certainly didn't want to fall back into that bad habit again. 'I'm sorry,' she said, chewing on her thumbnail. 'I didn't mean to come across so rude.'

'It's okay,' Max reassured her. 'You're worried, and I get it. I may not have had kids myself, but I put my old mum through some shit when I was young, so in a roundabout way I do understand and believe me, my poor mum had more than her fair share of worry over the years all because of me and the crap I got up to on a daily basis. I was a little fucker, and it's not something I'm proud of,' he said with a gentle smile. 'I put my mum through hell, and I have to live with that up here I mean,' he added, pointing to his temple, 'for the rest of my life.'

Tracey nodded. She could see the remorse in his eyes, and the way his shoulders slumped downwards was more than enough to tell her that he felt contrite for his past actions, that he'd give anything to be able to go back and do things differently. 'Did you not want children?' she asked, changing the subject.

Max shook his head and gave a light laugh. 'I'm hardly a good role model am I?' He shrugged. 'Besides, what could I ever offer a child?'

As she processed his answer, Tracey studied Max. He'd more than proved his loyalty to her and her sons over the past few weeks, he had morals, and from the limited amount of time she'd spent in his company, he'd made her feel safe. What else could a child possibly need?

Sensing her confusion, Max continued. 'I was in my mid-thirties by the time I was released from nick; I'd left it a bit late in the day to think about settling down. It was hard enough trying to rebuild my life without the added pressure of meeting someone and starting a family. I came out of nick with nothing other than the clothes on my back, my bus fare, and an address for a bail hostel.' He laughed. 'Let's face it, I was hardly a catch, was I? And I definitely wasn't the kind of man any decent woman would want as the father to her children.'

Tracey nodded again, wanting to kick herself. She'd totally forgotten that he'd spent the early part of his adult life locked up. At times she found it hard to imagine him as the ruthless murderer Kenny had claimed him to be. As for not being a catch, while he may not have had much when he'd left prison, he was a handsome man, he had a head for business, and she rightly guessed he could have had his pick of women.

'You still have time,' she said gently. 'I mean you're what, fifty now?'

'Forty-nine,' Max corrected her.

'Well that's still young enough to become a father; you hear of celebrities having kids well into their sixties and seventies.'

Shaking his head, Max laughed. He could think of nothing worse than having a son turn out just like him, and although some people may call it karma for the shit he'd put his own mother through over the years, he personally thought of it as a recipe for disaster. Besides, settling down wasn't for him, he was better off living alone. Maybe if his life had turned out differently, he would have loved nothing more than to have got married and one day have had kids, but what was done was done, he couldn't turn back time, no matter how much he might want to at times.

'How long did you go away for anyway?' Ricky asked. 'I know my dad said it was a lump.'

'Ricky,' Tracey hissed with a look of warning.

'No, he's all right.' Max laughed. 'I haven't got anything to hide,' he added with a slight shrug. 'I received a life sentence with a minimum tariff of eighteen years, so all in all, I served two years in a youth detention centre and then sixteen years in Belmarsh.'

'Fuck me,' Ricky said, whistling through his teeth. 'That's a lump and a half.'

'Well, some might say I deserved it,' Max answered with a small smile. 'At the end of the day I took a life, and it is what it is, I had to be punished for it.'

'But that must have made you' – his forehead furrowed, Ricky hastily calculated Max's age when he'd committed the murder – 'fifteen or sixteen.'

'Yeah,' Max sighed. 'I was sixteen, still a kid myself.'

'So what happened?' Leaning forward on the sofa, Ricky rested his forearms on his knees, his eyes wide. 'How did the old bill know it was you? I mean, like you said, you were a kid, so what made them even suspect you?'

Max shrugged. 'The same way most people are caught I suppose, some cunt grassed me up.'

'No fucking way.' Ricky's mouth dropped open, causing Max to give a half laugh.

'Yeah,' Max continued. 'An anonymous tip off. If it hadn't been for that I would have more than likely got away with it. I hadn't even been on the old bill's radar, and the only evidence they had to nail me was a bloody footprint. We didn't even have CCTV back in those days, not like we do today, and as young as I was, I knew enough to know that I had to dispose of the clothes I'd been wearing at the time. The only thing I didn't do was get rid of my trainers,' he said with a laugh. 'They'd been brand new at the time, I'd saved up for weeks to buy them, and I didn't want to throw them out all because of that ponce. In a way, I suppose my own pig headedness was my downfall.' He shrugged. 'Anyway, the filth found traces of the blood on the tread and that, coupled with the fact I had a motive, was enough to see me charged with murder. You see, I detested the bastard,' he said, screwing up his face, 'and I made no secret of that fact. The dirty ponce made mine and my mum's life a living hell, and I wasn't prepared to let him get away with that. Besides, it was only a matter of time before it came to a head between us. He hated me as much as I hated him, and if I hadn't done what I did, then sooner or later he would have ended up battering me to death and it would have been him up on a murder charge.'

'Fucking hell,' Ricky choked out. 'So who was it? Who grassed you up?'

'Now that,' Max said, pointing a finger in Ricky's direction, 'is the million-dollar question. And trust me, one I would very much like to know the answer to. If I ever get my hands on the grass he'll know about it, and believe me when I say this, I will have him. It might take me another eighteen years to find out who it was, but I will have my day with him.'

Kenny was grinning from ear to ear as he watched Jamie drag the big-mouthed blonde out of the room. He was so pleased with himself that if he'd been able to, he would have patted himself on the back for a job well done. All thanks to his quick thinking he now had Jamie exactly where he wanted him, and that was under his control. Although he had to admit that for a moment or two there he'd actually thought Terry's son was going to refuse his generous offer, that Jamie was going to make him look a fool in front of Kevin Murphy.

Sensing the mad man watching him, Kenny slowly turned

round, his head cocked to one side, and his dark eyes hard. 'What?' he snapped.

Kevin gave a carefree shrug, then relighting the joint he puffed on it for several seconds before blowing out a cloud of smoke and jerking his chin towards the open doorway. 'Are we giving out freebies now then or what?'

Agitation pumped through Kenny's veins, and waving away the pungent stench of the cannabis, he turned his head away, not bothering to answer. Murphy was beginning to get right on his tits, and as for those beady little eyes of his that followed his every movement, no doubt reporting everything back to his brother Michael, Kenny had had more than a gutful.

Still, he smirked to himself, the Murphys were on their way out, they just didn't know it yet, and as far as Kenny was concerned, the quicker they were gone the better.

* * *

Grasping the protesting girl by her upper arm, Jamie dragged her up the wooden staircase.

'Which one?' he asked, gesturing to the rooms on the upper floor.

The short red satin robe the woman wore came apart, exposing not only a lacy black bra but also a vast amount of smooth skin, not that she appeared to care or even notice as her hands flew at him, her fingernails ready and poised to scratch at his face and upper body.

'I asked, which one?' As he caught hold of her wrists, Jamie's voice became more urgent. He glanced over his shoulder at the staircase, his ears straining for any movement coming from down below.

Tears of frustration filled the woman's eyes, and in one final act of defiance she jerked her knee up, aiming for Jamie's groin, spitting into his face as she did so. 'Bastard,' she hissed at him.

His grip tightening, Jamie wiped the palm of his hand over his face, cleaning away the spittle. Considering her size, she was strong, a lot stronger than he'd been expecting and as he looked down at her, he fought the urge to laugh out loud, even though it would have been more so out of disbelief than anything else. He'd only chosen her because he'd thought she would be pliable and easier than the other women to deal with; now, he wasn't so sure. Maybe he should have picked one of the others, half of them had looked so drugged up that he doubted they even knew where they were, let alone that they would be able to put up a fight, unlike the little fire cracker in front of him, who at this precise moment in time looked capable of giving Muhammed Ali a run for his money.

The sound of footsteps across the linoleum flooring below spurred Jamie into action. His heart racing, in a blind panic he pushed the girl into the nearest bedroom, hoping it would be empty. He then slammed the door closed behind them, hastily locked it, then leant his back against the wooden panels. 'Fuck,' he muttered underneath his breath, 'fuck, fuck, fuck.'

This wasn't how events were supposed to have played out. Kenny was meant to show him the brothel, introduce him to Kevin Murphy, then allow him to go on his merry way. What he hadn't expected was for Kenny to actually tell him to take his pick of the women. He ran his hand through his dark hair, his gaze surveying the room, as he tried to think of a way out of the precarious situation he now found himself to be in. He was under no illusions that if he didn't think of something and fast then his cover would be well and truly blown.

From her position across the far side of the room, Georgiana yanked the satin gown around her body all the while watching Jamie warily, her body and mind on high alert, her breathing heavy.

After a few moments, Jamie propelled himself away from the door, his arms outstretched as he took a step in Georgiana's direction.

'You need to be quiet,' he told her as she backed further away from him, his voice slow and deliberate, before putting his finger up to his lips as a way of emphasising his request. 'Just play along okay?' He wasn't sure just how much she understood and he rubbed at his temples as he tried to think of a way to get his point across. 'Just stay there.' He pointed towards the window. 'And don't move.'

Fear shot down the length of Georgiana's spine. 'Stay away from me,' she warned. Turning her head from side to side, her gaze darted around the room on the lookout for a weapon that she could use against him. Spotting a ceramic lamp on the bedside table she made to lunge towards it.

'No,' Jamie said, his voice hard as he raced across the room and wrestled her away from the offending object. 'No, just stop, okay. I'm not going to hurt you.' He glanced over his shoulder; it wouldn't surprise him if Kenny was standing outside the door listening, the dirty bastard that he was.

There and then disgust filtered across Jamie's face. Think, he told himself, think. Looking over at the double divan bed, he manoeuvred the girl towards the window, ignoring her confused expression, then set to work.

Tearing the top sheet away, he thumped the pillows then yanked on the bottom sheet so that the bedding looked crumpled, or more to the point, used.

Straightening up, he tilted his head to one side and inspected his handiwork, then reaching out for one of the pillows, as an added measure he threw it to the bottom of the bed. Satisfied, he nodded. Should Kenny come knocking on the door, he wouldn't be any the wiser, or at least Jamie hoped he wouldn't anyway.

Georgiana continued to watch him warily. Holding up his hands, Jamie backed away from the bed and resumed his position in front of the door. He'd give it ten minutes, he decided, and then make his way back down the stairs.

'What happened to your face?' he asked, gesturing to the bruise.

Georgiana's fingers reached up to touch her eye, the tender, swollen skin surrounding it a mass of purple and black.

'Who did this to you?' he asked again. 'Was it them down there?' He pointed to the floor, not taking his gaze away from her face.

Her silence told Jamie everything he needed to know, and as she averted her eyes, his fists involuntarily clenched at his sides, anger surging through his body. Had his dad used brute force to keep the women under control too? Sickened, he glanced down at his watch, the urge inside of him to get out of the house so strong that he could almost taste it.

With a few minutes to spare he decided that he'd had just about enough, and after giving Georgiana one final glance he quietly opened the door and stepped out into the hallway. At the top of the staircase he paused for a moment to gather his thoughts, then plastering a wide smile across his face, he bounded down the stairs with as much swagger as he could physically muster.

'Here he is.' Kenny chuckled. 'I was about to send a search party for you!'

Jamie gave a light laugh in return, even though laughing was the last thing he felt like doing. No, what he really wanted to do was smash his fist into both Kenny and Kevin Murphy's faces and not stop until they were a bleeding, broken mess on the floor. 'I need to make a move mate,' he said through gritted teeth.

Still grinning, Kenny nodded. Jamie was like his old man all right, Terry had never wanted to stick around after getting his end away either. 'Come on then,' he said, slinging his arm around Jamie's shoulders.

Outside in the street, Jamie breathed in lungfuls of fresh air. He could still smell the house on him; it lingered on his clothes and skin, somehow tainting him in the process. All he wanted to do was go home, shower and throw his clothes into the washing machine – either that or burn them. Not that he could, at least not yet anyway; he had to report back to his mum, brother and Max first.

Shrugging Kenny away from him, Jamie gave a tight smile as he walked towards his car. After what he'd just witnessed, he didn't trust the man, and if Kenny was capable of harming a defenceless woman, then what else was he capable of doing? 'See you later,' he called out.

He didn't wait around for a response, and eager to get away, he put the car into gear and sped away from the kerb without giving Kenny or the house a second glance. As far as he was concerned, he and Kenny were done. He wanted nothing more to do with him, even if that meant walking away from everything he'd ever known, including his position in his dad's business.

* * *

Standing beside the window, Georgiana watched through the chink in the net curtain as Jamie and Kenny exited the house, her eyes narrowed and confusion spread across her face. Why hadn't he touched her? She looked down at herself, her forehead furrowing, then turning to look at the divan bed, she bit down on her bottom lip.

The bedding still lay in a crumpled heap just as he'd left it moments earlier. On autopilot she straightened out the bedsheets then tentatively perched her backside on the edge of the mattress. He'd tried to help her, he'd been kind, and his voice had been gentle when he'd spoken to her. Even when she'd lashed out at him, he hadn't retaliated; but why not, why hadn't he matched her slaps with punches of his own? And why had he asked about her blackened eye, why had he even cared? He didn't know her, and to her knowledge he'd never even set his eyes upon her before tonight. They were strangers, so why didn't he use her for sex? After all, that was why he'd been here wasn't it, the reason why any man would visit a brothel?

Standing up, she gave the room one final glance before taking a step towards the door, when something poking out from underneath the corner of the bed sheet that draped across the floor caught her attention.

It was a small steel flick knife measuring around ten centimetres long. Scooping down, she picked the object up, studying it, then glancing over her shoulder to check that the coast was clear, she cautiously flicked it open. From what she could tell the blade was sharp and as she gently pressed her finger to the tip she gave a startled hiss. Immediately blood pooled from the wound. Bringing her finger up to her lips, she sucked the blood away and looked around her, surveying the room, her gaze falling upon the ceramic lamp. The knife must have fallen out of his pocket during their struggle.

Unsure of what she should do with the blade, Georgiana

slipped the cool metal inside her bra so that it was hidden out of sight. She didn't want anyone to find it and certainly didn't want anyone else to know that she was armed with a weapon.

With one final glance around the room, she momentarily paused, then tipping her head forward she ran her fingers through her long blonde hair, making it look tousled. As an afterthought, she loosened the satin robe slightly and slid a bra strap off her shoulder. Perhaps the man had even left the knife for her to find, and as she made her way downstairs, she wondered briefly if he would come back, if he would help her and the other women to escape their prison. It was a long shot she knew, but one she was determined to hold on to, and as her fingertips slid over the hard metal at the side of her breast, a lone tear slipped down her cheek. He had to return, he had to help them; it was the only piece of hope she had left.

* * *

The bright headlights of a car pulling on to the drive was all it took for Tracey to leap out of her seat and fling the front door wide open.

'Thank God, you're home.' Relief flooded through her as her youngest son jumped out of the car. 'Are you okay?' she asked as she gave him the once over, checking that he didn't have any visible injuries. 'They didn't suss you out or anything?'

'Nah, of course they didn't.' Jamie shook his head, and slamming the car door closed, he made his way wearily across the drive. 'I'll explain everything once we're inside,' he said, nodding towards the house.

Moments later, he stepped inside the lounge with Tracey hot on his heels.

'Well,' Ricky asked cocking an eyebrow as he turned in his seat to look at his brother. 'How did it go?'

Taking note of the fact that they were all watching him, Jamie rubbed his hand over his jaw, his mind wandering back to the blonde girl and the black eye she was sporting. The bruise had looked painful, and despite her feistiness, she was so petite that he knew she wouldn't have stood a chance if he'd been the type of man who wouldn't think twice about putting his hands on a woman against her will. 'The brothel is in Ilford,' he said, 'and as far as I can tell, Kevin Murphy, the fucking psycho that he is, works there most days.'

'No-good cunt,' Ricky growled.

'Yeah, you can say that again.' Jamie nodded as he recalled just how easily Kevin had got his back up. Slipping his hand into his pocket, he felt around for the flick knife. He should have stabbed the fucker; as far as he was concerned he would have been doing society a favour by getting rid of the nutcase. At least it would have been one less Murphy in the world, which wasn't a bad thing in his opinion. His forehead furrowing, Jamie patted himself down. Where was the blade? He was sure that he'd had it on him when he'd entered the house in Ilford. He gave a slight shrug, perhaps it had fallen out in the car. 'And I think...' he sucked in his bottom lip, contemplating his next words. 'No, I more than think we were right. It was the Murphys who killed the old man.'

'What makes you say that?' Ricky demanded.

Jamie sighed and as he slipped off his jacket, he shrugged. 'Kevin Murphy made no secret of the fact that he didn't like him, he actually said that to my face. I think they killed him, and I think that Kenny either knew about it or was somehow involved.'

'No.' Tracey's mouth fell open. 'This is ludicrous. Kenny and your dad were business partners; they were the best of friends for Christ's sake. Kenny would never have willingly harmed a hair on your dad's head, neither would he have stood by and allowed the Murphy family to murder him. You know he wouldn't have; he was loyal to your father, he was in pieces when he died, absolute pieces.'

'Was he?' Ricky thought back to Kenny's reaction at the time of his dad's murder, and yeah fair enough, for all intents and purposes, Kenny had come across as sincere, he'd even seemed genuinely upset, at least at first anyway, but he'd never pledged his allegiance to find out who'd been behind the shooting, and he sure as hell hadn't gone out of his way to actively seek the culprit out. Ricky asked himself whether it was because Kenny had already known who had been responsible. Had he been in cahoots with the murderer all along?

'Yes, he was,' Tracey retorted. 'You were there, you saw Kenny's reaction for yourself, he was shocked, he—'

'I'm not being funny Mum,' Ricky interrupted, 'but we were a bit too preoccupied with Dad bleeding out all over the floor to scrutinise how Kenny or anyone else for that matter was reacting. Besides, this wouldn't be the first thing you've been wrong about would it? Not so long ago you were convinced that Max had killed Dad.'

'That was different,' Tracey protested, her cheeks flaming bright pink as she glanced across to Max in an apology. 'I didn't even know who Max was back then; how was I to know he and your dad had been childhood friends? In all the years we were together your dad had never mentioned him to me, not once. And Kenny was the one who told me that Max was dangerous, that he was a murderer and that he would think nothing of killing your father, and I...' Her voice trailed off as she realised what she'd said and as both her sons' and Max's backs stiffened, she slammed her hand over her mouth. Was there some truth to what her sons were saying? After all, it had been Kenny who had tried to convince her that she was on the right path, that Max had been guilty of Terry's murder, or at least he'd done nothing to put her straight on the matter. Neither had he come to Max's defence, and she suddenly wondered why Kenny would have led her to wrongly believe that Terry's eldest friend had been responsible for his death. Had he been trying to misguide her, or had he perhaps been trying to cover his own tracks?

'Oh my God,' she cried as the enormity of the situation finally hit home. Her sons had been around Kenny, she herself had been around him; could he have been plotting their murders too?

A sneer creased Ricky's face; Kenny had told them the exact same thing, that a war had been on the cards between his dad and Max. In fact he'd done everything in his power to try and make them believe that Max had been responsible for his dad's murder. 'I think you could be on to something,' he said, looking across at his brother.

'What, you only think?' Jamie answered with a sarcastic laugh. 'I'm right, and you know I am. And I'm telling you now, I'm done with the business,' he said, screwing up his face. 'Fuck Kenny, the bastard is sick in the head. Are you with me on this bruv?'

Deep in thought, Ricky nodded. It went without saying that he and Jamie would stick together. Kenny was sick in the head and as much as it pained him to admit it, their dad had to have been too.

'What do you reckon?' he asked, turning to look at Max. 'You know Kenny from old; do you think he could have had a hand in my dad's murder?'

Sitting forward on the sofa, Max rested his forearms on his

knees and laced his fingers together. He better than anyone knew just how sly Kenny could be, and even when they had been kids he'd known that Kenny couldn't be trusted. But murder? Would Kenny really have gone that far? And as for the businesses, or at least the debt collecting side of the business, Kenny wouldn't be able to handle that alone; it was only Terry's reputation which had made the business a success in the first place. Aware that they were waiting for him to answer, Max shrugged. 'That depends,' he said, 'on what exactly Kenny would have to gain from your dad being out of the picture?'

For a few moments they were all silent, each of them thinking the question over. Max had a point, how would Kenny benefit from Terry's death?

'Maybe Terry had wanted out of the prostitution business,' Tracey volunteered, ever hopeful that her husband hadn't been as guilty as Kenny had made him out to be. 'And so Kenny killed him?'

Jamie shook his head sadly. 'Dad was up to his neck in it, Mum. He would never have walked away; there was too much money involved.'

Tracey bit down on her lip and nodded, her heart clearly breaking that little bit more.

'Then it has to be about money,' Ricky piped up. 'I mean with Dad out of the way, Kenny and the Murphys would have a share of his profits, wouldn't they?'

It was possible, Max conceded, only it still didn't quite make sense to him, especially if the rumour about Terry and Bianca Murphy being lovers was true. Unless... no. He shook his head. There was no way Kenny would have been able to orchestrate Terry's murder alone, he didn't have the nous... did he?

'What are you thinking?' Watching the different emotions pass across Max's face, Ricky cocked his head to one side.

'Nothing.' Even as Max waved the question away, his mind was still working overtime. The only thing he knew for certain was that Kenny had lied to them all. Did that make him guilty of murder? Max wasn't so sure, but he was going to find out and with Kenny once again on his radar, he'd get to the truth of the matter even if that meant he had to kill all over again to get to it.

18

Michael Murphy was furious; in fact, he was so irate that steam was practically coming out of his ears. Not only had Kenny Kempton roughed up his little sister, an offence alone that was worthy enough to warrant a slow and torturous death, but to make matters even worse he now believed that he had the authority to bring all and sundry in on their business deal. Well like fuck he did; as far as Michael was concerned, Kenny was in no position to shout the odds.

'I'll have the arsehole for this,' Michael seethed as he lit a cigarette. 'I'm going to string the no-good cunt up by his fucking bollocks.'

A slow smile creased Bianca's face. She loved it when her eldest brother was like this: angry, brooding, and not forgetting downright dangerous. It was definitely a sight to behold and just one of the many reasons she was proud to be a Murphy. They weren't the type of family to take any shit lying down; no, they would fight until the bitter end, and they fought dirty.

Kissing his teeth, Kevin lounged back on the sofa. 'I should have smashed my fist into his face while I had the chance,' he said, referring to Jamie. 'I should have shown him exactly what happens when you cross a Murphy. He's got a big trap on him just like his fucking dad did, and he's another lairy little prick in the making if you ask me. I can tell you now that if Kempton brings him in on the deal then he's gonna try and run the show just like his old man.' He directed the comment towards his sister and there was a gleam in Kevin's eyes. Unlike his brothers, he didn't worship the ground Bianca walked on. In fact he didn't worship the ground anyone walked on, but in his mind Bianca was nothing more than a dirty whore, and the fact she had spread her legs for Terry Tempest was more than enough to prove his point.

As her hand automatically drifted down to gently caress the slight curve of her abdomen, the smile slipped from Bianca's face. Terry's child was nestled inside her womb, its very existence a secret that she held close to her heart. 'You know nothing about my Terry,' she snapped at her brother.

Kevin smirked. 'I know enough,' he said, pointing a nicotine-stained finger in his sister's direction. 'He was married for a start, and you' – he shook his head, disgust written all over his face – 'were nothing more than his dirty little secret, his side piece. As soon as he'd grown tired of you, he would have kicked your arse to the kerb and you fucking know it.'

Bianca jumped to her feet, her face red with anger. 'Well that's where you're wrong,' she screamed at her brother. 'I'm pregnant with Terry's child, and he loved me. He was going to give that stuck up bitch he was married to the elbow, he was going to kick her out of his house, and he was going to divorce her for me,' she said, stabbing a stiff finger into her chest.

A stunned silence fell over the room and as she looked around at her brothers, Bianca inwardly groaned. Fuck Kevin; if it hadn't been for him goading her she would have been able to keep her secret to herself for a little longer. Now, all thanks to her brother and his big trap, she had inadvertently spilled the beans.

'Well, well, well.' From the lounge doorway, Doris Murphy shook her head. 'I knew it,' she said matter-of-factly. 'Didn't I say that you looked peaky, that you were as white as a bleeding sheet. Although I've got to admit, I'm more surprised that you actually know who the father is, what with your track record.'

Tears sprang to Bianca's eyes, and as she silently cried, her hand reached down to touch her tummy again.

'Shut up, Mum,' Michael barked out, not taking his eyes off his sister. 'Is it true, are you up the duff?' he asked as he scrutinised Bianca.

Her eyes downcast, Bianca nodded.

'Are you keeping it?' he asked, his gaze drifting down to her stomach. After all, it wouldn't be the first time his sister had fallen pregnant over the years. In fact their mum had once remarked that Bianca had terminated more pregnancies than they'd had hot dinners, and considering their mother cooked for an army on a daily basis that was saying something.

Bianca nodded a second time and as she lifted her head there was a steely glint in her eyes, her expression once again hard. 'My baby is entitled to Terry's wealth,' she said with pure venom in her voice. 'My baby is entitled to everything that bitch he was married to has: the house, the cars, the businesses, everything. By rights it should belong to me. Terry didn't love her, he loved me, and I'm owed compensation; my man died and now my baby will be fatherless.'

Taking a puff on his cigarette, Michael chuckled out loud. 'Fuck me B, you don't do anything by halves do you girl?'

Wiping away her tears, Bianca let out a strangled laugh. She wasn't ashamed of her predicament, why should she be? She'd been in love with Terry and all that she had left of him was their baby. Helping herself to a cigarette from her brother's pack, Bianca lit up. 'The question is Michael,' she said, blowing out a plume of cigarette smoke above her head. 'Is what are we going to do about Kempton?' She looked around at her family, gauging their reaction. 'You told me that Hardcastle would obliterate Kenny, and so far he has done fuck all, so what exactly are we waiting for, eh, why haven't you taken control of this?'

The room fell silent, awaiting Michael's answer. It was an unwritten rule that as the eldest of the Murphy siblings what Michael said went, and it was more than any of their lives were worth to argue or go against him.

'What do you think I'm going to do?' Michael asked, stubbing out his cigarette in an overflowing ashtray. 'I'm going to see to it that you get everything you deserve, and if Kenny doesn't like it then fuck him. It's about time that he got it through his thick fucking skull that we run this show, not him and certainly not Terry's fucking sons either because let's not forget they also stand in the way of you getting what you're owed, your due.'

It was like music to Bianca's ears and as her brothers got to their feet, shouting out their approval, her heart skipped a beat. 'Thanks Michael,' she gushed, throwing herself into her eldest brother's arms.

'No need to thank me,' Michael said, kissing the top of his sister's head. 'We're family B, we're blood, and no one takes the piss out of us, no one, have you got that?'

Bianca looked up at her brother, her eyes filled with love for him. 'I've got it.' She grinned happily. She'd always known that they were a family to be reckoned with, and her child when he or she was born would also have the same respect bestowed upon them. After all, it would be their birth right, their legacy, one that they too would have to live up to one day. And not only would the baby have her blood flowing through its veins but also Terry's; it was a powerful mix, one that made her feel giddy with excitement. Her child would be strong, they would be a fighter, and they may just have what it took to lead the family one day.

'Right, come on then, let's pay Kempton a visit.' As they filed out of the house, Michael slung his arm around Kevin's shoulders. 'Get over to the house in Ilford,' he said in his ear, 'and if that trappy little prick Jamie turns up, give me a bell. It's about time we properly introduced ourselves to him, don't you think?' He winked.

Kevin's eyes lit up; now Michael was talking. He couldn't wait to get stuck in and show both Kenny and the Tempest boys exactly who was the boss. Whistling for the dogs, he opened the back door of his car and once the Rottweilers had jumped dutifully on to the back seat, he slammed it closed again.

'Oh and Kevin,' Michael shouted out.

'Yeah,' Kevin answered as his elder brother walked back towards him.

Michael smiled, then without warning, he smashed his fist into his brother's gut. 'You ever refer to our sister as some dirty slag again and I'll kill you, have you got that?'

As he clutched at his stomach, tears sprang to Kevin's eyes; he was so winded he could barely catch his breath, let alone retaliate.

'You might be the biggest nutter this side of the water,' Michael said over his shoulder as he walked away, 'but just you remember, you're a Murphy first and foremost, and we stick together – it's what makes us strong.'

Kevin stared at his brother's retreating back. It was just one of the many stark reminders not to get on Michael's bad side.

* * *

His eyes wide open, Jamie stared up at the ceiling. Sleep had evaded him and no matter how many times he'd tossed and turned throughout the night he'd been unable to drift off. His mind was plagued with thoughts and for the life of him, he couldn't get the little blonde fire cracker out of his head. She'd looked so tiny, so vulnerable, and so scared that his heart actually broke for her. He didn't even know her name and yet the notion that his dad and Kenny had been responsible for her fear was enough for him to want to kill them stone dead.

Finally giving in, Jamie threw the duvet away from him, sat up, swung his legs over the side of the bed, planted his feet firmly on the floor, then sighed heavily.

He should have done something to help the women; he should never have left the house knowing that they weren't safe. And how could they be when Kevin Murphy, the nutcase, was standing guard over them? Would Murphy even care if a punter was too rough with one of them? Or what if a fire broke out, would he leave them to burn to death or would he do the right thing and unlock the door so that they too could escape?

Riddled with guilt, he got to his feet, he padded across the bedroom, flung open the wardrobe and pulled out a fresh pair of jeans and a shirt. Tossing the garments onto the bed, he headed for the bathroom.

On some level he knew that he had nothing to feel ashamed of, yet he couldn't help but feel partly responsible for the women's plight. Not once but twice had he been in near proximity to the brothel, and on neither occasion had he lifted a finger to help any of them.

Thirty minutes later, Jamie left the house and climbed into his car. As he pulled away from the kerb, he lit a cigarette all the while contemplating his father's involvement in the prostitution ring. Not only had his dad had a reputation as a hard man but he'd also been both equally well liked and well respected within the community, and what an absolute fucking joke that was. In reality, his dad had been nothing but a scumbag, a bully, and a low-life pimp.

Shame washed over him and as his grip tightened around the steering wheel, he fought the urge to punch something. How could he or Ricky have not known what was going on right underneath their noses? How could they have been so blind? Were they really that stupid that they hadn't picked up on what their dad had been involved in?

Jamie's mind wandered to Shaun and his lips curled in disgust. What was the betting that Shaun had known what was going on? Shaun worked at the yard on a daily basis, he'd been around his dad and Kenny far more than he or Ricky ever had. The mere thought was enough to make him want to turn the car round and head straight for the yard; in fact, nothing would give him greater pleasure than to pummel his fists into both Shaun's and Kenny's faces. They deserved a beating and a lot more besides.

Instead of driving towards the yard however, Jamie pushed his foot down on the accelerator and headed in the direction of his brother's house. He and Ricky needed to talk about it; they couldn't carry on pretending everything was okay and ignoring the fact that their dad had bought and sold women. That the man they had looked up to their entire lives had been responsible for a crime so despicable that Jamie knew he could never forgive him. A tiny part of him even wondered if his dad had got what he'd deserved, if his murder had been the price that he'd had to pay for his wrongdoings. He swallowed deeply and pushed the thought away, the loyalty he felt for his dad once again rushing to the fore. He may not like what Terry had been involved in, but at the same time he still loved him, would always love him; he was his dad after all, and no matter how much he might want to at times, he couldn't just switch his feelings off.

Pressing his foot on the brake, Jamie switched off the ignition then looked over at his brother's house. In a lot of ways he and Ricky were alike; they were both strong willed, and neither one of them had the mindset to back down from a fight. He'd wrongly assumed that they took after their dad, but now he could see that it was their mum they took after, not Terry. Tracey had a quiet strength about her, look at how she'd handled her husband's murder. And yeah, fair enough, at one point he had thought that his mum had lost her mind, but who would blame her if she had? She'd been there to witness her husband's demise and had cradled him in her arms as he'd bled to death. But no, his mum had shown just how tough she was; she'd been determined to get to the truth, and it was only because of her persistence that they had done just that, even if the truth had broken her heart in the process.

His own heart heavy, Jamie stepped out of the car, locked up, then made his way down the path to his brother's house. At the front door he momentarily paused then, taking a deep breath, he thumped his fist upon the door.

With his dad now gone, all that was left was Kenny and the Murphys. As far as loyalty went, he didn't owe them anything, and never would.

When Ricky flung open the door, Jamie looked his brother in the eyes, his expression hard. 'I want them destroyed,' he said. 'Kenny, the Murphys, even Shaun if he was involved. They're not going to get away with this.'

Ricky gave a slight nod. 'I had a feeling you would say that.' He pulled the door open wider and motioned for his brother to enter the house.

* * *

Kenny was in the office and after switching on the kettle, he made his way over to the desk, took a seat, then tipped a copious amount of cocaine onto the back of his hand. Greedily, he snorted the coke, shook his head then licking his index finger, he gathered up the remnant powder and rubbed it ferociously across his gums. Within a matter of seconds, his heart began to thump wildly in his chest. As he gripped onto the desk so hard that his knuckles turned a deathly shade of white, a familiar sense of irritation washed over him. Once upon a time the coke had made him feel invincible, had made him believe he had the power to do anything he wanted, even to kill his long-term friend and business partner, but as of late all he felt was paranoia, and anger. He was forever chasing the high when he wanted to feel excitement run through his veins again, wanted to feel like he was on top of the world. He glanced at his watch. Where the fuck were Ricky and Jamie? It had gone eleven, and he'd expected them to turn up at the yard hours ago; Jamie had even said it himself – they had a busy day ahead of them, so why the fuck hadn't they shown up for work?

He snatched up his mobile phone, scrolled through his contact list and immediately pressed dial when he came to Jamie's telephone number. The call rang off. Narrowing his eyes, Kenny redialled a further three times, before scrolling through the list again to locate Ricky's telephone number.

By the time the call had been directed to Ricky's answering machine, Kenny was all but ready to throw the phone at the wall. Rage surged through his veins; the bastards were ghosting him, they had to be; what other logical reason could there be for the pair of them not to answer their phones? It wasn't as though he hadn't provided Jamie with a good night, and to his knowledge he had seemed happy enough when they had parted ways, or at least that had been the impression that Jamie had given him.

'Dad.'

The whine in Shaun's voice was Kenny's undoing and as he leapt to his feet, he clenched his fists, more than prepared to take his anger out on his son, not that he'd ever needed much of an excuse when it came to battering Shaun. 'What?' he spat as he charged around the desk.

Shaun flinched and as he raised one arm protectively over his head in a bid to ward Kenny off, he pointed a shaking finger towards the window. 'It's the Murphys,' he said. 'They've just turned up.'

The colour drained from Kenny's face and pushing his son out of the way, he peered through the barred window. 'What the fuck do they want?' he muttered under his breath. As he made his way back around the desk, the tiny hairs on the back of his neck stood up on end, and his palms became sweaty. The fact the Murphys had turned up at the yard didn't bode well, and despite his little speech about running the show, when it came to the crunch he was nothing but a coward. For the majority of his life, he'd chosen his battles well, and on the odd occasion when he'd found himself in over his head he'd had Terry to back him up. Snatching up the phone, he pressed redial, knowing full well that it was all the more imperative that he had Ricky and Jamie on side.

'Come on, you useless little fuckers,' he growled. 'Answer your poxy phones.'

19

Ricky took a seat on the sofa and kicking his legs out in front of him, he looked up at his brother. 'So how exactly do you want to play this?'

Before Jamie could answer, Ricky's mobile phone began to ring. Snatching it up he groaned out loud. 'It's Kenny, again. He's a persistent fucker I'll give him that.'

'Will you just switch that fucking thing off?' Jamie hissed. 'I told you last night we're done with him and the business.'

Ricky looked up again and seeing the look of anger on Jamie's face, he did as he was told and switched the device off. It wasn't often that he allowed his younger brother to bark orders out at him but under the circumstances he was willing to let the matter slide, at least for the time being anyway.

'Okay, done,' he said, setting the phone back onto the table. 'So, I'll ask again: how do you want to play this?'

Jamie was thoughtful for a moment and as his gaze settled on the television stand, he nodded to where his brother kept the baseball bat. 'We take them out, me and you together bruv, and then we...' He ran his hand through his dark hair and blew out his cheeks all the while shaking his head. 'I can't stop thinking about them; they're up here,' he said, pointing to his temple.

'Who?' Not taking his eyes away from his brother, Ricky tilted his head to one side as he studied him. 'Are you talking about Kenny... the Murphys?'

'No,' Jamie said as he slumped onto the sofa beside his brother. 'Fuck Kenny, I couldn't give two shits about that wanker, the bastard deserves everything he has coming to him.'

'Then who?' Ricky asked, throwing his arms up in confusion.

'The women... They looked...' He sucked in his bottom lip and turned his head away. 'I don't know, like they'd given up on life I suppose. I should have done something, I should have got them out of there, but I didn't. I walked away; I left them in the house with that fucking nutter Kevin Murphy.'

'Hey.' Ricky threw his arm around Jamie's neck and pulled him close. 'This isn't on you, this is on Dad and Kenny; they were the ones who put them there, not you.'

Jamie lifted his eyebrows but kept schtum all the same. It was easy for Ricky to say that he wasn't to blame, but Ricky hadn't been the one who'd walked away. That had been Jamie's choice, and one that he'd regretted ever since.

Releasing his arm from around his brother, Ricky picked up his mobile phone again and switched it back on. 'I'll give Max a call and give him the heads up.'

Jamie nodded. 'Just keep Mum out of it, I don't want her involved, because believe me, this is going to get messy.'

Ricky paused. It wasn't like Jamie to be on a downer. In any normal circumstances he didn't give a flying fuck about anything; he was easy going, a joker, until you upset him of course and then he kicked off in spectacular style. 'Are you sure that you're all right bruv?'

'Yeah of course.' Jamie shrugged.

It was a lie and not a very good one at that. Deciding to give his brother the benefit of the doubt, Ricky brought the phone up to his ear.

As he listened to Ricky fill Max in, Jamie flexed his knuckles, his mind drifting back to the house in Ilford. 'Change of plan,' he said, nudging his brother in the ribs. 'Kenny can wait; it's not like he's going anywhere, is it? We sort the women out first. They should be our priority; we need to make sure that they're safe.'

Ricky nodded, not that he could say he was overly surprised by the sudden turn around and as Jamie had stated, Kenny wasn't going anywhere, he'd get what was coming to him, and if he'd had a hand in their dad's murder then it would be all the more satisfying to see him brought down.

Kevin Murphy let himself into the house in Ilford and was met with pandemonium.

'Where the fuck have you been?' his elder brother Simon roared.

'Where do you think I've fucking been?' Kevin retaliated.

Simon blew out his cheeks, his gaze darting up the staircase. 'Sort them out, will you,' he said, referring to the angry shouts that came from one of the bedrooms. 'I've had it up to here,' he said, pointing to his head. 'All I've had is aggro from the minute I got here last night. Those bitches in there have been banging on the door every five minutes, doing my fucking nut in, and as for them up there' – he jerked his thumb in the direction of the bedrooms – 'the geezer is going fucking garrity. He's paid for her and she won't put out; she's been screaming blue bloody murder for the past ten minutes, I'm surprised the old bill haven't turned up on the doorstep yet.'

Before Kevin could open his mouth to answer, Simon headed for the front door.

'I don't get paid enough to deal with this,' Simon grumbled before slamming the front door firmly closed behind him.

His mouth hanging slightly open, Kevin swore under his breath then tore up the stairs.

* * *

Georgiana's chest heaved, and her heart thumped so loudly that she could hear the rush of blood in her ears. 'Stay away from me,' she warned.

White spittle gathered at the corners of Andrew Ellis's lips. He was a big man, tall and broad, with a thick bull neck. 'I paid for you,' he growled, his large hands darting out to make a grab for her. 'And I'm not leaving until I've had my money's worth.'

A scream escaped from Georgiana's lips, and as she clambered over the bed she reached out for one of the bottles of baby oil kept on the bedside table and launched it towards him. 'I said stay away,' she shouted.

His face turning bright red, Andrew ducked down, the bottle narrowly missing his head. He was so angry that he tore the mattress away from the base and threw it to the floor as though it weighed nothing. 'Get here you little bitch,' he roared.

Terror filled Georgiana and as he advanced towards her, she could barely breathe, so acute was her fear. 'No,' she cried as he yanked her towards him, ripping apart the satin robe she wore in the process and exposing a flash of bare skin.

They were so close that Georgiana could smell his hot rancid breath on her face and as his hands roamed over her body, she snapped her eyes shut tight and grappled behind her for something she could use as a weapon. Her fingers curled around the thick base of the ceramic lamp and using all of her strength she swung her arm around, crashing the heavy object into the side of his head.

A sickening thud filled the air and almost immediately Andrew released his grip. Stumbling backwards, Georgiana fell onto the bedside table, unsettling the bottles of baby oil and an array of condoms. Shock was etched across Andrew's face and as his eyes rolled to the back of his head, his lifeless body slumped forward, pinning Georgiana to the wall.

As panic washed over her, Georgiana cried out in fear and using what little strength she had left, she pushed Andrew's lifeless form away from her. As he dropped to the ground in a crumpled heap, Georgiana's heart began to beat even faster, her gaze automatically going to the lamp and in particular the smear of bright red blood still visible on the base.

In the commotion she hadn't heard the banging on the bedroom door and as the door crashed inwards, she jumped in fright.

As he took in the scene before him, Kevin's mouth dropped open for the second time in as many minutes. 'What the fuck have you done?' he yelled.

Georgiana's body trembled, her gaze dropping to the man on the floor. He was still, she noted, too still.

Charging into the bedroom, Kevin nudged Andrew's body with the toe of his boot. There was no response, not that he'd entirely expected one, it was more than clear to see that the punter was brown bread – the large dent in the side of his head, not forgetting the vast amount of claret that seeped into the carpet where he lay was a dead giveaway to that fact.

'You stupid bitch,' Kevin hissed. 'You've killed him.' Grabbing Georgiana roughly by the wrist, he pulled her out of the room then proceeded to drag her down the stairs. 'You're done for now,' he warned, his voice holding a hint of excitement. 'They'll tear you limb from fucking limb over this.'

Fear etched its way down Georgiana's spine, and as she lost her footing, she fell heavily, the small of her back taking the impact. 'No,' she cried out in pain. 'Let go of me.'

Kevin ignored her protests and as he continued to drag her down the last few remaining steps, he tightened his grip, his fingernails digging into her flesh. 'Maybe I should do everyone a favour and just kill you now,' he said matter-of-factly. 'Bury you in the back garden, or maybe feed you to the dogs.'

His words were enough to send Georgiana into a wild panic, and as her fingers reached inside her bra she slipped out the steel knife, flicked it open, then without hesitation plunged it deep into Kevin's back.

* * *

Despite the beads of cold sweat that broke out across Kenny's forehead, outwardly he appeared composed and in control which was a lot more than could be said for how he was really feeling. Not only were his palms clammy but his heart was beating so hard and fast that he wouldn't be surprised if he keeled over at any given moment from a heart attack.

'What do you lot want?' he said, waving his hand dismissively as Michael, along with his brothers and sister, entered the office.

Michael looked around him, a grin etched across his face. 'What do you think we want?' he answered as he pulled out a chair and sat down.

Kenny narrowed his eyes, not for the first time wishing that he'd never brought the Murphys on board. It wasn't as though he or Terry had even needed them, not really. After all, between them they had three sons to do the donkey work. 'I don't know.'

Careful not to let them see his fear, he wiped his clammy hands down the length of his trousers then reached out for his cigarette packet, took out a cigarette and brought it up to his lips. 'I'm not a fucking mind reader, am I?'

Michael laughed. 'Funny you should say that,' he said, the laughter dying as quickly as it had started. 'Because neither are we, and I don't recall you asking for my permission to bring someone in on our business deal.'

Lounging back in the chair, Kenny lit the cigarette and drew the smoke deep into his lungs all the while studying Michael with contempt. As far as he was concerned, the Murphys were all the same: thugs and as thick as two short planks. They didn't have the intelligence to run a business let alone believe they were in the position to shout the odds.

'You're forgetting something,' Kenny retorted. 'Without me, there would be no business. It was my idea, and it was only because of me,' he said, stabbing his thumb into his chest, 'that you were even brought in on the deal.'

A nerve at the side of Michael's jaw pulsed. 'And you think that gives you the right to bring in Terry's sons?'

There was an edge to his voice, one which Kenny immediately picked up on. More than aware that he was outnumbered, Kenny shot a glance towards Shaun, who was as much use as a chocolate teapot. Just one wrong look in his direction and he would fall apart, much to Kenny's disgust.

'What do you expect me to do?' he asked, spreading open his arms. 'I've got Terry's boys chewing my fucking ear off. They want their due, they want their old man's stake in the business.' Of course, it was a lie, but Kenny being Kenny would say and do anything if he thought it would get the Murphys off his back, and seeing as Ricky and Jamie were ignoring his calls, then it was exactly what they deserved. Let them deal with the nutcases;

they'd soon come running back to him with their tails between their legs.

Michael smirked and not taking his eyes away from Kenny, he gestured towards his sister. 'Looks like Terry's boys are gonna have some competition then.'

Sinking further into his seat, Kenny frowned. 'What are you talking about?' he asked as he looked across to Bianca.

'I'm pregnant.' Bianca's eyes lit up, and full of self-importance she stepped closer to the desk, a smug grin spread across her face. 'And that means as the mother of Terry's child I'm entitled to Terry's share of the profits, or to be more precise, my baby is entitled to everything Terry owned. He is the father after all, and he would have wanted our baby to be taken care of.'

Kenny's mouth dropped open and as he looked from Bianca to Michael, for the first time in his life, he could honestly say that he was speechless. In fact he was so dumbfounded that he could barely think straight let alone string a coherent sentence together.

'So you see,' Michael said, leaning forward, his voice beginning to rise. 'When it comes down to it, we own the majority of the business, and therefore that means you need our permission to even take a shit, let alone bring anyone else in on the deal.'

'No.' The blood drained from Kenny's face. No, it couldn't be true; Terry would never have been so careless as to knock up Bianca? Despite his womanising ways, Terry had loved Tracey. Not only that but he'd been adamant that he didn't want Ricky or Jamie to ever find out that he'd cheated on their mother, that he'd shag anything that moved. 'She's lying,' he said, screwing up his face. 'That baby could be just about anyone's.'

'Are you calling my sister a slapper?' Jumping up from the seat, Michael lunged forward and grasped the front of Kenny's shirt in his fist.

There and then Kenny's stomach dropped. 'No of course I'm

not,' he said, the words rushing out of his mouth so fast that he could barely catch his breath. 'I was just saying... maybe she made a mistake and it's not Terry's kid.'

'Well that's exactly what it sounded like,' Michael roared, pulling back his free arm and curling his fingers into a tight ball. 'And no one,' he snarled, 'calls my sister a tart and gets away with it and that includes fucking you.'

Kenny slammed his eyes shut tight, his body becoming tense as he awaited the assault, and from what he knew of Michael Murphy, it was bound to be savage.

'Wait.'

Slowly opening one eye, Kenny looked in the direction of his son's voice, his heart sinking that little bit further. Shaun was hardly man enough to stand up to the Murphys; he was the human equivalent of a snivelling mouse and was a constant embarrassment to his father.

'You're angry,' Shaun said, 'and I get it.' He glanced towards his father, the fear in his voice clearly audible. 'But' – he swallowed deeply then nodded in Bianca's direction – 'this isn't about us. What I mean is,' he said, shaking his head and beginning again. 'This is nothing to do with my dad, this is between you and Terry's sons; it's Ricky and Jamie who stand in your way. They have the claim to Terry's share of the business, not my dad.'

Kenny's eyes ever so slightly widened and as Michael dropped his arm to his side, for the first time in his life Kenny actually felt something other than anger and disappointment towards his only child – he felt pride.

'He's right,' Bianca said begrudgingly to her brother. 'You said yourself that Terry's boys stand in the way of me collecting my due, what I'm owed.'

Throwing Kenny away from him, Michael slumped back in the chair and rubbed his fingers over his jaw, thinking the situa-

242

KERRY KAYA

tion through. After an age, he flicked his chin in Kenny's direction. 'Get them here,' he said.

Kenny glanced wearily down at his mobile phone.

'I said get them here,' Michael roared.

'Okay, okay.' Holding up his hands, Kenny picked up his phone and as he scrolled through the contact list, he silently prayed that this time Ricky or Jamie would answer the call.

* * *

'You bitch.' Kevin Murphy yelped in pain. Releasing his grip on Georgiana, he reached out to touch his back. 'What the fuck have you done?' he screamed as his fingertips came into contact with sticky blood. Twisting his head to look behind him, he dabbed once again at the wound. 'What the fuck?' he cried as he brought his hand back around and stared down at the blood coating his fingers. 'You stabbed me.'

Georgiana saw this as her chance to escape his clutches and scrambling to her feet, she attempted to run past him, the flick knife slipping from her fingers as she grappled to unlock the front door.

'You fucking knifed me,' Kevin shouted again. Reaching out, he grasped a handful of Georgiana's hair in his fist and pulled her back towards him with so much force that the bones in her neck were in danger of snapping. 'You're gonna pay for this,' he spat into her face.

Oblivious to the blood that dripped onto the linoleum flooring, Kevin flung open the front door, scooped down to pick up the blade, then proceeded to drag Georgiana out of the house.

Tears streamed down Georgiana's face and as she bundled into a car, she continued to fight Kevin off. It was only the deep, ferocious growls that came from the two Rottweilers on the backseat that made her freeze with fear, Kevin's earlier threat that he would feed her to the dogs still fresh in her mind. And as the car sped away from the kerb, she resigned herself to the fact that her life was coming to an end, that she would never get to go home, that she would never see her mum again, and that she would never hear her younger siblings' laughter as they told their corny jokes. Her heart breaking that little bit more, she turned her head to look out of the window and as they drove through the streets the tears she silently wept blinded her vision.

20

Happier now that they were proactively doing something to amend their father's wrongdoing, Jamie allowed himself to relax as he gave Max directions to the house in Ilford. Ten minutes later they climbed out of the car, crossed over the road and came to stand in front of the house.

'Is this it?' Ricky commented as he surveyed the property.

'Yeah,' Jamie laughed. 'You would never think it's a brothel would you?'

Shaking his head, Ricky was actually at a loss for words. He could have passed the house a hundred times and would never have guessed the dark secrets hidden behind the front door. No wonder his dad and Kenny had been able to go undetected for so long.

All it took was two swift kicks to the front door before the rusting hinges gave way and the door swung inwards, crashing against the wall with a loud clatter.

Max shook his head; this wasn't like Terry. From what he'd seen of the yard it was obvious that he had taken security seriously; even the windows of the office and house had bars up at them, so why had he become so lax when it came to the property where he kept the women? Had he really believed that both his and Murphys' reputation was enough to keep intruders out?

'This way,' Jamie said as he made to step inside the house.

'Wait.' Max put out his arm, bringing Jamie to a halt. 'I thought you said that Murphy owns dogs.'

'Yeah he does.' Jamie screwed up his face, his wary gaze drifting back down the hallway. 'Rottweilers, two of them, big fuckers they are as well.'

'Well they're not here now,' Ricky said as he made to push past his brother and enter the eerily quiet house. 'And from the look of it, some nasty shit has gone down.' He nodded towards a large dark red stain on the linoleum flooring.

'Is that blood?' Jamie asked, his voice incredulous as he bent down to get a closer look.

'Looks like it,' Max said from behind them as he closed the front door.

Tearing his eyes away from the blood, Jamie straightened up and glanced up the staircase before looking back down the hallway. 'What the fuck happened here?' he asked. 'Do you reckon the dogs could have turned on the mad fucker?'

'Fuck knows,' Max answered. 'Just watch where you step, okay.' He gestured to where droplets of blood dotted the hallway. 'The last thing you want to do is leave any footprints behind.'

Careful of where they trod, they made their way inside the house.

'This is where they keep the women.' Jamie gave the door handle a hard tug, not that he'd been under any illusions that the door would miraculously open. From what he'd been able to gather, the door was kept locked at all times and only Kevin Murphy had the key. Taking a step back, he lifted his foot off the floor then kicked out at the lock.

'I'm going to check upstairs,' Max said, heading for the staircase.

As the door holding the women captive swung open, Ricky glanced inside. 'Yeah, I'll come with you,' he said, not wanting to venture any further into the room.

As he watched them go, Jamie shrugged, then, stepping forward, he offered the women inside the dingy room a warm smile. 'It's okay,' he said. 'We're not here to hurt you.'

'Jamie.'

Hearing the urgency in his brother's voice, Jamie gave the women one final smile before making his way back out into the hallway.

'What?' he called up the stairs.

'Get up here,' Ricky called back. 'You need to see this.'

* * *

With her fingers laced together and her elbows resting on the kitchen table, Tracey was deep in thought. Spread out in front of her was the glossy brochure offering memorial headstones. She'd wanted her Terry to have the best, she'd wanted him to be remembered and more than anything, even in death, she had wanted everyone to know just how loved her husband had been and still was.

Closing the brochure, she took a sip of her tea. It was hard to imagine that just two months earlier she had been so consumed by grief that she had fully believed that she wouldn't be able to carry on living without Terry by her side. Even the house didn't feel so empty any more. Of course, it was still quiet, but it was a comfortable silence, one that she was more than happy to be consumed by. She had even played her favourite David Bowie CD earlier that day and for a few short moments she had almost forgotten that her life had irreversibly changed forever.

Her thoughts wandered to Kenny. She'd known her husband's best friend for years and had always liked him. In her mind it was inconceivable that Kenny could have been involved in Terry's murder. Kenny had loved Terry like a brother and had wept like a baby at the funeral. Those weren't the actions of a man responsible for the death of his best friend... were they?

Determined to get to the truth of the matter, Tracey stood up and collected her mobile phone. She wanted to hear it from Kenny's own mouth that he hadn't been involved in the murder, for her own peace of mind she needed to know that he could never have carried out something so abhorrent. Heading towards the front door, she paused in front of the key rack, shrugged on her jacket, then snatching Terry's car keys off the hook, she left the house.

* * *

Entering the very same bedroom that he and Georgiana had hidden out in the night before, Jamie took one look at the body laid out on the floor and instantly rocked back on his heels. 'What the fuck?' he muttered.

'Yeah, what the fuck exactly?' Ricky said, nodding down at the man's very obvious erection that poked out from the waist band of his jogging bottoms.

'The stiff's got a stiffy.' Jamie laughed.

Narrowing his eyes, Max looked up. 'Sort it fucking out,' he ordered.

'What do you mean sort it out?' The smile slid from Jamie's face as his gaze went from Max to the corpse laid out on the floor. 'I'm not wanking him off.'

Screwing up his face, Ricky gave his brother a look of disgust. 'Are you for real?' he asked. 'He meant cover the fucking thing over.'

As the penny finally dropped, relief was clearly evident in Jamie's expression. 'Yeah I knew that,' he lied, 'I was only having a laugh.' Stepping towards the bed, he tentatively reached down to lift up the edge of the bed sheet then hastily threw it over the body.

'Right, now that I don't have to look at that monstrosity any more,' Max said. 'What have we got here?'

Jamie glanced around the dingy room. Not only did it stink of mould, but there was also a sour stench that permeated the room. Even the bed clothes looked grimy, the once white sheets now grey as though they had never been washed, something he hadn't noticed on his previous visit. 'Well, as you already know, it's a whore house,' he volunteered, his gaze going from the bedside table, to the surrounding floor that was littered with condoms and several bottles of baby oil.

Max rolled his eyes, fast on his way to losing his patience. 'Who's the stiff?'

Bending down, Ricky rifled through the man's pockets. Plucking out a wallet, he flipped it open and looked through the contents. 'Andrew Ellis. He was a bouncer from the look of things,' he said, holding up a security badge.

'I love a bouncer, me,' Jamie said with a laugh.

Ricky snapped his head round to look at his brother. 'Seriously, I'm starting to worry about you.'

'What?' Screwing up his face, Jamie's expression was one of concentration. 'Nah,' he said as he finally cottoned on to what his brother meant. 'What I mean is I love smashing them in.'

'Yeah like I said,' Ricky said with a shake of his head, the hint of smile creasing his face, 'I'm starting to worry about you.'

Max couldn't help but laugh and as he shook his own head at Jamie's obvious embarrassment, he turned back to survey the room. The name Andrew Ellis meant nothing to him, not that he'd actually expected it would; he didn't purposely socialise with men who used women as though they were nothing more than pieces of meat.

'Here, hold up a minute.'

Both Max and Ricky turned to look at Jamie, their foreheads furrowed.

Nodding towards the ceramic lamp on the floor that held traces of what looked suspiciously like blood, Jamie's face paled. The blood in the hallway hadn't trailed up the staircase. They had to be two separate incidents. 'I can't remember seeing her downstairs.'

'Who?' Max and Ricky asked in unison.

'The woman.' Racing out of the room, Jamie ran down the stairs, taking them two at a time.

'What woman?' they called after him.

Jamie ignored the question and as he charged into the room where the women were being housed, he looked frantically around him. 'Where is she?' he shouted.

The women looked up at him fearfully.

'Where is she?' Jamie repeated. 'She's this high.' He gestured towards his shoulder, then reached up to touch his hair. No, he shook his head then made a beeline for a blonde woman. 'This high,' he said again. 'And this colour hair.' He reached out to touch the blonde strands.

Recognition filtered across their faces and as they all spoke at once, Jamie held up his hands to quieten them down. 'You,' he said, pointing to the woman nearest to him.

'She go,' the woman said in broken English. 'He take.' She motioned with her hands towards the door.

'You mean someone took her?' Jamie growled.

The woman nodded, causing Jamie's heart to sink down to his boots.

'The bastard,' he shouted.

'What's going on?' Ricky asked.

Turning to look at his brother, Jamie rubbed the palm of his hand over his face. 'They took her,' he said as he pushed past Ricky.

'Who?' Confused, Ricky screwed up his face. 'What are you talking about bruv? Took who?'

Jamie made his way back out to the hallway and seeing Murphy's blood streaked across the linoleum floor, he grasped onto the banister rail and lowered his head. 'Jesus Christ,' he cried out. 'It was her blood, she was bleeding out; Murphy's fucking hurt her.'

'Jamie,' Ricky said, pulling his brother around to face him. 'What the fuck is going on?'

'There was this woman.' Swallowing deeply, Jamie looked away, shame engulfing him. 'They made me take her upstairs.'

Ricky narrowed his eyes and took a step away from his brother. 'What the fuck are you trying to say bruv?' he asked. 'Please don't tell me you actually... you know,' he gestured towards his brother's nether regions. 'You didn't...'

'No,' Jamie shouted. 'Of course I fucking didn't. I didn't touch her but I had to let them think I did. I couldn't blow the plan wide apart, could I? She was so tiny that I thought she'd be easier to manage, but it turned out she wasn't, she was a proper little fire cracker,' he said, giving a half laugh. 'But her eye.' He reached up to touch the skin underneath his own eye. 'It was bruised. Someone had really whacked her one, and now' – he turned back to look at the blood – 'she's gone, and they reckon he took her, that Kevin, the fucking nutcase, Murphy, took her somewhere.'

Looking down at the blood, Ricky took a sharp intake of breath. 'Fuck me,' he said, looking back up at his brother.

'I've got to get out of here.' Pushing his brother aside, Jamie headed for the front door. 'I have to find her.'

'Where are you going?' Ricky called after him.

'The yard,' Jamie growled over his shoulder. 'Where else would that nutter have taken her?'

Throwing up his arms, Ricky watched his brother go. Jamie in the mood he was in didn't bode well for Kevin Murphy, and as big of a nutcase as Kevin was made out to be, Ricky had a feeling that he may well have just met his match when it came to Jamie.

'Max,' he shouted out as he made to follow after his brother, 'we've got a problem. A very big fucking problem to be precise.'

Max bounded down the stairs, brandishing his mobile phone in his hand. 'Yeah, well whatever it is believe me it pales into comparison to this. Your mum has just been on the blower, she's on her way to the yard to have it out with Kenny.'

'For fuck's sake,' Ricky roared as he raced out of the house. 'This is all we fucking well need.'

21

Tracey climbed out of the car, then after locking up, she crossed over the road and walked through the open gates towards the office. Parked on the forecourt were two cars that she didn't recognise, and as she passed them by she gave the vehicles a quizzical glance. Perhaps they belonged to Kenny or Shaun? She wondered then about Kenny's wife, Sandra. She'd not seen her in years. They had been close once, or at least Tracey had thought they were until all of a sudden her calls to Sandra had gone unanswered and whenever she had popped over to Kenny's house there was never anyone home. Kenny had claimed that Sandra suffered with her nerves, that she'd become a recluse of sorts, and that she didn't feel up to socialising. Whether this was true or not Tracey had no idea, but maybe Sandra had simply decided that their friendship had come to an end. It happened, she supposed, and other than the fact their husbands were friends and that their sons were of a similar age, she and Sandra hadn't really shared that much in common.

Although she couldn't quite make out what was being said, as Tracey neared the office she could hear the sound of muffled voices coming from inside. Smoothing down her hair, she placed her hand on the door handle. Maybe she should have called ahead and given Kenny the heads up that she was on her way over?

Bugger it, she decided. Legally, half the business belonged to her anyway and seeing as she was Terry's widow, she shouldn't need to book an appointment to gain access to what was technically hers now. Without giving the matter a second thought, she pulled down on the door handle and pushed open the door.

* * *

'If that nutter touches a hair on Mum's head I'll fucking kill him,' Jamie raged from the back seat of Max's car.

'You don't know for certain that Murphy even headed for the yard,' Max said in a bid to calm both Ricky and Jamie down.

'No, but it still leaves Kenny doesn't it?' Ricky argued. 'And if he was involved in my dad's murder then I don't think it will go down too well if my mum barges in there and starts accusing him of shit.'

Max nodded. Ricky had a point. If he knew Kenny as well as he thought he did then he knew for a fact that he would think nothing of taking his anger out on a vulnerable woman, because let's face it, he'd only ever picked on people he believed were weaker than himself.

'Come on,' he shouted, thumping his fist on the horn when the car in front stalled at the traffic lights. 'Bollocks to this,' Max said as he hastily checked for incoming traffic then pulled the car out onto the opposite side of the road, pressed his foot down on the accelerator, and overtook the stationary vehicle.

Ricky glanced at his watch. 'We should be there in roughly

fifteen minutes,' he stated, turning in the seat to look at his brother.

As he chewed on his thumb nail, worry edged its way down Jamie's spine. What if fifteen minutes was too late? What if in the time it took them to get to the yard, Kenny or Kevin Murphy had already attacked their mum? What if she was already dead or was laid out on the cold floor taking her last breaths? 'I should have taken the no-good cunts out while I had the chance,' he spat. 'I should have done them over last night, stabbed the fuckers to death; it's not like I didn't have the opportunity, is it? I could have been in and out of the house in minutes and no one would have been any the wiser.' He paused for breath, the fear in his voice almost tangible. 'You know what Mum's like, she'll go in there all guns blazing and it won't take much for Kenny or Murphy to crack her one; they're more than capable of it, look at what they did to that little blonde bird.'

Both Ricky and Max shared a knowing glance. As much as they didn't want him to be, they knew Jamie was right. Kenny and Kevin Murphy had no morals when it came to women and they wouldn't think twice about lashing out. And as Jamie had stated, they were more than competent when it came to causing some considerable harm.

'Make that ten minutes,' Max said as he made a sharp left turn into a side street. 'I know a short cut.'

* * *

Stepping inside the office, Tracey instantly froze. The Murphys were the last people she'd expected to see at the yard, and as they all turned to look at her, an uncomfortable silence fell across the office.

'Am I interrupting something?' she asked.

Kenny waved his hand in the air. 'No of course not,' he lied.

'And you must be...' Michael slowly looked her up and down, the tip of his tongue snaking out and licking the length of his bottom lip. 'Tracey, am I right?'

'Yes.' Tearing her stare away from Kenny, Tracey pulled herself up to her full height. Even in her heels she would still be considered petite and as the occupants of the office towered above her, she lifted her chin in the air, hoping that the action would give her some much-needed added height, or at the very least that she would come across as a lot more confident than she actually felt. 'I'm Terry's wife.'

One or two sniggers went up and as Tracey looked around her she noted the smirk across Bianca Murphy's face, the same smirk she had seen when they had met previously in the pub.

'We were just talking about Terry,' Michael continued, throwing Tracey a wink. 'Nice fella.'

Tracey nodded. 'He was.' Although as much as she hated to admit it, Terry hadn't been quite as nice as she'd always believed him to be, not that she'd thought he was an angel to begin with.

Lighting a cigarette, Michael continued to watch her. His hard stare was enough to make the tiny hairs on the back of Tracey's neck stand up on end.

'Maybe I should leave you to it,' she said, backing away towards the door. 'I can always come back another time, when you're less busy.'

'No, stay.' Rising out of the chair, Michael Murphy flashed a wide smile, reminding Tracey of a predatory shark. 'We were just waiting for your boys to get here.'

Tracey's heart began to beat faster and as she turned back to look at Kenny she noted that he couldn't look her in the eyes. And if the damp patches which stained his shirt were anything to go by, then she had a pretty good idea that the Murphys were the source of his concern.

'Why don't you give them a call?' Michael continued. 'And tell them to meet you here.'

Swallowing deeply, Tracey gave a slight shake of her head. 'I thought you just said my boys were already on their way.'

'Slip of the tongue.' Michael grinned. 'Go on,' he coaxed. 'Give them a call. In fact,' he said, spreading open his arms, 'we have some news of our own, and believe me, they're not going to want to miss this.'

At her brother's words, Bianca laughed out loud. Snapping her head round to look in Bianca's direction, Tracey bristled. She'd just about had enough of the smug bitch, and as she looked Bianca up and down, she took in the patchy fake tan that looked more orange than brown, the thick layer of foundation that was far too dark for her skin tone and then the pale pink lips outlined in a darker shade of pink. She reminded Tracey of a nineties throwback, only back then they'd had more class and would never have been seen dead leaving the house resembling a clown. 'What's so funny?' she asked.

And there it was again, that smug smirk; it was enough to make Tracey want to pull back her fist and fell the younger woman to the floor. It was then that a memory sprang to her mind, and it suddenly dawned on her where she had seen Bianca before. 'You were at my Terry's funeral,' she stated.

'Of course I was.' Bianca rolled her eyes, and as her hand caressed her abdomen, Tracey's gaze followed the action. 'Terry would have wanted me to be there.'

Tracey frowned. Why on earth would Terry have wanted Bianca Murphy to be at his funeral? She opened her mouth to answer when Kenny interrupted her.

'Tracey,' he warned, his nervous gaze flicking towards Bianca.

'Just do as he asks and give the boys a ring. The quicker we get this over and done with the better.'

Tearing her gaze away from Bianca to look at Kenny, Tracey crossed her arms over her chest. She was in half a mind to tell them exactly what she thought of them, that they were despicable, that she thought they were nothing but scum, and the fact they bought and sold women only served to prove her point.

'Tracey,' Kenny shouted. 'Do as I fucking say and stop pissing about. Get on the blower and get the boys here, now.'

Tracey's mouth dropped open. In all the years she'd known him, Kenny had never once raised his voice to her, let alone actually swore at her and as she looked around at the occupants of the office the first prickle of fear coursed through her veins. Could it be true? Could they really be responsible for the murder of her husband? Feeling the blood drain from her face, Tracey took a cautious step backwards. 'Maybe it would be best if I leave,' she said, looking over her shoulder and gauging the distance between herself and the closed door.

'Nah.' Michael shook his head and as he leapt out of his seat and stalked forward, his tall, wiry body was suddenly taut. 'That's not gonna happen sweetheart.'

The coldness in Michael's voice chilled Tracey to the very core and as terror shot down the length of her spine, she spun round and ran for the door. As always, her sons were her one and only priority; she had to warn them to stay away from the office, and more importantly, to stay away from both Kenny and the Murphys.

Before her hand could reach out for the door handle, Michael yanked her back. 'Like I just said,' he hissed in her ear. 'You ain't going anywhere.'

From the corner of her eye she watched as Kenny made to push himself up from the chair, and a sliver of hope filled her.

Surely Kenny wouldn't allow her to come to any harm, would he?

One glance from Michael was all it took for Kenny to lower himself back down onto the seat, and as Shaun made to push himself away from the wall, the glare from his father was enough to stop him dead in his tracks.

The fact Kenny was clearly afraid made Tracey's heart beat that little bit faster. 'Don't touch me,' she warned as she fought to pull her arm free from Michael's grasp.

Michael tightened his grip and as he pulled Tracey further into the office, she swung back her arm and delivered a stinging slap to the side of his face. The impact was loud, and for the briefest of moments a stunned silence filled the room.

Her hand still smarting, the enormity of what Tracey had just done hung heavy in the air. She'd just slapped Michael Murphy, who along with his brother Kevin, was considered to be a bona fide nutcase. Not wanting to wait around for the backlash of her actions, she began to back away, her heart in her mouth.

'You bitch.' Bianca's face contorted with rage and, pushing past her eldest brother, she grasped a handful of Tracey's hair in her fist and pushed her face so close to Tracey's that Tracey could smell the stale stench of tobacco on Bianca's breath. 'You really think you're something special, don't you?' Bianca spat.

Clawing at Bianca's fingers, Tracey wrenched her hair free from the younger woman's grasp, her chest heaving.

'Well believe me, you're not,' Bianca goaded. 'He didn't love you,' she sneered, 'he loved me.'

Tracey's eyes widened and breathing heavily, she stared at Bianca, unable to get her head around what she was saying.

'He was going to leave you.' She smirked. 'He was going to leave you for me, for me and our baby.' Her hand drifted down to her tummy again; it was a calculated gesture and as Tracey stared at Bianca, she pushed her stomach out even further, emphasising the slight curve of her abdomen. 'I'm pregnant' – she grinned nastily – 'with Terry's child.'

'No,' Tracey gasped, stumbling backwards. 'No, you're lying.' She snapped her head towards Kenny. 'Tell me it's not true,' she begged of him. 'Terry would never have...' Her voice drifted off and she slammed her hand over her mouth in a bid to quash the sickness that washed over her.

Looking up, Kenny ever so slightly lifted his eyebrows. It was all the confirmation Tracey needed.

Tracey shook her head. After everything she had learnt about Terry, was she really surprised that he hadn't been faithful to her? As much as it pained her to actually admit it, the answer was no. Of course she felt hurt, why wouldn't she? After all, she'd given him everything there was of herself to give: she'd given birth to his sons, she made their house a home, she had devoted herself to him, and in all the years they had spent together she had never looked twice at another man. She had even put up with his mother, including the offhand, snide comments Patricia would often make about her capabilities as a wife and mother, and for what? For Terry to deceive her, for Terry to make a fool of her, for Terry to have taken a tramp to bed and impregnate her.

Revelling in Tracey's obvious shock, Bianca stalked forwards, her lips curling down in disgust. 'I'm going to take you for every penny you've got,' she gloated. 'You can say goodbye to your house, the cars, even this place,' she said, gesturing around her, 'because it's all going to belong to me and my baby, it's what my Terry would have wanted, for us to be looked after. We were his future.'

Too stunned to speak, Tracey's mouth dropped open. She thought back to how Terry's behaviour had changed in the months leading up to his death. Everything made sense now; no wonder he was never home, no wonder he hadn't wanted to touch her intimately, he'd already had his fill with the tramp standing in front of her. And as for Bianca getting her hands on her home, well over her dead body would Tracey ever allow that to happen.

'I was his wife,' she said, indicating to the heavy gold band on her wedding finger. 'And whether you like it or not darling,' she spat, 'that gives me rights.' She looked around her, disgust etched across her face. As for the so-called business, she couldn't care less if it burned down to the ground, she wanted no part of it. 'And let me tell you something else for nothing,' she continued. 'If Terry were alive then you would be welcome to him, he'd be all fucking yours. After what he's done I despise the man, and if you honestly think he would have stood by you, that you would have walked off into the sunset hand in hand, then you're deluded. In fact I pity you, and even more than that I pity that child you're carrying.'

Bianca's face fell. She'd been expecting a backlash of sorts and had fully expected Terry's wife to break down and cry – the twisted part of her had actually hoped for it. What she hadn't counted on was for Tracey to tell her she was welcome to Terry, nor had she expected Tracey to tell her that she felt nothing but pity for both her and her unborn child. Her cheeks flaming bright red, Bianca opened her mouth to answer when the office door burst open and her brother Kevin stumbled inside, dragging a kicking and screaming woman behind him.

'I'm bleeding,' he choked out, his face drained of all colour as he collapsed against the wall. 'She fucking stabbed me.'

22

Tracey took one look at the woman Kevin had dragged into the office and her heart immediately went out to her. Not only was she young and roughly the same age as her sons but she also looked terrified, so scared in fact that she physically shook.

'What the hell is going on here?' Tracey demanded as she shrugged off her jacket and draped it around the woman's bare shoulders. Even if what Kevin Murphy had said was true, Tracey knew instinctively that it would have been warranted, that Kevin would have deserved everything he'd had coming to him and more. They were animals, the whole bloody lot of them; was it any wonder the poor woman had lashed out?

Grateful for the jacket Tracey had placed across her shoulders, the young woman pulled the thin material around her slight frame and shivered. Her feet were almost blue with cold, and her eyes were red rimmed and puffy from the tears she'd shed.

Michael stalked forward, his expression murderous. 'That fucking bitch stabbed my brother,' he roared, spraying spittle in the air. 'And believe me, she's gonna fucking pay for it; she's finished.'

Tracey's pulse quickened and as she pushed the young girl behind her out of Michael's reach, she was more than aware of the fact that both she and the woman were in grave danger. 'I won't let you hurt her,' she stated, her voice surprisingly calm as she glanced towards Kenny and implored him with her eyes to help her out. 'You'll have to go through me first.'

Michael gave a chilling laugh and turning his head, he looked across at his brother. 'Are you okay?' he asked.

Kevin grunted out a weak reply, and as he gingerly eased his body to the floor, a streak of blood stained the wall he'd been leaning against.

Michael narrowed his eyes. Kevin was no easy target. At the best of times he could be a paranoid fucker, and he certainly wouldn't have sat around waiting for an attack on himself. Tearing his eyes away from the blood, he jerked his head towards his sister. 'Sort him out,' he ordered.

Bianca did as she was told and dropping to her hands and knees, she helped her brother to remove his jacket so that she could inspect the damage. A moment later she sank back on her haunches, looked up at her eldest brother and gave a slight shake of her head. The wound wasn't only deep, but it was still oozing blood, far too much blood for Bianca's liking, not only that but Kevin was subdued, his skin ashen and clammy, and his breathing had become laboured.

Michael screwed up his face, the anger he felt enough to make him want to pull back his fist and punch the women before him senseless. 'You fucking bitches,' he roared charging forward.

* * *

As they hit Dagenham, Max pushed his foot down on the accelerator. They were just minutes away from the yard and the only question at the forefront of their minds was whether or not they had arrived too late, not that any one of them wanted to utter the question out loud.

Just a few moments later, he brought the car to a screeching halt and before he had even switched off the ignition, Ricky and Jamie had flung open the car doors and jumped out.

'Wait,' he called after them. He didn't receive a reply, neither did they slow down, not that he'd actually expected them to. After all, their mother's life was in danger, and he knew himself that if it had been his mother he would have moved heaven and earth to keep her safe from harm.

Without even bothering to lock the car, Max cursed under his breath then charged after them. He was halfway across the yard when he heard the blood curdling scream that came from inside the office and as Ricky and Jamie bounded through the door he didn't need a genius to tell him that World War Three was about to erupt.

* * *

Tracey had never screamed so loudly in all her life, and as Michael Murphy's fist connected with the side of her face, an explosion of pain hit her. Dropping to the floor, she was so dazed that she could actually see stars dancing before her eyes.

She was barely aware of the tiny woman beside her trying to help her up, when her sons burst into the office, their large bodies dominating the already cramped space.

Within a matter of seconds they had begun an immediate assault on Michael Murphy, their heavy fists and boots punching and kicking out, while Bianca and her remaining brothers pummelled at their backs, their combined efforts to drag Ricky and Jamie away proving to be fruitless.

'That's my mum,' Jamie screamed as he repeatedly kicked out at the small of Michael's back.

'You no-good bastard,' Ricky added as he too kicked and beat the living daylights out of the eldest of the Murphy siblings.

Pushing herself into a sitting position, Tracey clamped her hand to her jaw and as Max entered the office she locked eyes with him. Across his face she watched a series of different emotions play out and when he turned his gaze on Kenny his expression became thunderous.

Kenny's face paled and before he could attempt to scramble away from the desk, Max was upon him, one meaty fist clenched into a tight ball, the other clasping the front of Kenny's shirt. 'It was you,' Max growled. 'You murdered Terry.'

A low laugh escaped from Kenny's lips and blinking rapidly, he shook his head, incredulous. 'You know I always thought that you had a bit of savvy,' he sniggered. 'Out of the three of us, you were the one who was more astute; you know yourself you could be a shrewd fucker when you had to be, but look at you,' he goaded, 'the big honourable Max, wanting revenge for his mate's murder, a mate who didn't give two flying fucks about him.'

Max narrowed his eyes and cocking his head to one side, he tightened his grip.

'I'm surprised you never worked it out for yourself,' Kenny continued. 'You must have wondered who it was that grassed you up all those years ago.' He laughed.

'What the fuck are you saying?' Max growled.

Kenny smirked, amusement lighting up his eyes.

'Answer the fucking question.' His grip tightening, Max yanked Kenny closer to him. 'Who grassed me up?'

'It was Terry.' Kenny chuckled. 'He knew you were done for, knew the filth would be all over you like a fucking rash and he was determined not to be dragged down the slippery slope with you.'

Shock edged its way down Max's spine. 'You're lying,' he spat.

Kenny laughed even harder. 'Am I?' 'Think about it, why was your name the only one ever put forward? Everyone knew that you and Terry were joined at the fucking hip and you and him made that pact.' He gave an infuriating grin, the type of grin that made Max want to repeatedly smash his fist into Kenny's face. 'If one of you were nabbed, you'd keep the other's name out of the picture. Terry was counting on your loyalty to him; at the end of the day, it was the only thing that kept him out of stir, and all along, while you were sweating your bollocks off in a concrete box, he was on the outside laughing at you. He hung you out to dry pal and you didn't have a fucking clue.'

Shaking his head, Max pulled back his fist. As much as he didn't want to admit it, it was true he and Terry had made a vow; the question was: how had Kenny known anything about it? Had Terry confided in him, had he told Kenny about his involvement in the murder and more to the point, could there be some truth to the revelation? Would Terry, his best mate, have really grassed him up?

'You put him up to it; there's no way Terry would have betrayed me. You got into here,' he said, stabbing a stiff finger into the side of Kenny's head. 'You always were a slimy fucker, from day one I knew that you couldn't be trusted.'

The smirk Kenny gave was enough for Max to see red. He pulled Kenny over the desk and Kenny landed on the floor with a loud thump. 'Admit it,' he roared as he grasped Kenny tightly by the jaw, his fingertips digging into the soft flesh. 'Just tell the fucking truth for once in your sorry life... you killed Terry!'

'It's over Dad,' Shaun said as he took a step in his father's direction. 'Just get it over with and admit what you did, what we did.'

'Shut up,' Kenny hissed, his dark eyes flashing with rage.

'No.' Shaun took another step forward. All of his life he'd been afraid of his father. Kenny was a bully who'd terrorised his family rather than protect them; his poor mum had suffered at her husband's hands, and he had suffered too. He'd lost count of how many times Kenny had beat him, and for what, all because he didn't conform to what he'd wanted from a son. He stood up a little straighter, determined to get it off his chest, determined for the first time in his life to stand up to his father even though he knew the repercussions would be huge, that Ricky and Jamie may very well kick his head in, or even kill him. But he deserved it, he conceded. After all, he had murdered their father.

'My dad made me kill Terry.' He turned to look at Tracey. 'I'm sorry,' he said, his voice cracking. 'I had no other choice; he would have hurt my mum if I didn't do as he said.'

'You stupid little fucker,' Kenny roared as he tried to fight his way out of Max's grasp in a bid to reach his son. 'You stupid, stupid little fucker, I'll fucking kill you over this.'

'No you won't,' Shaun retorted. 'Like I already said Dad, it's over.'

'You bastard.' Ricky and Jamie made to advance forward, and Max put up his hand, warning them to stay back. It was understandable that they wanted revenge for their father's death, but even he could see that battering Kenny's son wasn't the answer. Only one person was responsible for Terry's demise and that was Kenny himself.

Pulling back his fist, Max repeatedly smashed it into Kenny's face. 'I should have done this a long time ago,' he snarled. 'You're poisonous, always have been.'

'Max, no, stop.'

The fear in Tracey's voice was enough to make Max pause, and with one fist still raised in mid-air, he snarled, 'You know what, you're not worth it.' He shoved Kenny roughly away from him. 'I'll leave that honour to the filth. What is the sentence for sex trafficking anyway?'

'It's got to be at least fifteen years,' Jamie said from behind him.

Max grinned into Kenny's face. 'Do you hear that? Fifteen years,' he repeated. 'And that's without the murder charge on top. You'll be lucky if you get anything less than, oh I don't know' – he pretended to think it over – 'thirty, or maybe even forty, years.' He shrugged. 'And then when you get out, that's if you ever get out of course, I'll still be there, waiting for you.'

Kenny groaned in pain. His left eye was so swollen that he could barely see out of it, and from his eyebrow blood trickled. 'I've got shit on you, don't you forget that,' he wheezed. 'Your feet won't even touch the floor before they fling you back inside.' A craftiness lit up Kenny's face; he had the bastard now, and the knowledge he had on him was enough to guarantee that Max wouldn't step foot outside of prison again; they'd lock him up and throw away the key and good riddance to the cunt as well. All he'd ever been was an irritation to him.

Max laughed, a cold laugh that was enough to chill Kenny to the very core. 'Yeah maybe you do,' he admitted, 'and just maybe we'll end up in the same nick, because let's face it, there won't be anything to hold me back then, will there? In fact, everywhere you turn I'll be there, watching, biding my time. A constant reminder of what you did to me.'

Kenny blinked rapidly, his heart beating ten to the dozen. He'd rather die than spend years of his life locked up, constantly looking over his shoulder, waiting for Hardcastle to take him out.

'Just get it over and done with,' he whimpered. 'Kill me now, finish me off.'

'Nah.' Getting to his feet, Max sneered. 'You're going to get exactly what you deserve.' Drawing back his foot, he executed a swift kick to Kenny's ribs, the bones cracking beneath his boot, bringing Max nothing but immense pleasure. 'See you inside, pal.' Turning to look over his shoulder at Ricky and Jamie, he jerked his chin towards them. 'Phone the old bill.'

'What?' Ricky's mouth fell slightly open. He'd actually thought that Max was winding Kenny up. Ever since they were kids it had been drummed into them that they didn't snitch, that they didn't go running to the filth at the first hint of trouble. Instead, they took the law into their own hands and dished out their own form of retribution. 'Are you being serious?' he asked, glancing towards his brother.

'Make the fucking call,' Max growled. 'These cunts are going down even if it means I have to drag them there myself.'

'I'll do it,' Tracey said, getting to her feet and giving Kenny one last look of contempt.

'You can't do that,' Bianca screamed from across the office, panic clearly audible in her voice. 'I'm having a baby; I can't go to prison.' She looked helplessly around her. 'Michael,' she cried. 'Do something; stop them.'

Groaning out loud, Michael rolled slowly onto his side, spitting out a mouthful of blood as he did so.

'Please Michael,' Bianca continued to wail, 'you have to help me.'

In no fit state to even help himself, let alone anyone else, Michael clutched at his gut. Not only did his stomach muscles feel as though they were on fire, but he had a feeling he would be pissing blood for the foreseeable future. 'We're done for B,' he said, his swollen lips and jaw making his voice sound thick.

'No!' Bianca's cries reached a crescendo and as tears rolled down her face, she wiped them away, smearing the thick foundation and black mascara across her cheeks. 'I can't breathe,' she cried as she jumped to her feet and looked around her for an escape route. 'I need to get out.'

'Sit down.'

Hearing the low growl in Max's voice, Bianca immediately dropped to the floor and silently wept.

Ten minutes later the wail of police sirens could be heard in the distance and turning towards Tracey, Ricky and Jamie, Max nodded towards the door. 'Time for you lot to get out of here.'

'What?' Tracey's jaw dropped. 'No.' She vehemently shook her head. 'We're not leaving without you.'

'Yes you are,' Max answered as he indicated for Ricky and Jamie to get their mother and the young woman away. 'I've got nothing to lose, no family of my own to worry about, and if I end up back inside it won't be the end of the world. I've done it once and survived and I'm pretty sure that I can do it again.'

'But.' As she looked around her, Tracey's breath caught in the back of her throat. The injuries to both Kenny and the Murphys was more than enough to ensure that Max would stay locked up for the duration, maybe he would even be charged with attempted murder. At the very least he was looking at ABH, a crime that would still warrant a lengthy sentence to be bestowed upon him. Guilt ate away at her; it was only because of them that he had even become embroiled in finding out the truth behind Terry's murder.

'No buts.' Max gave a gentle smile. 'Go on, get out of here.'

'And what about her?' Ricky asked, his voice low as he glanced across to Bianca. 'What if she tells the old bill that we were here?'

Max glanced over his shoulder. 'Then it will be her word

against mine.' He glanced down at his bruised knuckles. 'Besides I've got the evidence right here to prove it,' he said with a grin as he lifted his fists for them to see the blood and grazes.

'It will be my word too.' Getting to his feet, Shaun lifted his chin in the air. 'You were never here, and I'll take an oath to that fact. Besides, it's the least I can do after what I did.'

Taking a deep breath, Ricky nodded. Shaun, it appeared, was more of a man than his father could ever be.

'Now, go on go, take your mum home.'

Not needing to be told twice, Ricky and Jamie bundled their mother and the young woman out of the door.

As he watched them go, Max took a seat, and leaning his forearms on his knees he hung his head down low and breathed heavily through his nostrils. He hadn't exactly been lying, he had survived prison once and he knew he could do it again, and as much as every fibre of his being told him to get up and run, he wouldn't, he would see it through to the bitter end, he would go down and do his time with the minimum of fuss, only this time it would be on his terms, by his own admission, for no other reason than to make sure that Tracey never had to suffer in the same way that his own mother had suffered.

The sirens neared and as the walls of the office were swathed in flashing blue lights, Max took a deep breath and readied himself.

Just moments later, police officers entered the office and standing up, Max lifted his hands in the air, surrendering himself to them. 'It was me,' he said, gesturing around him at the aftermath of the assaults which had taken place. 'I did it all.'

EPILOGUE

Sitting at the kitchen table, Tracey looked down at the glossy brochure in front of her. Six months Terry had been gone and as of yet he still didn't have a headstone. Some days she barely even thought of him at all and other days the grief she felt would hit her like a tidal wave.

She glanced down at the brochure once more, her mind wandering to the women Terry had trafficked into the country. They were safe, and although they would always carry the scars of the trauma they had been through, Tracey knew that they were strong, that they would find a way to rebuild their lives. She smiled then as she thought of Georgiana. She had returned home to her family in Romania, but Tracey had a feeling she would be back, she'd seen the way that she and her youngest son had looked at one another, there had been an attraction there, a spark that neither one of them could deny.

'Tracey.' The kitchen door swung open and Max stood in the doorway. 'They're about to crack open the champagne,' he said, giving her a gentle smile.

Tracey returned the smile. Ricky had finally got down on one knee and popped the question, and Kayla had immediately said yes to marrying him as Tracey had known all along that she would. As for Max, her and her sons owed him their freedom. Just as he'd promised them he would, he'd taken the rap for the assaults on Kenny and the Murphys, and Shaun had backed up his claims that he had acted alone. Even Kenny had unbelievably kept their names out of the frame. Perhaps he was too afraid of Max's wrath to say or do anything else. In the coming weeks, Max was due to appear in court and his solicitor fully believed that any custodial sentence handed out would be minimal, perhaps even as little as a few months, or if he was really lucky he would walk free from court, which in Tracey's eyes was exactly what Max deserved, seeing as he'd given the police information about people trafficking. But if the worst came to the worst and Max was sent down, he had reassured her time after time that he could deal with it. His only request was that she keep the car dealership going for him in his absence. Of course she had readily agreed and as it was, her sons had begun working for him.

Getting to her feet, Tracey gave the brochure one final glance before picking it up and walking across the kitchen. In front of the pedal bin she paused. Terry didn't deserve a memorial; he didn't even deserve a wooden cross to bear his name. No, the only thing he deserved was to rot in an unmarked grave. As she pushed her foot on the pedal, the lid opened and she dropped the catalogue into the bin. In that instant she slung back her shoulders and took a deep breath. Already she felt as though a weight had lifted off her shoulders.

'Come on Mum,' Ricky called from the lounge.

Tracey smiled. 'I'm coming,' she called back good-naturedly.

Without giving the bin a second glance, Tracey left the kitchen and joined her family. It was time to be free, she decided. Time to enjoy her new life as a single woman.

As the cork was popped, she laughed happily and as her glass clinked against Max's in a toast she took note of the wink he gave her and smiled to herself. Yes, it was time to rebuild her life, and who knew which direction she would find herself being taken in. The only thing she knew for certain was that she would enjoy every moment of what life had to throw at her, and along the way she would cherish the new memories she and her family made, memories that wouldn't include Terry, his mother, or the despicable crimes her husband had been embroiled in. They were free from their old way of life and Tracey was determined to keep it that way.

ACKNOWLEDGMENTS

A special thank you to Boldwood Books for continuing to believe in me.

Thank you to Sarah Warman, Joana Castro and Elizabeth Tyler for your support.

And also a huge thank you to the readers of NotRights Book Club for your continued support over the years.

MORE FROM KERRY KAYA

We hope you enjoyed reading *Betrayal*. If you did, please leave a review.

If you'd like to gift a copy, this book is also available as an ebook, digital audio download and audiobook CD.

Sign up to Kerry Kaya's mailing list for news, competitions and updates on future books.

http://bit.ly/KerryKayaNewsletter

Explore more gripping gangland reads from Kerry Kaya.

ABOUT THE AUTHOR

Kerry Kaya is the hugely popular author of Essex based gritty gangland thrillers with strong family dynamics. She grew up on one of the largest council estates in the UK, where she sets her novels. She also works full-time in a busy maternity department for the NHS.

Follow Kerry on social media:

 twitter.com/KerryKayaWriter

 instagram.com/kerry_kaya_writer

 facebook.com/kerry.bryant.58

PEAKY READERS

GANG LOYALTIES. DARK SECRETS.
BLOODY REVENGE.

A READER COMMUNITY FOR
GANGLAND CRIME THRILLER FANS!

DISCOVER PAGE-TURNING NOVELS
FROM YOUR FAVOURITE AUTHORS
AND MEET NEW FRIENDS.

JOIN OUR BOOK CLUB
FACEBOOK GROUP

BIT.LY/PEAKYREADERSFB

SIGN UP TO OUR
NEWSLETTER

BIT.LY/PEAKYREADERSNEWS

Boldw∞d

Boldwood Books is an award-winning fiction publishing company seeking out the best stories from around the world.

Find out more at www.boldwoodbooks.com

Join our reader community for brilliant books, competitions and offers!

Follow us
@BoldwoodBooks
@BookandTonic

Sign up to our weekly deals newsletter

https://bit.ly/BoldwoodBNewsletter

Printed in Great Britain
by Amazon

37288457R00159